By the same author

The Courier

Beaver to Fox

Beaver to Fox

DEREK KARTUN

St. Martin's Press
New York

Library of Congress Cataloging in Publication Data

Kartun, Derek.
Beaver to fox.

I. Title.
PR6061.A78B43 1986 823'.914 86-3978
ISBN 0-312-07059-4

First published in Great Britain by Century Publishing Co. Ltd.

First U.S. Edition

10 9 8 7 6 5 4 3 2 1

For Henry

Chapter 1

'Fox to Beaver, Fox to Beaver. Anything to report? Over.'

'Beaver to Fox. Nothing here except for a smashing piece sunbathing. She looks restless and lonely, too. Over.'

'Fox to Beaver. Keep your mind on the job, Jacquot.'

'Beaver to Fox. Sorry, chief. Over.'

'Leopard to Fox. I've a hunch about a black 402 travelling north along the Route des Lacs. I only caught him briefly in my rear mirror, but I'd swear I saw him twice. Cruising. And black isn't that common. Over.'

'Lizard to Fox. Jo-Jo's seeing things. It wasn't black: it was grey. And anyway, it was a Bordeaux number plate. Christ, it's hot. I'm stretching my legs. Maurice will take over for five minutes. Over.'

'Fox to Lizard. Okay, and keep away from the women. There's only another four hours of this. You fellows don't know when you're on a cushy assignment.'

The man in the car which was designated Fox handed the mike to the young man next to him and pulled out a large and grubby handkerchief to mop his brow. He was sweating heavily in the broiling July sun, sticking to the seat, thirsty, irritable. 'The *patron* is too damn keen on these random stake-outs. Eight cars and sixteen men on overtime for a whole Sunday in the Bois – for what? A chance in a million. My wife's livid.'

'Wasn't Nikichev caught this way, chief?'

'That was two bleeding years ago and the *patron* has been hooked on the system ever since. You don't get lucky twice. Not in this game. Maybe once in a lifetime. Not twice.'

The radio crackled. 'Bison to Fox, Bison to Fox. Any of

you gentlemen mind if I take a piss? Nothing elaborate, you understand, just a little quick relief.'

'Fox to Bison. Don't waste air time with your stupid chat. Find a tree and hurry up. Over.'

'Bison to Fox. Find a tree, he says. Christ, there's nothing *but* trees and he says find a tree. Over.'

The big man sweating in Fox laughed and took a swig from a half-empty can of lemonade. He glanced in his rear-view mirror, narrowed his eyes, pulled himself upright in his seat and grabbed for the mike. As a black Peugeot passed them, cruising at thirty or so, he was already snapping into the mouthpiece.

'Fox to all. Fox to all. Black Peugeot 602, Soviet Embassy number plates, heading west past me on the Route de Longchamps. Driver alone. We didn't recognise him. Note the number 99772 AR75. Bison and Wolf, you're further along the Route de Longchamps. Report when he gets to you. Over.'

'A fish in the net at last,' the driver of Bison said to his mate.

'Red mullet.'

'About bloody time.' He had his eyes fixed on the mirror, waiting for the Peugeot to come up behind him from the east. 'Here he comes.' He pulled the mike to his mouth. 'Bison to Fox. He's coming up on me now. Doing about forty but slowing down. Now he's turning left into the Route Sablonneuse. I got a good look at him, chief. I think it's Galievich. Not sure. Now he's turned and travelling south away from me along Sablonneuse. Over.'

The big man in Fox was following the progress of the Russian diplomatic car on a map spread awkwardly on his lap. 'He's heading for Lizard,' he said to his companion. 'Tell him.'

The other man took the mike. 'Fox to Lizard. Jean or Maurice, he's heading your way. Unless he's turned off on the Route de l'Etoile, he'll be with you . . . about now. Over.'

'Lizard to Fox. This is Maurice. No sign of him. He must have turned off. Over.'

'Fox to Panther. He has to be coming your way. The rest of you, be ready to move. He may be heading right out of the Bois de Boulogne. Over.'

'Panther to Fox. No sign of him. If Maurice hasn't seen him he's stopped somewhere up the road, between the two of us. Not sure, but I think I can see something a couple of hundred yards back. Over.'

The big man in Fox threw his map aside and seized the mike. 'Fox to all. Fox to all. Right, *scramble*! And mind how you go. We don't want to blow it. Now listen. Beaver to move down to the Route de l'Etoile at a decent lick, as if you were heading somewhere. And keep your eyes skinned in case he's pulled off the road. Panther turn round, keep your engine running and stay where you are in case he's just stopped for a piss and is moving on. I want Bison to move forward as soon as we locate him. I'm waiting to hear from you Beaver. And if you see him, don't do anything stupid like stopping or slowing or looking at him. Just keep going, right? Over.'

A few moments later: 'Beaver to Fox. Beaver to Fox. I've just passed him. He's parked by the roadside about three hundred yards north of Panther on the Route de l'Etoile. There's a couple of other cars and a van parked nearby and a few people about, not many. He's not in the car, and if anyone's covering for him, I never saw them. No one looking like a Russki that is. What shall I do now chief? Over.'

'Fox to Beaver. You can stop next to Panther. Some of us will move in closer. I want Leopard to move up to the Route de l'Etoile. When you're all in position, operate foot surveillance. And don't forget the movies. Over.'

The big man in Fox threw the car into gear and moved it fast up the Route de Longchamps and round into the Route Sablonneuse, acknowledging the men in Bison at the corner. There was the trace of a smile on his fleshy face. He was enjoying himself. 'Perhaps I was wrong,' he said. 'Maybe you do get lucky twice. Thank God these gits at the KGB are as stupid as we are. Christ, what is it about the Bois de Boulogne which pulls them back here every time?'

'The birds,' his companion said. 'There's a lot of it about this afternoon, too.' He was trying to dissolve the tension in macho humour. A recent recruit from the regular police in Nantes, it was what he'd heard others do in the DST squads. He liked the style. He was having a marvellous time.

The big man drove Fox fast past the point where the Soviet car had parked, without so much as glancing at it. A couple of hundred yards further up the road, he pulled off into the trees and stopped. He turned to his companion.

'Now, I don't want any fumbling, right? We're after big game, my lad, and when you're after big game you don't go advertising the fact. You're dressed all right for the job so off you go, wandering about looking for skirt, right?'

'Right, chief.'

The young man got out of the car, hitched up his jeans and sauntered off between the trees. There were few people about in that part of the Bois de Boulogne. The big crowds were round the lakes, further west, and in the larger open spaces, where sunbathing could be a communal sport with a chance of making intriguing contacts. In this part there were few clearings among the limes and silver birches. Lovers with more on their minds than getting bronzed were coupled here and there while, parasitically, *voyeurs* meandered through the trees hoping for entertainment.

Jean and Maurice, equally dressed for a Sunday in the Bois, were sauntering slowly up the Route de l'Etoile, seemingly deep in conversation. Three or four other men had advanced from their cars to within a hundred yards or so of the parked Russian car. All carried nicely miniaturised transceivers in their pockets. Three of them had movie cameras. It wasn't the most discreet and professionally competent stake-out in the annals of the French counter-intelligence Service, but it was reasonably fit for the purpose, provided the quarry was not alerted and had had a good lunch on this sleepy day. The big man had been on worse-run jaunts than this and was feeling quite good about the prospects.

In a clearing, a dark girl in a bikini lay face down on a rug, her bra undone, a youth by her side tickling her with a twig and trying to make her turn over. They were laughing and the girl was making no great effort to keep her breasts covered. A little beyond, a middle-aged man was walking though the trees arm in arm with a slight girl with long blonde hair. They were deep in conversation, paying no attention to the couple on the rug. The young recruit from Nantes first caught sight of the Russian among some bushes close to the clearing. He was standing still, looking intently in the direction of the couple. The girl, now, had turned over. 'Smashing tits,' the young man said to himself. Then he pulled his mind back to his quarry. 'The dirty little devil, he's spying on them! But perhaps that's a form of cover and he's going to make a contact in a minute.'

He felt a gripping sensation in the pit of his stomach. This wasn't dangerous but it *felt* dangerous. The perfect feeling. He moved carefully round behind the Russian, whose absorption appeared to be total. Then he glanced round, as he'd been taught, to see whether another Russki was covering for the first one. It was an unbreakable rule on contacts: a second man to watch the contact man's rear and warn him if anyone was on his tail. But the young man from Nantes couldn't see anything resembling a KGB field man. There they all were: Galievich, if it was him, the randy couple on the rug, the couple wandering about deeply involved with each other – probably someone's husband cheating with his secretary – and further off, a few Sunday afternoon strollers along the Route de l'Etoile. All that, and the carefully kitted-out inspectors of the DST as they moved in slowly from both ends of the road with their transceivers and cameras. It was straight out of the movies and he was loving every minute.

Maurice had picked up the Russian and was using his camera. The big man snapped into his mike: 'What the hell are you shooting him for? He isn't doing anything. Wait till he makes contact.'

Maurice took his finger off the button. The chief was right: he'd been wasting Government issue ultra-fast movie stock.

'We're in too close,' the chief said. 'Get back, all of you

except Luc. Move around. Look as if you're enjoying your Sunday, for Christ's sake.'

The young man from Nantes was flattered to be picked out to do the close surveillance. He mustn't blow it. Keep calm. Look nonchalant. Pretend to be interested in the girl's tits. God, he *was* interested. They were smashing. He envied the youth playing around with her. The Russian seemed to be taking a similar view of the situation. He hadn't moved from his spy-hole among the bushes for some time. But now the girl was fastening her bra and the lucky devil with her was pulling on his T-shirt. They were packing up. What would the Russian do? Where was his cover? Above all, where was his contact? He turned away from the clearing, the spectacle over. Luc saw his face – the high cheekbones and narrow eyes of a man from east of the Caucasus. It betrayed nothing, neither pleasure nor disappointment, anxiety or impatience.

It suddenly dawned on Luc that the DST had mounted this whole elaborate stake-out – eight cars and sixteen men on overtime – to catch a randy Russian from Novosibirsk idling away a hot Sunday at a favourite pastime. Maybe there *was* no contact. What a joke! Mireille would laugh when he told her. She loved stories like that. Something with a sexy edge to it and a laugh.

The Russian was walking back to his car now. He was getting in. He was driving away, eastwards along the Route de l'Etoile and fast out of the Bois de Boulogne.

'Sod it,' the chief said into his transceiver. 'It certainly was Galievich. That's the second time we've caught him at the peeping Toms. Okay, all of you, back to your cars. There's three hours to go.'

André Bastien looked at his watch for maybe the tenth time in fifteen minutes. Six-twenty. He was running late, would have some fast talking to do when he got home. By now he should have been with Claudine over on the Left Bank for their drink. But, God, the traffic! Worse than ever. And in August, too, when half Paris was away for the summer. He'd been crawling forward parallel to the river along the Cours

Albert Ier and then the Cours la Reine for nearly twenty minutes. There must be a holdup somewhere ahead. Maybe a car had broken down – overheated as it crawled in the stifling heat. Or maybe the trouble was the usual Friday rush to get some air in the countryside. *La sortie du weekend*.

He glanced to his left. The pretty girl in the Mini was still abreast of him. They had exchanged glances ten minutes ago and now he smiled at her and shrugged expressively. She smiled back, slightly. He found the tentative, modest smile inviting. Maybe there was some way of extracting a little joy out of this Godforsaken traffic jam by talking to her. Shouting, rather, in the din of idling engines and the periodic outbursts of angry hooting.

He remembered that that was how he'd actually met Claudine, two years ago in just such a traffic snarl-up in the Avenue de l'Opéra. He'd smiled, she'd smiled back with the boyish smile he'd come to know, to love and lately rather to dislike. A driver ahead had lost his temper and started cursing and he'd shrugged towards Claudine just as he'd done now with this girl in the Mini. And Claudine had shrugged back. Then he'd had the idea of trying a pick-up. Why not? The worst that could happen would be a short, fruitless wait over a drink. He'd scribbled on a scrap of paper: 'Please excuse the cheek, but I'll be in the bar of the Crillon at six this evening and tomorrow. Please come and celebrate our escape from this traffic jam.' He had read it, thought of better ways of enticing her, decided it would have to do, underlined the first 'please', then the second, and rolling it into a ball, he'd thrown it into her car – neatly, he thought – and bowed in her direction. Claudine had picked the ball off the seat, placed it in the tray before her and hadn't even unrolled it.

André Bastien thought it was a non-starter, but the following evening, at 6.30 (he learned later that Claudine was not punctual) she had turned up.

It had been going for two years now and he was, frankly, tired of it. That was why he'd planned only a quick drink with her and had promised his wife he'd be home by 7.30. But the way this was going, he wouldn't make 7.30. Not unless he stood up Claudine and faced the tears and complaints that would follow. He decided he'd prefer to be late home and hide behind a late meeting in the office, plus this traffic jam. After all, the jam was real enough.

He glanced at the girl again. Although she was looking ahead, he knew she was aware of him. Her chin was tilted a shade higher than it needed to be and a slender hand came up and brushed a loose hair back. That was unnecessary too. Perhaps he'd try the note gambit again. What splendid irony, if he was going to abandon Claudine, to start up something new in exactly the same way. It appealed to his sense of style.

The traffic was still crawling forward. Now they were approaching the underpass beneath the Place de la Concorde. It looked as if the two lines of cars were converging into a single stream in the tunnel. It was where the breakdown must be. It was his last chance.

He tore a page out of his diary, wrote quickly on it, rolled it up. But her offside window was closed against the fumes. He signalled to her to wind it down. She looked surprised but did as he bade her. Then he leaned over and tossed the ball of paper just as the traffic moved forward again and she pulled ahead of him in the single file. But the paper had landed inside her car. André Bastien felt a sense of impending adventure. She'd been a very pretty girl. He was very interested.

The time was 6.32. Now he could see what it was all about. A green Volkswagen Beetle was parked inside the tunnel. It must have broken down. Presumably the driver had gone to phone for help. André Bastien noticed that it was old, battered, unkempt. He cursed people who went out in unroadworthy cars and put everyone else to such inconvenience. The thought struck him that the chocolates he'd bought for Claudine, lying on the seat beside him, had probably melted in the appalling heat. Next to them was the electronic game for young Robert's birthday tomorrow. That would be nice. He loved his kids' birthdays. He'd get home early from the office and join in some of the fun.

He was level with the Volkswagen now and it was the last

thought vouchsafed to André Louis Marie Bastien, thirty-four, father of two, lover of Claudine Martial, unfaithful but loving husband of Laure Bastien, and worthy citizen of Paris. For at that moment the green Volkswagen was pulverised by the sixty pounds of explosive lying in four carrier bags behind the driver's seat. The explosion, in the confined space of the underpass, created pressure waves of immense force which flung André Bastien's car, and the pretty girl's Mini, and some forty other cars, against each other and the walls of the tunnel. It brought heavy slabs of masonry crashing down from the roof, collapsed the lungs of virtually every man and woman in the tunnel, tearing some of them to shreds or smashing them beneath masonry and twisted metal, and started fires as petrol spurted from punctured tanks.

It was all done within seconds, leaving a roaring blaze, billowing black smoke and choking dust. The screams came not from the victims but from those further back along the road who were aware of what had happened.

At 6.42, almost precisely ten minutes later, came the second explosion, on the first floor of an office building in the Cours Albert ler. By then the traffic stood in a solid block all the way back to the Place de l'Alma and beyond, and on both sides of the river. Similarly, it was solid beyond the Concorde, along the side of the Louvre as far as the Châtelet. No fire tender managed to get within a quarter of a mile of the fire in the underpass or the blazing building.

A reporter at *Le Monde*, searching later for a lead for his story, hit on the phrase:

> Last night, Paris was the victim of technology – the technology of the modern terrorist explosive device and the technology of the internal combustion engine which creates the ideal conditions for the promotion of unmanageable terror in the heart of a great city. A car carries the bomb and countless other cars prevent the ambulances, the fire engines and the police cars from reaching the holocaust. Ladies and gentlemen, we are vulnerable.

This sobering thought was published in the Saturday 8 August issue of *Le Monde*, which date happened to be six days after the abortive DST expedition to the Bois de Boulogne.

Later on the same Friday evening in casualty at the *Hôpital Beaujon* things were quiet. There had been many dead but relatively few injured in the two explosions, and other hospitals had been used. Beaujon had sent a surgical team: a number of motorists outside the underpass had been cut about the face by glass from their windscreens and a call had gone out for help with eye surgery. But at Beaujon things were pretty average for a Friday evening: a few road casualties, what looked like a burst appendix, a woman rather nastily beaten about the face by her man. The young doctor in charge had been on duty for fourteen hours and felt like it. The night nursing staff had just come on, dreaming of day duty and a decent night's sleep. There was a bit of trouble with a noisy drunk who had fallen into a fire of some kind and burned most of his hair off.

When they brought the youth in, the young doctor got wearily to his feet. 'What's the gen?' he asked the ambulance men who were carrying the stretcher.

'Riding his motorbike. Hit by a truck. No helmet. Looks like concussion but could be worse. Very faint pulse and I don't like the look of his skin.'

'Let's take a look at him, then.'

They put the stretcher on a couch and the doctor pulled the youth's eyelids up, felt his pulse, loosened his clothing and put a stethoscope to his heart. It didn't look good and the doctor, being still in his first post-graduate year, was frankly frightened. He'd never met a fractured skull and judging by the youth's general condition and the deep abrasion on the side of his head, a fractured skull was what he seemed to have here.

'Damn! We'd better get him up to a ward and notify the super. Got his details?'

The ambulance man pointed to the youth's jacket lying across the end of the stretcher and a leather satchel which had been picked up next to him in the road. Between them they emptied his trouser pockets, the pockets of the jacket and the satchel.

'Better get this recorded,' the doctor said.

The clerk at the desk wrote it all down on a card.

Contents of pockets and one leather satchel: identity card, driving licence, 122 frs 30 cash, six Metro tickets 2nd cl., one white handkerchief, one notebook, one ballpoint, one envelope sealed, wallet with three photographs.

Then she filled in the details from the identity card.

Name: Guido Ferri

Address: 127 Rue Blanqui, Alfortville

Date of birth: 10 August 1964

And so on . . .

The doctor looked the list over, checked the items and signed it, adding: 'Patient unconscious on arrival. Sent to Mandé Ward.'

The stretcher was put on a trolley and a hospital porter wheeled it away to the lifts.

'Put him in a side ward for the super to see,' the young doctor said. 'It looks serious. He'll have to go up to X-ray and maybe the theatre right away.' Then he phoned the ward sister and slumped in a chair with the idea of dozing for a bit.

'What about next of kin?' the clerk asked. She was new and didn't know the drill.

'Our ambulance must have beaten the police to it. I suppose they've all been mobilised to deal with the bombings. Call the local *Préfecture de Police* and ask them to get in touch with the family. Give them the address on his identity card, right? They're to say "seriously injured".'

The girl nodded and did what she was told.

But an hour later the police were on the phone.

'What was that address of the motorcyclist again?'

She repeated it.

'According to the police in Alfortville he's unknown at that address. Is he still with you?'

'I'll say. Looks as if he'll be here a long time yet.'

'All right, we'll get a man over right away. We want to take a look at his things.'

A quarter of an hour later two young men in mufti came in through the swing doors, bringing with them the unmistakable smell of police station. They were polite, businesslike, self-consciously bored. The clerk handed over the youth's few possessions and everything was noted down again, this time in a police notebook. When the senior of the two policemen came to the sealed envelope, he hesitated for a moment, examined the name and address typed in capitals, with the words STRICTLY PRIVATE beneath, then tore it open carefully along a short edge and extracted a sheaf of papers. They were photocopies. As he read he tried to control his expression of studied *ennui*. It was an expression he was cultivating carefully since he had been translated to the plain-clothes branch. The change of attire signified in his mind that the force now cherished him for his brains rather than his brawn and it behoved him to act accordingly. Hence the expression. But what he was reading wiped the studied look off his face. He looked up at his side-kick.

'I'll be damned.' It was all he could think of.

'What is it?'

'What is it? It's dynamite, that's what it is. Come on.'

He stuffed the sheets back into the envelope and collected up the odds and ends. 'We'll be taking this little lot,' he told the clerk. 'And we'll be keeping in touch. Meanwhile, don't let that young man out of the place. That's an order.' He repeated it to the young doctor and beckoning his colleague with a new note of authority in his gesture, marched out.

The terror campaign which had been growing in intensity for the past three months had attracted the attention of the anti-terrorist experts in West Germany and Italy, where political terror was well understood. They were struck by the efficiency of the French terrorists, by their seeming ability to do as they pleased, and by the fact that they appeared to be exceptionally well supplied with explosive devices of the latest types. They seemed to have no money troubles. And the French police had been making no progress against them. Offers of help, made via Interpol, from the Germans, Italians and Dutch had not been taken up. This, at the time, was ascribed to the well-known national pride of the French services.

Chapter 2

Despite the multiplicity of police forces and the habitually savage rivalry between them, the French system sometimes works with surprising speed. In the present case, the two plain-clothes men bore their find triumphantly back to the *Préfecture* of the 6th *arrondissement*, where there happened to be an intelligent young Sergeant on duty. He looked at the documents in the envelope, decided that this was a hot one and called the duty officer at the main *Préfecture de Police* on the Boulevard du Palais.

He explained the circumstances.

'What are these documents of yours?' the headquarters man asked.

'The first one is a photocopy of the minutes of a meeting. It's on official letterheading.'

'What letterheading, man?'

The young Sergeant gulped. It was his big moment. 'The Ministry of National Defence.'

There was a low whistle at the other end.

'Do you want me to read it to you?

'No, I don't. I want you to put the whole lot back in its envelope, seal it securely – and I mean securely – and give everything to the despatch rider I'm sending over to you now. He'll be with you in fifteen minutes.'

'Right, sir.'

'You did the right thing to call us.'

'Thank you.'

The Sergeant did as he was told, priding herself on not having taken a further look at the documents. What he'd seen already was enough: this was the big time. When the despatch rider came, he handed everything to him in a large sealed envelope and collected a signature for it. Then he turned his mind to the humdrum affairs of the night.,

Meanwhile, the duty officer at the *Préfecture* was trying to get the Prefect of Police on the telephone. But that important personage was dining out. He had better luck with his deputy, Commander Roisset. The Commander had been watching late television with his wife and was not pleased to be disturbed, but he listened to the duty officer.

'It isn't for us,' he said. 'That kind of thing's for the DST. Put the stuff in your safe when you get it and I'll call you back with your instructions.'

'Yes, chief.'

It so happened that Commander Roisset in his younger days had shared an office at the *Police Judiciaire* with Georges Wavre, now head of the *Direction de la Surveillance du Territoire* (DST), the body responsible for counter-intelligence on French soil and currently rather keen on exhausting Sunday stake-outs in the Bois de Boulogne. Now he hesitated between calling his old friend or waiting for his own boss to get back from his dinner party. He was unaware of the fact that his decision to call Georges Wavre – a virtual toss-up in his mind – was to prove of absolutely decisive importance in all that was to follow. It just seemed a sensible way of cutting a corner. But he would wait until the stuff reached him, to make sure no one (himself included) was making a fool of themselves. So he called the duty officer back and told him to send a despatch rider out to him at St Cloud.

When he had the motorcyclist's modest possessions spread on the dining table he worked his way up, as it were, from the Metro tickets to the contents of the buff envelope, heavily encrusted now with sticky tape. The sergeant in the 6th *Préfecture* had appended a note to say that the identity card appeared to be false and the youth was unconscious with no time indicated for him to come round. A uniformed man had been posted outside the hospital ward. There would be no release on the accident to the local press. The two plain-clothes men had been told to keep their traps shut.

It was close to 1 a.m. when Commander Roisset came to examine the documents. He spent a quarter of an hour reading them: he freely admitted that he had an inquisitive nature. All the sheets were copies of Ministry of National Defence letterhead. Roisset, whose temperament verged towards the apocalyptic, decided that suddenly he had become involved in procedures that were the very stuff of history. He would certainly not call his boss, the Prefect, and have everything taken out of his hands. If kudos was eventually to be had, then it was only right that it should be his – for recognising the importance of all this, the urgency, the need to involve the DST without delay, the State nature of the whole thing. He reflected that nowadays it seemed to be one damn thing after another. Terrorist bombings had been on the increase for the past four months and no one had got a lead worth having. Today's gruesome double bill somehow crowned it. Was the country cracking up? Was there something at work which went beyond sporadic lunatic bombings of the kind most of Europe had tasted for the past ten years? Having this penchant for the apocalyptic, the melodramatic even, Roisset thought there was. It was a view he couldn't get the Prefect to share with him. That cynical and worldly man would shrug and talk disparagingly of Red Brigades and tell the Minister of the Interior that the police needed time, a lucky break, something to go on. In Roisset's view, the Prefect placed too much faith in the Bomb Squad. What was needed here was a national effort – a few thousand policemen turned onto the problem, country-wide, and to hell with cannabis and illegal whores in the Avenue Foch. And now this modest buff envelope, a bomb of a different kind. And surely the detonator was that name typed in capitals on the front: Armand Seynac. The Editor in Chief of *l'Humanité* and a member of the political bureau of the Communist Party. He allowed himself five minutes to ponder all this and then he dialled Wavre's number and waited until the sleepy voice answered.

'*Cher ami*, I'm sorry to wake you. Roisset here. I'll not

waste time. I'm sending a messenger with some stuff taken off a motorcyclist who crashed his machine this evening and is in a coma at the Beaujon. The Prefect wasn't at home. This is direct from me to you.'

Wavre grunted. 'Thanks. I hope it was worth waking me, that's all. But I expect you know what you're up to.' And he rang off.

Baum's digestion had been troubling him again and he knew what it meant. Normally he could eat like a true Frenchman and never a murmur from his liver (being a true Frenchman he attributed all digestive and most other disorders to the state of his liver). Last night his wife had cooked a simple *ravioli au gratin* with a salad, followed by cheese and a little fruit, and washed down with a not excessive quantity of *rouge*. Nothing there to upset a man's liver. Yet this morning he felt liverish. Decidedly so. Reflecting on the fact, he realised that he'd felt much the same for the past couple of days. And he knew the signs. He was worried, and when he was worried his liver always played him up like this. 'Other people,' he reflected, 'worry with their minds, while I worry with my liver.'

He poured a little water into a tumbler from the jug on his desk and took a pill. 'Useless,' he said to himself, 'but I suppose a pill is better than no pill.' The box carried encouraging messages about dyspepsia and heartburn. He had never known them to do him any good and taking them was more of a ritual than a medication. It was a small superstition that he allowed himself. Perhaps the only one.

He looked at his watch. It was just after 9 a.m. and he'd already been in the office for an hour and a half. He always made an early start like this when he was aggravated by a problem. And his aggravation this time, he reflected, should have got him to the Rue des Saussaies before dawn – probably would have done if the trains from Versailles had run that early.

He had spent the past hour in the archives and he had brought one of the grey files back to his desk, not because he expected it to reveal more here in his office than it had down in archives, but because he wanted somehow to soak himself in it again, touch it, feel its wavelength, read between its lines – in short, get out of it what was patently not there in the lines of typing and handwriting which had accumulated in the *dossier* over the years. This unyielding, uninformative and exasperating file now lay open before him. There were perhaps twenty separate sheets in it. They were of varying dates, sizes and characteristics. All were numbered in the top right-hand corner with the DST's reference number for the individual whose file it was, plus a sheet number which had then been listed on the inside of the file cover so that the absence of a sheet could be detected.

Baum checked the sheets against the list. They were all there. He knew they would be, since he had played thus with the file every day since Wednesday, and now it was Saturday. It was just a way of playing for time, of toying intuitively with the *dossier*, of doing something more or less mechanical while he allowed the problem to mature in his mind. But this one was a long time ripening. He hoped that somehow what he thought he'd seen in the clip of film would turn out to be something else, or that, if he was right, then that there was a laughably simple and harmless explanation for it. The only trouble with this line of reasoning, however, was that Baum was certain with the certainty of thirty years' experience that he had interpreted the film correctly, and that there was not a simple, innocent, absurd explanation. And though the first of these certainties was a physical thing – his unerring eye for a face, for the physical dimensions and characteristics of a man – and the second was a kind of metaphysical certainty – the certainty of hunch, of experience, of 'feel' for an *affaire* – yet if he had to choose where his conviction was strongest he would have to say it was in the second instance.

And so he toyed listlessly with the sheets in the *dossier*, his mind too distracted by his liver to be able to lead him into any areas of hope, let alone certainty.

When his intercom buzzed it was a relief. It was the rapid frequency which signalled the *patron*.

'Baum here.'

'Alfred, I want you in my office. Right away. We may be some time.'

'Yes, *patron*.'

He locked the file in the grey metal safe in the corner of his room, went out, locking the door behind him, and trudged gloomily along the corridor to the lift. Georges Wavre sounded pretty sharp – usually a sign of a new *affaire*. He hoped he was only wanted for an opinion. He needed to be left alone to nurse his special problem. He'd have to plead pressure of work.

On the fifth he left the lift and trudged back down an identical corridor. Wavre's head of secretariat waved him through the Director's outer office. 'The old man's onto something. I know the signs.'

'I could have told you that. I got it from his tone on the intercom.'

He went into Georges Wavre's office and sat down.

'Alfred, *mon vieux*, we have work to do.'

'That's not new, *patron*.'

'I mean real work. Here, look at these.' He handed over Commander Roisset's photocopies and Baum glanced through them. As he read he shook his head in a manner that all his colleagues knew. It was as if he were sorrowing at the foolishness, or maybe the incorrigible wickedness, of man, manifested yet again in the text before him.

'How did this reach you, *patron*?'

Wavre explained the night phone call and passed over the Sergeant's note. 'Here, take a look at the rest of the stuff.' He had the contents of the motorcyclist's pockets spread out on his desk. Baum pulled his chair closer, spent some time examining the identity card. Then he lingered over the three photographs. Two were of the same good-looking girl, both portraits. The other was of an older woman. She looked like someone's mother: possibly it was her son who carried her picture, taken in front of a nondescript house, out of focus, yielding nothing.

Wavre waited while Baum took his time over the pictures, the card, the envelope and the sheaf of a dozen photocopies. He was careful to hold everything by the edges, though by now all this must be heavily decorated with police fingerprints. 'All our people, all of them, are inadequately trained,' Baum often said, 'and none more so than the mob at the *Préfecture*.'

'What do you make of it?' Wavre asked.

'It's intriguing, you must admit. A young man carrying a presumably false identity card, biking across Paris with a photocopy in his satchel of the minutes of the June meeting of the National Defence Committee and other goodies from the Ministry of Defence, all addressed to a leading member of the PCF. Stuff which isn't even likely to be shown to the Cabinet. Or to us, come to that.' Baum was shaking his head again. He seemed to be chuckling to himself at the enormity of the thing. 'As I say, intriguing. Who knows about all this?'

'Only the policemen.'

'The Prefect of Police?'

'No, unless Roisset's told him by now.'

'Any Ministers?'

'I have told no one yet but I've asked to see the President this morning.'

'And Mallard?'

'Not yet. But the Minister of the Interior has a right to know what goes on in our outfit, considering it's part of his Ministry.'

'A pity.' Baum said it quietly, almost mischievously.

'Why do you say that?'

Baum shrugged. 'I would have thought, *patron*, that something so sensitive . . . the makings of a national scandal . . . security of the State and so on. Maybe the fewer the better?'

Wavre shifted his great bulk in his chair and stabbed absently at a blotter with a paperknife. 'It strikes me,' he said, 'that two things remain unknown at this moment: the fact that there has been a leakage is unknown to the members of the Defence Committee and, presumably, to everyone else at the Ministry save the person responsible for the leak. That's the first thing that's unknown. And the second, of course, is that these documents have fallen into our hands – a fact that is unknown to whoever conspired to obtain them. We should remain the only ones to know *both* of these things as long as we can.'

'But you'll have to tell the President since you're by-passing the PM.'

'Obviously. But maybe I can get him to agree that no one else should know.' He picked up the phone. 'Get me Roisset at the *Préfecture*.'

A few minutes later: 'Roisset, old man, I've read that stuff. Very interesting. Yes, yes absolutely. Yes, the President of the Republic. That's my view too. In that connection, can I rely on your complete discretion? Good. But I mean complete. I think it important that you mention it neither at a lower level nor, my friend, at a higher one. You will? Splendid. Thanks, I shall keep you informed as far as I am able.'

He replaced the receiver and looked up at Baum. 'Roisset's reliable. There's nothing in the world he likes better than a secret, provided he's in on it. If we feed him a crumb or two, he'll keep his mouth shut.'

'What do you want from me?' Baum asked. He knew what was coming.

'To take charge, of course. Who else?'

'Allembeau would do well.'

'Not as well.'

'You flatter me. Also, I have a lot on my plate.'

'We all have.'

'Do you want me to come to the Elysée with you?' Baum knew he was defeated.

'Please. I'll let you know when we have a time.'

Back in his own office two floors down, Baum sighed, fetched the folder out of the safe, opened it, closed it again, and took it back to archives. Although it couldn't wait it would have to wait. More dramatic events were displacing it. And that seemed to be something of a pattern lately. Life had become more dramatic, more tense, as if the whole nation were moving towards a destiny that no one had willed and no one wanted – a movement punctuated by bomb explosions, mysteries of the kind that Baum had been wrestling with for the past three days, and now this. Unconnected but worrying events. Clouds no bigger than a man's hand, they said. The quiet before the storm. A strange, intangible restlessness in the nation's collective mind? Baum's thoughts, had he known it, paralleled those of Commander Roisset earlier that morning as he had pondered what to do with the documents.

With his usual impatience, the President of the Republic listened to Wavre and after glancing at the photocopies, looked over his glasses at the men from the DST as if they were to blame for the whole thing. He was famous for failing to distinguish between the messenger and the message, with the result that he rarely heard anything but the good news and thus was singularly ill-informed, for a head of State, on what was happening in the country. On the other hand, he was no fool, and what he saw in the photocopies was two quite distinct things, related but separate: two different kinds of trouble.

The first was self-evident: a blow to the security of the State if a foreign power was sitting back comfortably and reading the minutes of France's highest military committee. The second, less obvious, was political: a first-rate scandal only three months before the coming elections, with the press baying for victims and the Opposition asking for the name of the mole in the Government. So that Wavre's news filled him at once with alarm, irritation and hostility towards the men who were bringing it to him and thus complicating his life.

'These documents were addressed to Seynac at *l'Humanité*?'

Wavre nodded.

'Well, what do you advise?'

Wavre had been dealing with Ministers and Presidents for years and understood their problems. He knew that they invariably felt deeply threatened by events, since most events were uncontrollable and liable to interfere with what had been painfully put together during the political process. They were hag-ridden by the knowledge that to the extent that they controlled anything at all, it was achieved through a long chain of command, down through the civil service, where treachery, duplicity, incompetence or sheer personal hostility anywhere along the chain could bring their plans, and sometimes their careers, to naught. Understanding all this, Wavre knew that one talked to politicians as to fractious children, telling them no more than was good for them, arguing not at all, persuading, cajoling, mystifying always.

His voice now was low, reassuring, almost offhand. 'I recommend that you entrust this matter to the DST and the DST alone, *Monsieur le Président*. We will know how to take it out of the hands of the *Préfecture* without alarming anyone, and whereas they will not succeed in keeping the press away, we most certainly will. That, I believe, is important.'

It was important - overwhelmingly important to the President. A palpable hit.

'Also, we will need to know certain things about the working of the Defence Committee - the membership, where and when it meets - basic things like that; only as much as is necessary. I must ask you to put us in touch with an absolutely reliable man who can inform us and also act as liaison with you so that we do not have to take up your time. I believe this, also, is important.'

Hit two. The President was currently more interested in the upcoming meeting of EEC Heads of State and the elections than he was in news of this kind. It was bad karma and he wanted no part of it.

'Finally, I must ask you, sir, to speak to none of your colleagues about this - even those closest to you.'

The President looked hard at Wavre and said nothing. Obviously, the fewer people who knew about the wretched business, the better. Any one of his ministers was capable of leaking the thing to his favourite journalist if he reckoned thereby to win a shred of political advantage. The elections were coming: not a time when loyalties, political or personal, were specially conspicuous among the ambitious men and their rival parties who made up the uneasy alliance in the Cabinet. It was all very well for these two fat policemen to ask for a security blackout. It made their task easier, of course. But there were other considerations. What if they failed to uncover the culprit? What if it emerged, maybe months from now, that the only politician in the know had been the President of the Republic? What if the Opposition newspapers held that lonely politician responsible? Even hinted, as they might well hint, that he had engineered a cover-up together with the DST? That, surely, was the greater risk. It was not one he was prepared to take.

'It seems to me,' he said, 'that in a case involving the Ministry of Defence, it is constitutionally appropriate that the Minister should be aware of what has happened in his Ministry and what is being done about it. You will therefore inform Monsieur Pellerin.'

Wavre considered arguing, thought better of it, nodded his head. 'And the Minister of the Interior?'

'I suppose that is necessary too.'

'And the Prime Minister.'

'I mentioned no one else.'

'Very good, *Monsieur le Président*.'

The President looked hard at Wavre. Then he turned and looked at Baum. He pointed a thick finger at him. 'This man will do the work?' he asked.

'Yes, *Monsieur le Président*.'

'Is he any good?' The President was not noted for his tact.

'Yes, *Monsieur le Président*.'

The President sat motionless and absolutely silent for perhaps half a minute. Then he took his spectacles off his nose and used them to tap out on his blotter an *obbligato* to his words.

'I require absolute secrecy. I demand speed and I demand answers. If one word of this gets out without my approval, I shall want your resignations on my desk. You can work with Vallat, my *Chef de Cabinet*. He regards the reading on his watch as a State secret.'

He picked up the telephone on his desk. 'Vallat, these gentlemen are coming in to see you now. You will answer their questions. And what you do not know, you will find out. Discreetly.' He replaced the receiver. 'Good day, gentlemen. I hope I shall have some answers quickly.'

And the President opened a folder before him on the magnificent desk, leaving his guests to find their way across the immense Savonnerie and out of the room.

Vallat, a cadaverous, pinstriped figure with the sorrowful look of a man who had worked too long with the President of France and would shortly die of it, looked at Wavre and Baum dispassionately. He did not want to know why they had questions to ask. He was totally devoid of curiosity and quite without the normal human desire to impart what he himself knew to others.

'Your questions, please,' he said drily.

'I would like to know the composition of the Defence Committee,' Baum said. 'Also the dates of its last two meetings and the proposed date of the next one. I want to know where it met in June – not only which building, but which room. I may wish to inspect the room. I also need to know who attended.'

Vallat was making notes on a pad. He showed no signs of interest in what Baum was saying.

'Anything else?'

'Yes, I want an exact description of what happens to the Committee's minutes. Who takes notes, who composes the minutes, who types them, who at the Ministry or elsewhere has access to them, what happens to the rough notes, who receives copies – the lot.' Baum paused. 'Can you do that?'

'Of course. When do you want it by?'

'It's very urgent.'

'Very well. Where can I reach you?'

'At the Rue des Saussaies. Just say you have something for me and I'll walk over at any time.'

'Very well.' Vallat rose from his chair, shook hands with both of them and saw them to the door. There was no expression of any kind on his face.

As they went down the stairs, Wavre said: 'What do you think of our friend Vallat, the President's gothic amanuensis?'

'I think he'll do what his master tells him. No more, no less.'

'Extraordinary,' Wavre said, shaking his head, 'Jesus Christ to the President's God.'

'More like Hitler's barber, I'd say.' And Baum chuckled.

'And our friend Pellerin?'

'I suppose we shall have to see him.'

'A pity. Though I can think of more dangerous Ministers from our point of view.'

'I'll fix it up. And I'll see Mallard later.'

They walked across the courtyard of the Elysée, signed out at the gate and walked the 200 yards back to the Rue des Saussaies. Both were overweight, and in the oppressive midday heat of a Paris August even the short walk had left them sweating and out of breath.

With every foreign correspondent in Paris filing stories on the bombings, the tourist trade was suffering heavily and the powerful tourist lobby was making a nuisance of itself. Paris hotels were half empty, restaurants were in trouble and the stores reported lower sales. Travel agents around the world were switching their clients to Italy, Spain and North Africa. The Times *in London ran a solemn editorial asking whether the days of the Gaullist Republic were numbered and making much of the political instability of France since the year 1789.* Il Corriere della Sera *asked: 'Why cannot the French do what we did with the Red Brigades?'*

Chapter 3

'This evening,' Alfred Baum said to his wife, Estelle, 'I think I must have a bottle of that special *Export*. Is there some in the fridge?' He said this in the hall, before kissing her in his usual manner, very firmly on the left cheek and then on the right. The walk from the station at Versailles to the flat had exhausted him. There was no let-up in the day's stifling heat even though it was close to 9 p.m.

'Of course. But you're running low. There's only a few bottles left.'

'I'll have to get some more.'

He went into the living room, with its oversize, heavy furniture and oppressive drapes, dropped his jacket on a chair, took off his tie and allowed himself to drop heavily into one of the two armchairs. He was too tired to fetch his slippers or even to have a wash until he had something cool inside him. Both cats came and rubbed against his legs and one of them went through the familiar motions of getting ready to spring into his lap.

'Not tonight, old fellow,' Baum said to the cat. 'I'm too hot. How you manage in this heat with that splendid coat of yours I've no idea, but that's your problem. I have my own just now.'

Estelle brought in the beer and sat on the edge of the chair opposite. She was a darting, anxious little woman, narrow where her husband was broad, and seemingly for ever poised to anticipate his next requirement.

'A hard day?'

'Very. And it's the start of a hard week, month, maybe a year for all I know.' He took a draught of the ice-cold beer and let out a sigh of satisfaction. Discouraged, the cats went about their business.

'What's for supper?'

'I did a couscous.'

'How did you know I fancied couscous tonight?'

'You always say that, whatever I prepare.'

'You always know.'

'You tell lies, Alfred. All the time. I never know what you really think.'

He smiled at her and tapped a finger twice on the side of his nose. 'I'm not in the truth business, you know. But I do actually fancy a couscous. Any of that Reblochon left?'

'Yes, and I got a nice piece of Roquefort today, so you can choose.'

He grunted and drank some more beer. They always exchanged gastronomic news like this, as others might exchange views on the weather. It provided some kind of substitute for the news from the office that most men would come home with. Baum rarely said a word about his work, simply because it was not the kind of work to talk about, and Estelle never asked questions. 'Was it a hard day?' was the full limit of her curiosity.

Over the couscous they did not talk. Twice Baum said 'delicious – excellent' and once he said 'go away' to one of the cats. For the rest, he ate in silence and because his wife knew the signs, she said nothing herself. After the cheese, when Baum had said 'excellent' again, she busied herself with making the coffee in a red enamel pot with a hinged lid and clearing away, while he went back to the living room, pulled a sheet of paper out of his pocket and settled down to make notes.

The notes were brief and infrequent – maybe a line of writing every ten minutes or so. For the rest, Baum was indulging in that concentrated, unrelenting thought that was his particular talent: the ability to take a grip on a problem, exclude all else from his mind, and analyse it in ten different ways like an antiquary assessing an ancient vase or a really expert bridge player carrying in his head all there was to be known about the game in progress – the significance of his hand, the probabilities in the hands of the others, what had gone before, the chances, the tactics and the psychology of the four interdependent wills gathered round the card table.

That afternoon he had put the investigation under way. The motorcyclist's possessions had gone down to forensic with strict instructions on what to do and in what order. Also, he had obtained from the police fuller details of the accident in which the young man had been injured, asking for copies of any statements by witnesses. There had been no witnesses, he was told. He suspected the police were too busy to bother and had sent one of his own men down to the Place Maubert, where the accident had occurred. It was a long shot: maybe a café had been open and a waiter or someone had seen what happened.

The enigmatic Vallat had phoned from the Elysée to say that he would have something by tomorrow morning and Baum had arranged to be in his office at ten. Also, he had had a short but satisfactory conversation on the telephone with the administrator of the hospital. In this, he had pretended to be a police inspector.

'What matters here is time.' He kept repeating this simple slogan to himself now. 'Tonight, here and now, in this room with the cats and the noise of washing up from the kitchen and my dwindling stock of decent beer, I must decide what to do so that tomorrow morning, from eight onwards, we start to do it. And I have to get it right because there will be no turning back and no second chance if we balls it up the first time round.'

He had noted so far:

1: Forensic: Report on origin of photocopying paper and envelope.
What type photocopier? Traceable?
Fingerprints (unlikely!).
Handwriting on envelope.
The photos.
2: Archives.
3: Data from Vallat, which must lead *somewhere*.

Then he wrote 'Possible action', and beneath this heading the following grew gradually:

1: Interview Seynac, to whom documents were addressed?
2: Take over from the police at hospital.
3: *Mystification*!

He underlined the word and added the exclamation mark. After writing it he sat for a long time with his eyes closed, looking more than ever like a hibernating hamster, and stirring himself a couple of times to drink the strong black coffee that Estelle had brought him. Knowing the signs, she had retreated to the kitchen with a mass of pink knitting.

'*Mystification*!' Baum repeated the word to himself several times, like some incantation. He appeared to be half asleep. In fact, his brain was racing too fast and he repeatedly had to tell himself to slow down, re-examine his ideas, consider the consequences of something going wrong, assess what advantage there could be if, on the contrary, things went as planned.

'Mystification is all very well,' he told himself, 'as long as I remain the one person who isn't mystified by my own cleverness.'

At eleven Estelle looked in. 'I'm going to bed,' she said. 'Don't forget the lights when you've finished. You can reheat some coffee if you want it.'

'Good night,' Baum said. 'I don't expect to be too late. I have to be up by six.'

It was shortly after midnight that he added the words: 'Urgent: set the trap' to his list. Then he spent ten minutes looking at what he'd written in the past two hours. His lips were moving, like an actor learning his lines. Then he tore the sheet of paper into small fragments which he deposited in the empty coffee cup, turned out the light as instructed and retired to the bedroom where Estelle was fast asleep on her back and snoring gently. Soon he joined her and managed rather to his surprise to get quite quickly to sleep.

He had called a meeting of three of his men for 8.15 next

morning, disregarding the fact that none of them was due for Sunday duty. He always said that if a man joined the DST for the extra excitement he would have to take his thrills on whatever day of the week they were available. Those who wanted a thirty-six hour week had best join the traffic police.

They sat round his bare metal desk on hard chairs – Léon, the heavy man who had led the stake-out in the Bois, Luc, his young assistant from Nantes who had been with him in Fox, and another inspector, a veteran of numerous *affaires* in which Baum had been involved. These three had not been told any more than they needed to know. The Ministry of Defence had not been mentioned. Baum had brought coffee in a flask: the canteen did not open on Sundays. Four paper cups on the desk contained the steaming blackish liquid, already heavily sugared. The day promised to provide another scorching instalment of the heat wave that was trying to bring life in the city to a standstill but at this hour one could still breathe and two of the men still had their jackets on.

'No notes,' Baum was saying. 'I want no notes unless authorised by me. And I want no chatting with the others. If anyone asks you what you're on, say we're looking for a Soviet cat which has been trained to read our codes.'

The three men grinned.

'Now here is what I want.' He turned to the Inspector. 'Marcel, what are your contacts with the press like these days?'

'Not bad.'

'Anyone owe you a favour?'

'Several.'

'I shall want to use whatever rain checks you're holding.'

Marcel nodded. He was not a man who spoke a lot.

'Do you think you can get *France Soir* and some of the dailies to run a story tomorrow on a simple street accident with no sensational angles apart from the fact that the victim has been in a coma for over twenty-four hours and no one knows his next of kin?'

'Not thrilling, is it?'

'That's why I ask.'

'I'll try.'

'You'll have to do more than try, Marcel my friend, you'll have to succeed. It's at the heart of what I'm trying to do.'

'Give me the gen,' Marcel said doggedly, 'and I'll try.'

Baum told him as much about the accident as he needed. 'Now off you go. I want it particularly in tomorrow's *France Soir*. And it has to be in all editions, right?'

'I'll see what I can do, but you know they have a habit of throwing out crap like this in the later editions.'

When Marcel had gone, Baum turned to the others. 'This young man, one Guido Ferri, is in intensive care at Beaujon. There's a cop from the local *Préfecture* on duty outside the ward. Regular replacements. Twenty-four-hour surveillance. They put it on because his papers weren't in order. After I've done some telephoning I'll want you, Léon, to get over to Beaujon. Your young colleague here can stay on call in his office but both of you had better warn your wives or whatever you have at home that they can expect you when they see you and you don't know how long that will last, right?'

The two men nodded.

'All right, I'll let you know when to go and what I want you to do when you get there.'

At nine he called the hospital again. 'That young man, Ferri,' he said to the administrator. 'How is he?'

'Hold and I'll check.'

He heard a brief exchange taking place on an internal system. Then the administrator came back. 'No change in his condition, I'm afraid.'

'Will he recover?'

'We don't know. It's a fifty-fifty thing.'

'Can you put him in a side ward on his own?'

There was a pause. 'Is it important? He's linked up to a lot of life-support systems, you know. It's easier to keep him where he is.'

'I'm sure it is, and I'm sorry to interfere with your routines, but believe me, it is important to us.'

'Very well, we'll do it.'

'Thank you. Oh yes, a detail.' Baum's tone was inconsequential. 'We hope to get some relatives in to see him quite soon, even if he hasn't regained consciousness. Would you please see that his possessions are in the room with him, just in case anything is needed.'

The administrator sounded surprised by this outbreak of thoughtfulness on the part of the authorities. 'Certainly, you can leave it to me.'

Baum called Léon back to his office. 'Right, my friend, you're off to Beaujon.' He told him carefully what he had to do. 'Oh, and take a couple of reliable lads in another car – good tails – and have them handy outside the hospital. If there's no one about, put out an emergency call on my authority.'

'Very good, chief.'

Next, Baum called Commander Roisset at home. 'Make him feel he's in on everything,' Wavre had said. 'Don't actually tell him anything worth knowing, of course, but let him have some titbits and he'll eat out of your hand.'

'The *patron* told me you could help us,' Baum said now. 'I have a favour to ask, Commander.'

'How is the enquiry going?'

'We're getting into it. The President is very cooperative.'

'You've seen him?' Roisset's sense of history was being pleasantly tickled.

'Yesterday. He asked who we were in touch with at the *Préfecture* and Georges Wavre told him it was you.'

'He told him that?'

'Yes.'

'Good. Very good. So what can I do for you?'

'Can you get the police watch over the young man at the hospital removed without provoking any questions?'

'Of course.' Roisset was enjoying the image he felt himself to be projecting. 'No problem at all. I can do it right away.'

'Thank you,' Baum said. 'It is important and urgent.'

'What do you have in mind?'

'Perhaps I can tell you that some time in person rather than on the telephone.'

'Quite, quite,' the Commander was saying as Baum rang off.

Down in forensic there were four men working and wondering what all the hurry was about. This was fishing weather and quite unsuitable for analysing paper samples and trying to track down xerography experts and graphologists. When Baum came down, little progress had been made beyond confirmation of the fact that both photocopying paper and buff envelope were standard commercial types, available in any adequately stocked stationer's.

'Fine,' Baum said. 'Just what I wanted to hear. So one of you will get me a dozen or so sheets of identical paper and a packet of identical envelopes.'

'On a Sunday, Alfred? You have to be joking.'

'I wish I were, but I'm not. I don't mind how you do it. I don't mind if you break into a stationer's shop. But I want them by tonight, right?'

The senior forensic man scratched his head. 'I could do it for you first thing.'

'Too late.'

'Hell, Alfred, I simply don't know where to look.'

'Nor do I.' Baum's voice was matter of fact. 'But I'll say this to you. This little business is probably the most important job you've had to do in the dozen years or so that you've been in the department, my friend. So please treat it as such. I don't mind what you do but I want that stuff here by tonight, and if you think you can't do it then say so now and I'll go out and do it myself.'

'All right, chief,' the senior man said. 'All right, we'll do it somehow.'

'Good lad.' And Baum waddled off to archives, where he asked for the file of one Alexandre Antoine Vallat, civil servant. When he had the grey folder – identical to the folder that had been aggravating him since Wednesday – he signed for it and carried it up to his room. There he settled down and spent fifteen minutes reading it carefully. He found nothing to interest him and returned it to archives. 'Pretty dull, the stuff you have here,' he said to the man in charge. 'I haven't had a really good one for ages.'

'We do our best, Alfred. They can't all be best-sellers.'

Back in his room he pulled a key from his pocket and after turning it in the lock of the grey safe which stood in the corner, heaved open the heavy door and extracted from the safe's innards two files identical in appearance to the one he had just returned. He spent a further fifteen minutes scrutinising them, appeared satisfied with what he read there, and returned them to their place in the safe, which he then locked carefully.

It was time to walk round to the Elysée again.

'I hope I didn't bring you into the office on Sunday simply on account of this enquiry of ours?'

Vallat ignored the friendly gambit. He clearly did not regard the plump little man from the DST as anything more than an intermediary, taking orders from someone else just as he was taking orders from the President. If he had known that this intermediary was fresh from reading his own life history, put together over the years by the security services and updated whenever Wavre decided that the higher echelons of the civil service needed a fresh look, he would no doubt have taken Baum a shade more seriously. And if he had known, further, that his dossier contained remarkably accurate details of an escapade of his youth involving not a girl, which is what it should by its nature have involved, but an unusually handsome youth, then perhaps his frozen demeanour and profound sense of his own worth might well have been shaken. Not that Baum attached much importance to such peccadilloes. And in any case, whereas the file was reasonably well informed on Vallat's marriage and subsequent infidelities, it reported no further episodes of that dubious kind. Nevertheless, it would be difficult to maintain a stance of unshakable hauteur if your interlocutor knew your own darkest sexual secret whereas you did not know his.

'I have what you require,' he said. He was unlocking the centre drawer of his desk as he spoke. He removed a plastic folder and opened it on his desk. It contained several sheets of plain paper. He passed the top sheet to Baum.

'That is the composition of the Committee. I have placed a cross against the names of those who were present at the June meeting. Is that satisfactory?'

'Perfectly. I see you have indicated rank and function in each case. That is very useful.'

'Here are the dates of the last two meetings, the projected date of the next one, and, as you will see, the meeting place. In fact, it is the Cabinet room at the Matignon, since the Prime Minister takes the chair.' He handed over the second sheet.

'You don't meet here at the Elysée?'

'Only when the President chairs the proceedings, which he does from time to time.'

He passed a third sheet across his desk. 'This gives you what you need to know on the minutes of the meetings. Only two people take notes: the Permanent Secretary of the Ministry of Defence and myself. My own notes are for reference in case the President wishes to check on what took place and finds the official minutes inadequate. They are not typed up but kept in my private safe. The Permanent Secretary's minutes are typed in his private office at the Ministry of Defence. No carbons are taken but the typed sheets are photocopied eight times for the permanent members of the Committee but only four receive the sheet containing the decisions.'

'Why is that?'

'Because that is by far the most sensitive material and so only goes to those who have to have it.'

'What happens to the Permanent Secretary's own notes?'

'I do not know. I can ask.'

'I think not,' Baum said.

'Each of those receiving copies of the minutes is required to read and initial them and return them to the Permanent Secretary's office, where they are filed in the safe in his room. The only exception is the President's set. I keep them here.'

He pointed to a squat safe in a corner behind his desk.

'If someone told you, Monsieur Vallat, that a photocopy

of a set of minutes had turned up in the wrong place, how surprised would you be?'

The gaunt and ascetic face betrayed no interest in the question. Baum imagined that it had probably never betrayed anything stronger than faint disgust in all the years that it had been looking out upon the world of high politics and the dubious procedures of the State machine.

'It is altogether possible. There would be no reason for me to be astonished. It would be highly irregular but when documents travel around Government circles as these do, there is always the risk.'

'If it were said that the copy for which you are responsible was the errant one, what would you say to that?'

'That is impossible.' Vallat said it simply, without emphasis. He was secure, impregnable in his self-regard.

'I see. But as for the other copies . . . not impossible, you say?'

'Not impossible.'

'Do you have a view as to which copy would be the most likely to . . .' Baum left the sentence unfinished.

'I have no such view, Monsieur.'

'Does each copy have the names or initials of the relevant person on it?'

'The initials. In the box at the top of the first page. Thus AP/MD signifies Ambroise Pellerin, Minister of Defence, and so on. Then, below that will be the reference of whoever composed and typed the minutes. So that you have two references on each set: the first one different for each photocopy, the second one always the same. You will have concluded that the first set of initials is typed individually on the photocopies.'

'Can you show me this on the copy you have in your safe?'

'No, I am not authorised to show you State documents.'

'Quite.' Baum looked through the sheets of paper, lingering over the list of members of the Committee. 'I see that the Prime Minister and Ministers of Defence, Finance and the Interior were at the June meeting, together with the

Chief of the General Staff, another general, the Permanent Secretary at Defence and yourself. Is that typical of your usual attendance?'

'We usually have ten to twelve people. That was only eight. Others come in for an agenda item as required. It so happens that no one was brought in in June.'

'Why?'

'That arose out of the nature of the agenda. I have not been instructed to tell you anything on that topic.'

The President had been right. This was not a man who would willingly give you the time of day without a signed chit. Not that it mattered: Baum knew precisely what had been discussed in June. No underlings had been brought in because the meeting had been entirely devoted to a review of French relations with the NATO powers and her nuclear policy, in preparation for a major policy meeting later at which the President of the Republic would preside. It was a very nice set of minutes to convey to the Soviets if one's heart's desire was the retirement rank of colonel in the KGB and a dacha not too far from the bright lights of Moscow.

But there had been more than the minutes in the motorcyclist's package.

'I understand the Committee discussed the appointment of the successor to General Lapointe as Chief of the General Staff and had before it the Minister's short-list of four possible candidates with a recommendation attached.'

Vallat allowed a reluctant 'correct' to emerge from his thin lips.

'Were those two sheets circulated to the members in exactly the same way as the minutes?'

'They were.'

It was all Baum needed. 'Thank you, Monsieur,' he said, rising and extending a pudgy hand to be shaken.

Vallat rose from his chair, briefly shook hands and gave a slight bow. 'If there is anything else that lies within my competence and authority . . .' He said it without enthusiasm.

Again on the way down the great staircase of the Elysée Baum found his thoughts wandering back to the twin disasters at the Concorde and the Cours Albert ler. The press was now in full cry. There was, for once, a consensus: Red Brigades of some kind were responsible. Not that any known ultra-Left organisation had claimed the glory as yet (no one attached too much importance to a phone call received by *l'Aurore* from the *Recall 1968 Movement*, since it had never been heard of until then). But the internal evidence was there. The building burned down was the headquarters of the Iron and Steel Federation, the employers' body which had been locked in often violent combat with the unions over wages and redundancies for the past six months.

'I must keep my mind on what concerns me, on what I can do, and not on what I fancy myself to have opinions on,' Baum said to himself.

As he crossed the courtyard the gates opened and the Prime Minister's gleaming black souped-up Citroen swept in, escorted by four outriders. 'Little does he know,' Baum reflected as the PM alighted and mounted the steps, 'that he and his Government are sitting on a powder keg which will most certainly explode under their bottoms if I, poor old Alfred Baum, make one false move.'

He grinned as if, buried somewhere in this sombre fact, was a very good joke.

Later that day, Georges Wavre was in the imposing office of the Minister of Defence over on the Left Bank near the Parliament building. It was, in a sense, an expedition into enemy territory, since the Ministry had overall command of the Ministry of War, and that great bureaucracy had always guarded with the utmost jealousy its famed *2e Bureau* – the Second Bureau of its intelligence arm, responsible according to statute for military intelligence but often arrogating to itself counter-espionage activities with which it had no business under law. A fiefdom within a military empire, the *2e Bureau*, with its faceless colonels and majors and their obscure and frequently libellous archives, was a worthy opponent and rival of the DST. It possessed the advantage of age and long tradition – the power, and the ability to inspire awe, of a national myth; whereas the DST was an upstart wartime creation which had always worked in the dark and liked it that way, and had more enemies than friends in high places. Conversely, the *2e Bureau* had a long catalogue of scandals, grotesque incompetence and unseemly internecine warfare to its discredit, whereas the DST had managed never to wash any of its dirty linen in public.

Ambroise Pellerin, shaggy and slow-moving, a veteran of the political battlefield, looked carefully at Wavre from under bushy brows. A phone call from Vallat had asked him to receive the head of the DST urgently *en tête à tête*. More likely, Vallat reflected, eyeball to eyeball. For this reason the head of the Minister's private office, a sallow, eager man named Pichu, was not sitting in the chair by the side of his desk. Recognising Georges Wavre on his way in, Pichu had raised an eyebrow when, contrary to his expectation, he had not been called into the room. Unlike Vallat over at the Elysée, he was a man who desperately wanted to be involved.

'What can I do for you, Wavre?' The Minister's voice might not be hostile, but nor was it exactly forthcoming.

'A matter of some delicacy and of the utmost confidentiality.' Wavre's aim was a rather complex one: to tell the Minister what he was now obliged to tell him, but to minimise as far as he was able the impact of his news, so that the Minister would not be tempted to hand the matter over to his own *2e Bureau* on the principle that if there was any glory here, better that it should accrue to his own outfit rather than to the Minister of the Interior's DST. Between Pellerin and Mallard at the Interior, no love, no respect and no trust were lost.

'Please tell me then.'

Wavre proceeded to say what he had to say, de-emphasising where he could, skating over details where he dared, and insinuating that the President's instructions regarding the responsibility of the DST were even more imperious than they had in fact been.

A grandiloquent painting of the young Napoleon on the bridge at Arcoli hung behind the Minister's chair and Wavre had some difficulty in keeping his gaze away from the heroic scene and on the sceptical and motionless face of the Minister. When he had finished there was a brief silence.

'Whose initials,' the Minister asked carefully, 'were on the copy of the minutes which were leaked?'

Wavre was ready for the question. 'You will forgive me, *Monsieur le Ministre*, if I do not discuss details of the case at the present early stage. I am under the strictest instructions from the President.'

Ambroise Pellerin shrugged his great shoulders and allowed a smile to crease his mouth. 'I suppose you will want to make enquiries in my Ministry?'

'We may come to that,' Wavre said. 'For the moment, however, I am simply informing you of the facts. I know that I can count on your cooperation should we wish to speak to any of your staff.'

'Of course. Please come through to me personally.'

'Thank you.'

'This is a serious business,' Pellerin said as he rose and offered his hand. 'I hope you fellows at the DST are alive to the *political* implications . . .' He allowed his voice to trail off, and again the slightly enigmatic smile was there.

'We are, sir.'

They shook hands and Wavre was escorted through the outer sanctum and into the lobby by the head of the private office, on whose face chagrin or something like it could be read.

Later, Wavre said to Alfred Baum: 'I simply don't feel comfortable over there at Defence. If we ever reach the point of going in with a full-scale investigation it will be rough, my friend. Like someone said, they'll be slapping us on the back in order to locate the best place to insert the knife.'

'That was Lenin,' Baum said with a smile.

At forty-six Guy Mallard was the youngest of the senior ministers and possibly the brightest of them. He had been given the Ministry of the Interior despite the angry protests of the lesser Communist ministers in the Government. For in Guy Mallard the Communist Party recognised an implacable foe, and it had subjected him accordingly over the years to a campaign of vilification which had left him unmoved. His was the anti-Communism of the man who had flirted dangerously with Marx and Lenin in his youth, before the revelations of Khruschev and his personal political ambitions had come into happy juxtaposition, turning him overnight into a Social Democrat with an enormous respect for policemen. 'I do not expect the members of my bodyguard to read Proust and visit the sick in their spare time,' the President said when the less attractive aspects of the Minister's personality were drawn to his attention, 'so why should anyone expect a sensitive and compassionate soul at the Interior?'

When Georges Wavre had finished his report on the leakage, Mallard asked exactly the same question about initials as Pellerin had done over at Defence, and got exactly the same answer.

'You forget, my friend, that your department heads to this Ministry, to me,' he said.

'I do not forget it for a moment, Minister. But with respect I must ask for a certain professional latitude. My findings will of course be submitted to you as soon as possible, in toto.'

Mallard appeared to be contemplating a little pressure but thought better of it.

'Very well, *Monsieur le Directeur*. I await your report.'

The unions in the steel industry had issued a statement deploring the bombings but pointing out that the employers' intransigent and callous policy of plant closures and cuts in real wages was bound sooner or later to favour extremist elements and lead to violence. The somewhat lukewarm tone of the unions' disapproval did not satisfy the Right-wing press, which now began to develop the line that 'objectively' the stubborn and inflammatory statements of the unions were responsible for the outrages. 'Morally,' announced the leader-writer of a distinguished daily, 'the unions are therefore responsible. If they did not plant the bomb, they provided the climate and the motivation for those who did.' Replying in kind, newspapers under Left influence accused the Right of hoping to benefit from the public backlash against those responsible for the terror and, by extension, the entire Left.

Chapter 4

The man with red hair walked down the Faubourg St Denis, past the cinema which had recently been divided into three and was showing three blue double-bills, and on past a row of cafés frequented exclusively by North Africans. At the news-stand on the corner of the Rue du Désir he stopped and asked for all the daily papers and the early edition of *France Soir*.

'All?' The ancient lady peeking from among the mass of multi-coloured print looked at him as if he'd asked for *Porno-Libre*.

'I said all.'

She scratched arthritically at the piles of newspapers and managed to gather up a half dozen or so. 'Here, just eighteen francs.'

The man was looking at the colourful display of magazines printed in Arabic as if they had offended him in some way. He pulled a purse out of the hip pocket of his jeans, counted out the eighteen francs, and took the small bundle of papers. He did not say 'thank you'.

He strode on past a half dozen food stalls by the roadside, kicking at the cabbage leaves underfoot and taking up a firm central lane on the narrow pavement, allowing those coming towards him to step aside as best they could. He was tall and well built and he walked like an infantryman who had not had the benefit of transport and had marched to his battles. Despite the heat he wore a black bomber jacket over his T-shirt. He had lace-up combat boots.

He turned right into the Passage St Denis, a short cobbled lane bordered by buildings most of which had been put up in the eighteenth century and all of which would have fallen down had one of them decided to go missing. The street was lined with the kind of shops which could not afford even the modest rents of the Faubourg, where rents had been steadily falling as the blue movies prospered and the old buildings were invaded by the North Africans – many of them 'illegals'.

In the Passage the man with red hair stopped at the fourth shop along on the left and swung in through the glass door, the bell clanging discordantly as he shut it behind him. The shop's fascia proclaimed *Teinturerie*, and beneath that *Réparations*. In the window to the left of the door was a low platform with a wooden chair and a low table on it. It was where, maybe forty years ago, some girl had sat all day, invisibly-mending stockings. No one had bothered to move the chair and its table since nylons had killed this strange peep-show craft. In the window to the right a long garment rail was laden with coats, suits and dresses, labelled and ready for collection by their owners. In the back of the shop a German machine throbbed and whined as it tumbled clothes and suffused the shop in the sickly-sweet smell of trichlorethylene.

Behind the counter a middle-aged man in a grubby white coat looked up at the man with the red hair and nodded. Then he pressed a button beneath the counter. The man walked round the counter, past the machine and on to a door at the back which he opened with a key. He found himself in a small room with a window high up on one wall which let in neither air nor daylight. The naked 100-watt bulb hanging from the ceiling shed a harsh white light on the room's sparse contents and on the three people – a girl and two men – sitting round a centre table. They had been talking, but fell silent when he appeared.

'Did you get the papers?' the girl said.

He threw them down on the table and went over to a low divan, saying nothing. The three at the table divided up the papers and started searching – running their eyes down the columns without speaking. The girl had *France Soir*. She had searched through the first three pages. At the foot of the first column of page four she stopped.

'*Voilà!*' Her voice was quiet, educated, and the tension was under control. 'Listen.' She read the story, a three-paragraph account of a young motorcyclist, Guido Ferri, of Alfortville, found unconscious by his motorbike in the Place Maubert and now in the *Hôpital Beaujon*. The heading read: *Hit & Run Driver Injures Youth, Escapes*.

'At last. Why the devil did they take so long to report it?'

'It doesn't smell good,' one of the men said. He was still searching through *Le Matin*.

'I don't agree.' The girl spoke like someone who had acquired the habit of being obeyed. She had closely-shaped blonde hair, showing darker at the roots. Her eyes were an intense blue and her gaze was compelling. Her beauty was chiselled, the lips thin, the cheekbones clearly outlined beneath the very fine skin, the nose straight and well moulded, the neck slender. She wore no make-up and there were shadows beneath her eyes as if she needed sleep. She was twenty-six.

The man with red hair stretched back on the divan, his head against the wall, legs apart, and scratched carefully at his crotch. He had lighted a *maïs* which hung now from his lower lip, wreathing his face in smoke. 'The stupid sod,' he said. 'About time he learned to ride that fucking bike.'

The girl ignored him. 'I shall go,' she said.

'I don't think you should, Ingrid,' one of the men said. 'It's too risky.'

'We've been over all that. You must learn not to keep trying to go back on collective decisions. When do the hospitals have their visiting hours? I asked you to check.'

'Two till four. But I still think –'

'The subject is closed,' the girl said. She looked at her watch. 'Eleven thirty. Now I want to go over this evening's action. Jean-Paul, come here.'

The man with red hair pulled himself reluctantly off the divan and sat down at the vacant side of the table. He sat well back, leaning his chair onto its back legs and stretching his long legs out in front of him. It was his way of complying, since he wanted to be in the discussion, and not complying, since he did not wish to take orders from the girl – any girl. He pulled at his crotch again and allowed the ash from his cigarette to fall onto his stomach. He smelt very bad in the airless heat of the small room. The girl ignored the demonstration.

'Victor, have you checked the guns?'

The man called Victor nodded. He was short and thickset, with a mass of wiry black hair. The intelligent eyes peered through thick, heavily rimmed lenses as if in constant surprise at what he saw. When he spoke the accent was faintly *méridional*, perhaps from the south-west. 'I still think we'd do better with the automatic pistols. They're easier to handle and get rid of.'

'And far harder to hit anything with,' the girl said. 'Especially a moving target at five yards or more, which is what you reckoned it might be.'

'I don't like the Kalashnikovs,' Victor said. 'They jam. The Russians are lousy engineers.'

'And you are lousy marksmen. With the Kalash you can spray the target and you can't miss. So let's have no more argument, right?'

'Right.' Victor shrugged his shoulders. 'But Serge feels the same, don't you, Serge?'

'I could do it with the 9-mm Firebird,' Serge said. 'Easy. It gives you nine shots at high velocity and it's accurate. I've practised plenty.'

He was pale, with a bad complexion, his face eaten up (as the French express it) by his eyes – the intense eyes of a believer. He spoke ponderously like a man who found speech difficult, preferring other ways of expressing himself.

'You will use the Kalash,' the girl said. 'We agreed on that in the Command and that's final. Now let's check on the other points. Disguises?'

They nodded.

'The cars,' she said to the redhead. 'Are they in perfect order?'

'Of course.'

'Who checked them?'

'Berenger. And me. We even changed the fucking plugs. If you want new engines put in by tonight you'd better tell me now.'

The girl ignored it.

'Look,' she said, the colour on her high cheekbones rising slightly, 'none of you seem to understand the *politics* of this. You are all behaving like little technicians who are trying to prove themselves while what we need is political activists with technical competence, not the other way around. It's absolutely pathetic. And what are the politics of the thing?' She paused and no one said anything. 'I'll tell you, then, as if you haven't been told already. The political objective is destabilisation, correct?'

They nodded and Victor said: 'We all know that, Ingrid, for God's sake.'

'Well, do we all know that? I doubt it. Because if we knew and *understood* it, we'd know that two things are required of every one of our actions. Not one, but two. The first is an event which achieves the maximum disruption, shock – I don't mind what word you use. The second – and here is where all of you lack politics – is that we give an impression of *invincibility*. That whatever we set out to do is always and inevitably *done*. The public has to feel that we can do whatever we want whenever we choose and the State machine is powerless to stop us or protect them. And that means no failures. None. Ever. *That's* what I mean by the politics of the thing. And if it takes Kalashnikovs to achieve certainty – even if it makes the job riskier – then Kalashnikovs are what we shall use. So let's have no more nonsense about how good we are with automatic pistols and how smart we are as garage mechanics.'

'You're swapping one kind of risk for another,' Serge said. 'Of course we mustn't abort the mission. But by using Kalashnikovs you're increasing the danger to the mission itself. If the car's stopped afterwards we can't get rid of the weapons half as easily as we could if they were pistols. And that's another kind of risk.'

'The Command is less interested in your personal fate than it is in our mission,' the girl said. 'You have to understand, if we merely wound the target tonight and fail to finish him off, we'll have achieved exactly the opposite effect to the one we're after. There'll be a wave of popular support for him. What we need is a corpse, not a wounded idol of the masses. In any case, if you do your jobs properly there's no reason why you should have any trouble afterwards. Our diversion will have emptied the local *Préfecture de Police* and I can guarantee you a good ten minutes for the getaway.'

'Who needs that much?' Jean-Paul said. 'The second car is two minutes away from where they do the job. It's in place already. The set-up's neat: no traffic problems. Once they're in the second car no one will know who the hell they're looking for, will they?'

'Jean-Paul's right,' the girl said. 'Now I want to check the timing.'

'We've had him under observation for three weeks,' Victor said. 'Every Monday he attends some party committee out at Vincennes and drives himself home afterwards. His times of arrival for the last three Mondays are ten forty-seven, eleven twenty-eight and eleven nineteen.' He reeled off the figures, out of his head. 'When we thought we were going to do the job a couple of months ago we found his arrival times then ran between ten fifty and eleven thirty. So the time-span is reasonable. We'll be in position by ten forty.'

'Make it ten twenty,' the girl said.

'It increases the risk.'

'It increases the chance of success.'

Serge shrugged. 'We're expendable,' he said sarcastically.

'Precisely,' the girl said. 'All of us. We're dealing with causes, with the nation's survival, not with people.'

Jean-Paul had lit another cigarette from the stub of the first one, throwing the stub into a saucer on the table where it continued to burn for a while. He leaned back again on his chair, looking at the hard outline of the girl's breasts through her T-shirt and wondering what it would be like to tame her. These conferences always ended by boring him stiff. It was mostly rubbish anyway, chewing the cud over ideology, whatever that meant, and fussing with details which were best left to people who knew, like him and Berenger. This stupid cow knew nothing about cars or guns so why didn't she shut up and let them get on with it. What she needed was a good –

'Jean-Paul, where's the first car now?' She had interrupted his thoughts with another of her damn-fool questions.

'In Berenger's lock-up. Where the hell do you expect it to be, outside the Elysée?'

'Where's Berenger?'

'Taking a shit, I shouldn't wonder.'

'All right, Jean-Paul,' Victor said, 'you don't have to be like that. This is a team job. Cool it.'

The girl got up. 'Try to keep your friend in order, Victor. I've a couple of things to do, then I shall go on to the hospital. I expect to be back here by three thirty at the latest. You'll follow the usual rules before an action. No one goes out for the rest of the day. No telephoning, no drinking. Right?'

The others nodded. She picked up a worn leather shoulder bag and let herself out. On the way through the shop she nodded to the man in the white coat. 'I'm not happy about Jean-Paul,' she said.

'He's all right,' the man said. 'A bit raw, that's all. Flatter him a bit.'

'I don't flatter.'

'Perhaps you should. Maybe you don't make allowances enough.'

'If we made allowances we would all be dead by now,' the girl said. 'If only we could do this thing without these animals from the great French proletariat.'

'We can't.'

'I don't want him on any more jobs after this one.' The thin voice was hard.

The man shrugged. 'It's up to you lot in Command. But he's the best car thief in Paris. And he doesn't get drunk.'

'He smells,' the girl said. 'Tell him at least to take a bath, even if he won't wash his mouth out.'

The man grinned and shook his head as the door closed behind her and the sound of the bell died among the rows of clothing.

Alfred Baum had been in Wavre's office soon after eight that morning, sipping black coffee and wearing the mischievous expression that the Director knew well and, on the whole, viewed with alarm. It was an expression which invariably heralded some ingenious, always unorthodox and frequently risky scheme. Baum referred to these baroque ideas of his as mystifications. Wavre called them dirty tricks. Neither man was overly scrupulous in dealing with unscrupulous opponents. The only difference between them was that Wavre had to carry the ultimate can and make the end-of-term excuses to the Minister of the Interior should anything go wrong. It tended to reinforce his native caution.

'You agreed with the President, *patron*, that secrecy was of the essence,' Baum was saying.

'I did.'

'And that by secrecy we mean that neither the guilty party nor the rest of the community should know what has happened – at least until we have identified the culprit, and quite possibly *after* we've identified him.'

'Correct.'

'Indeed, you and I know, *patron*, that our masters will want this one buried. Solved but subsequently buried.'

Wavre nodded and looked up at the framed photographs of de Gaulle and the current President on the wall behind Baum. Nothing was being said that would have alarmed either of them. Not yet, anyway.

'My little plan,' Baum was saying, 'is designed to achieve that end.'

'Whenever you refer to a "little plan", Alfred, I get worried for my job, not to mention yours.'

Baum smiled, more than ever the mischievous hamster. 'I must admit,' he said, 'that this one has its risks.'

'Come on, out with it.'

'It is simple, really. I want these people to regain possession of the envelope and deliver it to its destination.'

Wavre shifted his bulk in his chair and let out a groan. 'My God, you must be crazy.'

'Audacious perhaps, but not crazy. It seems to me we have only two ways of making progress in this *affaire*. One is by opening an investigation at the Ministry of Defence and among the members of the Defence Committee and their staff. After all, there must be a couple of dozen senior people at Defence and in the other Ministries who had access to the papers and could, one imagines, have organised a little photocopying. But that would mean putting the whole thing into the hands of an examining magistrate at some stage and certainly guaranteeing that the newspapers get onto it long before we're ready with our answers. And that in turn means a more or less lengthy period of public sniping at us and the Government – exactly what the President doesn't want. I only have to ask Pellerin at Defence, say, to let me talk to his staff, and we are immediately at risk.'

'True. There's as much solidarity in the Cabinet as there is in the average cockpit.'

'So that we have to approach it by another route. We have to get the operators at a lower level, whoever they are, to reveal themselves. Interrogation at such a level won't make any headlines.'

'You mean the man in hospital?'

'If he recovers. The hospital has its doubts. Anyway, people can stay in comas for weeks. And even when he comes round, we won't be able to put much pressure on him for some time.'

'So?'

'So we have to find others at such a level who can either be interrogated quietly, with no fuss from the media, or better still, may lead us to whoever set this thing up.'

'But you dare not risk this material getting to Seynac or anyone else.'

'I agree. And I therefore propose to substitute another set of documents for the first one. The substitution is not perfect, but the paper and envelope are identical and the handwriting people have done a passable imitation of the writing on the front of the envelope. As for the photocopies, we've done a careful scissers and paste job, and though the typewriter face is unfortunately not identical to the original, we have a set of minutes and other documents on Ministry letterhead which reveal nothing of what was decided but do include a certain amount of highly interesting rubbish. I put the text together myself with Allembeau's help – he's good at this sort of thing – and I'd like you to read it side by side with the original. The chance we take is that someone knowledgeable will open the envelope to check the contents before delivery, but I'd be surprised if they do.'

'And what happens when Seynac gets this stuff? What then?'

'Does it matter? I'd say we would be happy to let him pass it over to the other side. Of course, we'll cover him on a twenty-four-hour basis in order to trace his contacts with the Soviets because that will be useful anyway. But if we don't want scandals there's no reason for us to do anything about it.'

Wavre sat in silence, looking hard at Baum. He saw the twinkle in the intelligent eyes, the slightly cocked head, the trace of a smile, even, at the corners of the mouth.

'Risky,' he said.

'Not really, *patron*. But of course, I would be happy to consider any safer scheme you may have in mind. But don't forget, the initials on the copy of the minutes which leaked are GM/MI. Will you go in to our friend Guy Mallard and tell him that, or shall I? Investigating our own boss next door at the Interior on the Place Beauveau? And a man like Guy Mallard – bitterly hostile to most of his colleagues and puffed up with his own importance? Can you imagine him being either discreet or sensible?'

'Let me see what you've concocted, damn you,' Wavre said.

Baum handed him a folder. 'Perhaps you'd call me back when you've read it. You'll find the true and false texts side by side in there. I don't think we did too badly.'

Back in his room two floors down, he called on the intercom for the man who had been sent to find a witness at the scene of the accident in the Place Maubert. 'I want you in my office right away.'

The man stood and Baum did not ask him to sit down. 'Well?'

'I found two people from a café nearby who came out after the accident but by then the truck was speeding off down the Boulevard St Germain and they only saw the back of it. They didn't get the number. It was a Simca pick-up.'

'No one who saw the accident happen?'

'No, but my mate and I could go down there this evening and hang about at the same time. There must be regular weekday passers-by who saw something. We'll chat some people up, see what we can dig out, if you think it's worth it.'

'It is. Take three men with you. You'll need them. Tell the duty officer I said so.'

'*Oui, chef*.'

Baum's telephone rang and he picked it up. 'Reporting from the hospital.' It was the voice of Léon, the big man.

'Anything, Léon?'

'No. He's still unconscious. I just relieved my mate, who reported all quiet during the night.'

'Now listen carefully. I shall be sending someone over later today with an envelope for you. I want you to put it in the leather satchel that you'll find with Ferri's things in his room, right?'

'Yes, chief.'

'And this is important. It's the meat in the sandwich, *mon vieux*. Ferri may have a visitor today during the normal visiting hours. I want the visitor turned away. They are to say that the patient cannot be seen today because the doctor has ordered no visits, but that it can be arranged for the same time tomorrow. Got that?'

'Got it, chief.'

'And I want the visitor tailed when he leaves the hospital. If he becomes aware of the operation I shall fire everyone involved, starting with you, my friend. Is that understood?'

'Understood. But we'll need more than the four of us out here.'

'I'm sending another car. You are in charge. Dispose your forces sensibly around the hospital and have some of your men on foot as well. I don't need to teach you how to carry through this sort of thing, do I?'

'No, chief.'

'Good lad. And good luck. I'll buy you a beer if you pull if off. But remember this: I'd sooner lose our quarry than have him know we're after him, right?'

'Right, chief.'

Then Baum's intercom sounded and he went back to Georges Wavre's office two floors above.

'We'll do it,' Wavre said, handing over the folder. 'But it's on your head. I never saw this thing. Are you willing to go ahead on that basis?'

'I am.'

'You understand, I shall swear you exceeded your responsibilities. I shall not be able to support you, Alfred.'

'I understand, *patron*. I would say the same if I were sitting in that chair.'

Chapter 5

At 2.15 the blonde girl got off a bus and walked the 300 yards to the main entrance of the *Hôpital Beaujon*, paying careful attention to the cars parked along her route. She walked with a springing athletic stride and she carried her body as any young woman of her beauty would, but on the crowded pavement she was not specially noticeable: Paris was full of healthy, long-legged blondes in tight jeans and T-shirts.

Inside the lobby of the hospital she stopped at the enquiry desk. It was manned by two men in grey nylon work coats. 'I have come to visit a patient,' she said to the younger of the two.

'Name, please.'

'Guido Ferri.' She spelt it.

'And you are?'

'Adrienne Ferri. His sister.'

'Which ward?'

'I don't know.'

The man looked down a list. Then he looked up at the girl. His companion was searching for something in a drawer, failed to find it and started cursing to himself.

'Monsieur Ferri is in intensive care,' the younger man said. 'There's usually no visiting in there without special permission.'

'I'm his sister and I only just heard he was here. We've been very worried about him. Please can I see him?'

'I'll have to find another one of those damned stamps,' the older man said to his colleague. 'You carry on for me.' And he got up and walked across the lobby. Half way across he brought his right hand up to his ear and scratched it, and a man with a briefcase who had been waiting among the crowd in the lobby nodded almost imperceptibly and went out through the glass doors into the street.

'I'll try, Mademoiselle,' the younger man said, and picked up the internal phone.

'A young lady to see Monsieur Ferri,' he said. 'Yes, his sister. You can't? She says it's important. Oh, I see. Yes, I'll tell her.'

'I'm sorry,' he said to the blonde girl. 'There's no visiting in intensive care without the special permission of the doctor in charge of the case, and I'm afraid he isn't at the hospital today. The ward sister says she can speak to him in the morning and if you'd like to come back at the same time tomorrow, she thinks there won't be any objection. I'm sorry.'

'But isn't there another doctor who can give permission?' The girl was clearly annoyed. 'After all, it's just bureaucracy, isn't it? If they know I'll be allowed to see Guido tomorrow, why can't they be human and let me see him for a moment today?'

'I'm sorry, Mademoiselle,' the man said. 'I have no authority.' She was a terrific looker and he would have been glad to help. But rules were rules and he'd been given extra instructions on this particular case only that morning. He wondered why and was tempted to tell the girl as much – to make it clear that it wasn't his fault. Then the other man returned with his stamp – the man they'd put on the desk an hour ago – got him from God knows where – and the younger man thought better of it.

'I'm sorry,' he said again. 'I'm afraid you'll have to come back tomorrow. I'm sure they'll let you see your brother then. But the ward sister asked me to take your name and address as we have no record of next of kin.' He took a form and passed it to her. 'Perhaps you'd fill it in – there.'

The girl seemed nervous. Perhaps it was irritation at not being able to see her brother. He could understand it. She kept looking round the lobby as if she were searching for someone. Then she took a ballpoint from her bag and quickly scribbled a name and address on the form. She struck through 'telephone'.

'Thank you,' the young man behind the desk said. 'I'm sorry.'

The girl hesitated, as if she were about to make a fresh plea. Then she shrugged, turned on her heel and walked out through the glass doors. A closed van was parked outside the entrance, and as she appeared on the step a camera with motor drive, its lens pressed against a small hole in the van's side, was started up. It kept running until she was out of shot.

'Got her,' the operator said. 'Beautiful.'

'The shots?'

'The girl. Both.'

A man in blue overalls, carrying a tool bag, emerged from the hospital and turned left like the girl, walking some fifty yards behind her. On the opposite side of the street a cyclist mounted a bicycle and started cycling slowly down the street, keeping well behind the girl. Once she had reached the bus stop around the corner and it was clear that she did not have a car, two men got out of a car parked nearby and made their way to the bus stop, arguing rather noisily with each other about some business deal. The man in overalls also waited at the stop. All this looked quite natural among the early-afternoon crowds. No one looked at the girl.

A few moments later a 73 pulled up at the stop. The girl showed no interest. She must have come on a 192, the young man from the Nantes police said to himself. He was wearing the overalls, carrying the rather heavy bag and cursing the heat. But at the last moment, after the driver had closed the door the girl suddenly darted forward and banged at it. The driver would not have operated the opening mechanism for anyone but a good-looking girl, but this was a good-looking girl. The door opened. The girl climbed aboard. The young DST man from Nantes had to think faster than was his normal custom. If he climbed in after her now, would it not be obvious that he was tailing her? And hadn't he been told that under absolutely no circumstances should their quarry be alerted? 'Better lose 'em than let 'em know,' Léon had said. On the other hand, how would it look if he had to report sheepishly that at the very outset this slip of a girl had outsmarted him and got clean away? The other two – the ones who were talking business so seriously – hadn't a chance. It was him or no one.

'Hey,' he shouted to the driver, 'you don't go to the Boulevard de Clichy, do you? Or is that the 192?'

The driver signalled him with his head to get aboard. The young man climbed on as the bus moved away, confident that the girl had heard the exchange, which had sounded perfectly natural. He was proud of the way he had handled it and remained proud of himself for all of two minutes, until it dawned on him that if the girl got off the bus before the Boulevard de Clichy, he would somehow have to get off without being seen, whereas if she went past the Boulevard and he was still on the bus, she would guess why he was there. Clearly, she was smart. The ploy of getting on the bus at the last minute like that showed she knew how to look after herself. He had a sickening feeling of impending failure. But looking back he saw two of the DST cars following behind. If he lost her, one of the lads should be able to pick her up.

Two stops further on she got up from her seat and stood by the door. He was afraid she would suddenly get off, leaving him no time to follow her. In any case, if she alighted before the Boulevard de Clichy, wouldn't she know at once that he was tailing her? Of course she would! So he was helpless. He felt thoroughly miserable. Thank God the cars were still behind. They were taking it in turns to overtake the bus and then wait to be overtaken. They were talking to each other on a police wavelength.

'Leopard to Beaver, Leopard to Beaver. Your turn to overtake. Over.'

'Beaver to Leopard. I am overtaking now and will slow down three hundred metres ahead. Over.'

'Leopard to Beaver. Remember the drill. If she gets off the bus, Jacquot gets out of your car and Marc gets out of this one to carry on on foot. And I repeat: better lose her than let her know she's being tailed. Over.'

At the following stop the girl alighted briskly and crossed the road to the *Louis Blanc* Metro station, darting through the fast-moving traffic.

'Leopard to Beaver. Leopard to Beaver. She's off the bus. Crossing the road now. Looks as if she's heading for the Metro. Jacquot double back here. Marc is leaving me now. Remember the drill in the Metro. Over.'

The girl reached the entrance to the Metro in long strides without glancing around her and ran down the steps. The DST man, Marc, was a few feet behind and fumbled with his money at the ticket counter to give her a chance to choose a platform. She turned left onto the platform for the *Porte d'Italie* trains. A moment later he sauntered down the platform and stood near the edge. When the train drew in, she did what he had feared: nothing. She just sat on the bench, staring. He had no choice but to get onto the train. She was certainly a smart one, but Jacquot would see her when he reached the platform and with luck she'd take the next train.

Jacquot, a plump middle-aged man who was not built for chasing young women around Paris in a heat wave, reached the Metro station just as the *Porte d'Italie* train drew out. Having to choose a platform, he chose this one since its trains were heading into town and it seemed likely to him that she would go that way. When he got down onto the platform he saw the girl at the far end, still sitting on her bench. Marc was nowhere in sight and he realised that he was now on his own: she had shaken off everyone else. He did not feel good about it. She was more athletic than he was and he foresaw discomfort and trouble. But he had been lucky with the platform. His luck might hold.

He did as Marc had done – moved to the centre and waited. When the next train came in the girl got up from her seat and climbed aboard. Jacquot moved down the platform and got into the carriage next to hers. He stood by the door and prayed for a little more luck.

The next stop was *Château Landon*. The doors opened. The girl did not move. He could see the back of her head as she sat in a seat facing forward. The following stop would be the *Gare de l'Est*. There would be a great crush of people getting aboard from the main line station. It would be the worst possible place for her to alight. He could lose her within seconds in a crowd like that. Hell, if only he had a back-up man. Maybe Marc was somewhere ahead of him and they'd make contact again at the *Gare de l'Est*. Then again, the girl might not get out there at all. But the train would be crowded and things could only get more difficult.

As the train came to a stop at the *Gare de l'Est*, the girl got up quickly from her seat, opened the door and darted out onto the platform. Then she sprinted the few yards to the exit, raced up the steps two at a time and made for the tunnel leading to the main line station. Panting and desperate now, Jacquot lumbered after her along the ill-lit and deserted tunnel. But soon there was a bend, and shortly afterwards, two alternative flights of steps into the station concourse. By the time he was round the bend she had chosen a flight and was out of sight. He could only choose one at random and pray that he'd hit the jackpot this time too. Damn Marc, where the hell was he?

Maybe he'd chosen the wrong one, or perhaps she had simply been swallowed up in the crowd. At all events, five minutes later Jacquot confessed himself beaten and gave up the chase. The little bitch had got clean away, made fools of all of them. He set off miserably to find a phone.

Meanwhile, the girl had emerged from the station, crossed the Place and was walking at a measured pace down the Faubourg St Denis, stopping occasionally to look in a shop window, when she would glance back along her route before continuing on her way. At the Passage St Denis, she looked back for the last time, and once round the corner, covered the remaining few yards to the drycleaning shop at a run.

She paused for a moment in the shop to regain her breath. She knew the importance of always appearing calm before the others. Morale was important – one of the three important things in the underground: first ideology, second morale, third technique. The claustrophobia got on people's nerves. Being together nearly all the time with the same people, taking risks almost daily, keeping the nerves stretched to snapping point – all this made for irritability, personal rivalry, paranoia even. Often nauseating fear.

The leadership had to set an example. Always calm. Always objective. Personal feelings submerged for the sake of the cause. Putting up with impossible comrades, often. Comrades with limited understanding, like Jean-Paul. She thought him unreliable, immature, undisciplined. Something would have to be done about it soon.

She had regained her composure now, and taking her key from her bag, she opened the door and let herself into the back room.

'Well,' Serge said. 'How did it go? Did you see him?'

She shook her head. 'No problems, but I can't see him till tomorrow. He's in intensive care.'

'Will he pull through?'

'I don't know. I expect the doctor will tell me tomorrow.'

'Christ, fancy getting himself clobbered on a job like that,' Jean-Paul said. 'Putting the whole damn operation at risk.'

'I'm surprised,' Serge said. 'He was a very careful rider. I never knew him to take risks. That's why we sent him, after all.'

The girl shrugged. 'Anyway, I shall go back tomorrow afternoon to check on whether the envelope is there. As far as we can tell, they aren't wise to it. I took care on the return journey but no one was after me.' She looked at her watch. 'Now I must go. I'd better change.'

She went to a cupboard and took out a pale yellow blouse, a brown skirt and high-heeled shoes. Then she opened a low chest next to the cupboard. It was full of wigs. She selected a dark, shoulder-length one. Ignoring the three men, she slipped off her T-shirt and slacks. She wore the skimpiest of briefs and no bra. Jean-Paul's eyes were on her. The others looked away. Jean-Paul was telling himself that she was a cock-teasing bitch who treated men as if they didn't exist. One of these days . . .

Soon she was dressed. She pulled the wig over her short blonde hair, adjusting it in a mirror hanging on the wall. She applied eye make-up and lipstick. The transformation was complete. Then she transferred the contents of the old leather bag to a smart bag in black patent leather. The small revolver made the smaller bag bulge but she managed to close it.

'I'm off,' she said. 'Is everything in order for tonight?'

The three men nodded.

'I shall be at Command headquarters,' she said. 'We have these two operations in Paris tonight and there's more in the provinces. Good luck!' And she went out through the shop, nodding to the man in the white coat as she went past.

The events of that evening, Monday 10 August, were as follows.

Just before 9.30 p.m. a good-looking, youngish woman, wearing dark glasses and trendily dressed to match this affectation, presented herself at the reception desk in the National Radio and Television Centre in the Place Clément Ader and asked for Paul Morhange, the TV newscaster. Morhange was not in his room and she asked for him to be paged. She was told to wait and sat in the row of divan chairs along one wall of the lobby. She was carrying a handbag and a briefcase of the attaché-case type.

After a few moments, the receptionist signalled to her to come back to the desk and she did so, leaving her attaché case at the side of her chair. In this position it was out of sight of anyone who was not sitting down.

'Monsieur Morhange is not in the building.'

'Thank you. I'll contact him at home.'

The woman walked out of the building and round the corner into the Rue Raynouard where she climbed into a car, removed her dark glasses and drove away in the direction of the city.

Shortly after 10 p.m. a cleaner doing his regular rounds of the building's public spaces came across the briefcase and carried it over to the receptionist.

'Looks as if some fool's left his briefcase. Will you lock it up, Jeannine?'

The receptionist said 'damn' and held out her hand for it. It seemed surprisingly heavy.

'Must be full of books.'

'I expect so.'

'Unless it's –'

At that moment the minute hand of the clock mechanism stowed inside the briefcase reached its appointed place, completing the simple electrical circuit, thus activating the detonator. The charge of explosive in its metal casing did its work. The receptionist and the cleaner were killed instantly, quite literally blown to pieces. There was no one else in the lobby, but four passers-by were slashed by the shards of flying glass from the glass wall surrounding the building at street level. The lights went out in the lobby, which had been completely devastated.

Just after 10.15 a Volkswagen Polo drew up outside No. 18 Rue Jasmin and parked across the drive-in entrance, ignoring the official *no parking* sign on the building. The two men in the Polo remained in their seats. Neither spoke. They were about ten minutes' drive from the Television Centre and the wail of sirens could be heard in the distance as police cars and fire tenders raced to the Place Clément Ader.

At 10.28 a car came up the Rue Jasmin, intending to turn into the courtyard of No. 18. Finding the way blocked, the driver stopped and flashed his lights. The Polo did not move. Impatiently, the driver gave a quick blast on his horn. Getting no response, he climbed out, leaving his engine running, and walked round the front of his car and towards the Polo, lying slightly ahead of him. As he did so, Serge poked the snout of the Kalashnikov automatic through the open window and directed a short burst at the man in the road, aiming chest-high and then at the head. As the man fell, the Polo drove away at full speed.

'Got the bastard,' Serge said. He was smiling in the dark as Victor took the car rapidly down the street and round two blocks. 'I enjoyed that.' He was trembling slightly and his bowels were giving him their usual trouble after an action. He hoped he wouldn't shit himself again this time and tried to wrench his mind onto some soporific topic. It did not work.

In the Rue Bazin, two streets away, the Polo stopped and the two men got out with the Kalashnikovs wrapped in pieces of cloth under their arms, entered a Renault which had been left unlocked, and drove off in the direction of the river. It was just after 10.30. With two bullets through his lungs, one lodged in the thorax and one in his head, the man in the Rue Jasmin died a few moments later as neighbours hurried out to see what the commotion had been about.

During the further course of the evening there were bomb explosions in Brest and Douai. In the explosion at Brest, in an expensive restaurant frequented by the bourgeois families of the town, fourteen people were killed or injured. It was the first incident in Brittany since the bombings had started four months before.

Soon after midnight the President of the Republic phoned the Prefect of Police at his home. He was not in a mood to observe the niceties and go through either the Prime Minister or Guy Mallard.

'Have you heard the news?' he asked. He did not feel the need to start with a greeting.

The Prefect had been out all evening with his socially ambitious wife and had only just come home. The duty officer at the *Préfecture* had been trying to get him ever since 10.30 and was dialling his number again when the President came through.

'No, *Monsieur le Président*. What news?'

'A bomb at the Television Centre and Aristide Laborde shot down, and you ask what news.'

'My God! I was out. I've just come in and was about to phone the –'

'Never mind any of that,' the President said. 'I want you here at the Elysée right away. What I shall want to know is why we are unable to protect the citizens of Paris from these maniacs.'

'Of course. I am coming at once.'

The Prefect turned to his wife. 'The President,' he said.

'That bloody ape is on the warpath. There've been more incidents.'

He called the duty officer, obtained a brief report on what had happened, and went down to his car.

The President had meanwhile called the Prime Minister, who had now joined him, finding him in a brutal mood. Convinced that he had in the Minister of the Interior and the Prefect of Police two incompetents, if not worse, he was determined to start fixing responsibilities. This would be for the record. It might also help to effect a little progress against the organisations which were plunging the country into fear and instability.

The attacks were all on 'establishment' targets – employers' organisations, banks, smart nightclubs, the TV Centre, police stations, even the expensive hairdressing salon where his wife usually went. True, this night's assassination of a leading Communist broke the pattern, but pattern there undoubtedly was. It was likely to mean that the extreme Left, with its contempt for anything that might come out of the polls, had fallen back on the politics of physical confrontation favoured by the Italian and West German lunatic fringe. And what worried the President was not that such isolated gangs of youngsters with too much undigested ideology in their heads could succeed, but that they would provoke the classic reaction: a swing to the Right, to the law and order generals, policemen and Catholic authoritarians who were never far from the surface of politics in France.

The President was a genuine enough republican – as ambitious and possibly as venal as the next politician, but a patriotic Frenchman and republican all the same. He had demonstrated as much in his youth under the Nazi occupation. He was not going to allow the country to fall into the hands of the maniacal Left or the maniacal Right. It was to stay with the blundering, dubious but reasonably civilised Centre, where it belonged. But nothing, absolutely nothing, had been achieved so far against the bombers.

In Vallat's office the Prefect of Police joined the others: the Minister of the Interior, the Mayor of Paris and the

Minister of Information. No one said anything. They were like guilty youths about to get a ticking-off from their headmaster.

'We may now go in to the President, gentlemen,' Vallat said, and led the way into the next room, where chairs had been set round a table. The Prime Minister was already sitting in one of them, next to the President, studying some papers. He did not look up. It was as if he felt ashamed of his presence there. For whose side was he on? It was a question repeatedly posed by the ramshackle French Constitution.

'I don't suppose it will be any use asking the Prefect to give us a report,' the President said sourly, 'since I understand he was out this evening and knew nothing of these latest outrages until I told him myself on the telephone.'

It was unjust but the Prefect felt it unwise to say so.

'Perhaps you, Mallard, as Minister of the Interior, are briefed on the events of the evening?'

Guy Mallard was not briefed. He had heard two news bulletins, tried unsuccessfully to contact the Prefect on the telephone, failed also to find the Director of Radio and Television, and decided that it would have to wait until morning. The President's call had interrupted a game of chess with a friend. He had presumed that the Prefect was getting himself into the act. The presumption had clearly been wrong.

'I am not briefed,' he said, 'I was busy all evening.'

'So was I,' the President said, 'but I will now tell you gentlemen what you should have been in a position to tell me.'

He then referred to notes which the tireless Vallat had put together by phoning the *Préfecture*, the headquarters of the Paris Fire Brigade and the head of the news department of the television service.

'The bomb at the TV Centre killed two and injured four. Some ten minutes later, Aristide Laborde was shot down outside his home nearby and the assassins got away without being seen by anyone. What appears to be their car was found two streets away and so far has yielded nothing in the way of clues. So I am informed, Prefect, by your department, though one may well have reservations about its competence in the matter.

'It seems clear to me that the two incidents are connected, since a bomb explosion ten minutes before a carefully planned assassination would be a good way of immobilising the local police and thus improving the chances of a successful getaway. And so it has proved.'

He looked round the table and there was a long silence.

'I will not discuss here what is happening in the rest of the country beyond expressing my conviction that the concerted nature of these outrages bespeaks a carefully orchestrated and politically sophisticated campaign. But that is a matter for the Government as a whole. Here and now I am concerned only with the capital city, which has become an unsafe area in which to live, gentlemen – an intolerable situation!'

The President brought a heavy fist down on the table and treated the others to the scowl which he had long since made famous, both in committee and on television.

'It is a total and absolute police failure,' he said. 'It is also a total failure on the part of the Ministry of the Interior and thus has serious political consequences for the Government.'

Since the Government had been mentioned, the Prime Minister felt impelled to contribute to the proceedings. Having been pulled from relative obscurity into the prime ministerial chair by the President of the Republic on the understanding that he would be the President's man without an independent thought of his own, he was anxious now to reflect the President's thinking. But he was equally anxious to preserve a semblance of calm and civilised discourse within his Cabinet. It was not an easy feat and he had met with only moderate success in attempting it in the past. He looked forward to the end of the Government's life, three months hence, with something approaching relief. But meanwhile life must go on.

'It is difficult, my dear colleagues,' he said, 'to quarrel with the President's assessment of the situation. If I myself had not been entertaining the President of Gabon this evening I would have made it my business to intervene in these matters. However . . .'

No one deemed it expedient to say anything, and the President appeared not to be interested in the Prime Minister's alibi. He resumed his monologue.

'I am not fool enough to believe that anything useful can be done in a meeting of this kind, in the middle of the night, without adequate information or preparation. But the Prime Minister and I sent for you now because I propose to call a meeting tomorrow morning at nine and I want you all in my office at that time with clear and comprehensive proposals on how to galvanise our counter-measures, which so far have been pathetic. Have they not, Prefect?'

'I would hardly say that, *Monsieur le Président.*' The Prefect was acutely unhappy.

'Oh, then I must be misinformed,' the President said. 'You must tell me, how many arrests have we made?'

'Several, but they were abortive, I am afraid.'

'And that is not pathetic?'

The Prefect of Police shrugged. 'I will give a full report in the morning,' he said.

'I shall also want reports on what we are doing about public morale,' the President said.

The Minister of Information and the Mayor nodded. The Prime Minister was also nodding and made a show of taking a note, as if his memory might fail him overnight. The Minister of the Interior said nothing and did not allow his head to move in unison with the others. Dirt was flying. Movements of any kind might attract some of it.

'And I shall want to know what precautionary measures we have taken to protect the more obvious targets, though I must confess that I would not have regarded Aristide Laborde as a likely risk.'

The others nodded again and the President got up and marched out of the room, leaving the Prime Minister to the mercy of his associates.

'*Voilà, Messieurs,*' Vallat said, '*et à demain.*'

Chapter 6

The Ministers were in conference at nine the following morning. At 13 Rue des Saussaies, Baum was with his Director. Whereas the President was still in a dangerous mood, Georges Wavre's mood could best be described as an unhappy blend of apprehension and misgivings: misgivings about Baum's eccentric methods and apprehension about the result of allowing him to apply them. But Alfred Baum, perched on the edge of one of Wavre's uncomfortable chairs and clutching a file of papers, seemed the very embodiment of confidence and good nature.

'It is all too complicated, too risky. I do not like complex solutions,' Wavre was saying. 'I have always found, Alfred, that the simplest lines of enquiry lead to the speediest results. Tried and trusted stuff – the archives, interrogation . . .'

'I agree entirely,' Baum said. 'But once we had abandoned the possibility of interviewing the Defence Committee members – quite rightly, in my view – we abandoned any possibility of following a simple route. And so we are thrown back on mystification. And I know how distressing you find that.'

He chuckled and shook his head, as if to say Wavre had to be humoured in his neurotic objection to roundabout methods.

'So where are we, Alfred?'

'The envelope and the young man's effects have been put in place at the hospital,' Baum said. 'We now have a good photographic record of the woman who called to see him, claiming to be his sister and giving a false address. My men lost her after her visit yesterday, but today we will be making far more elaborate arrangements and she won't slip through the net. Yesterday was a very useful dry run.'

'What if she does?'

Baum brushed the question aside. He had concocted a plan to deal with such an eventuality which he was not disposed to reveal to the Director at this stage. When you were embarked on a course of action which struck fear into the breast of your boss, and something resembling it into your own, you didn't throw the whole thing at him in one go. No, you revealed it in consecutive layers, like peeling the proverbial onion, and he had peeled enough layers for one day.

'Leave it to me, *patron*,' he said. 'The way I have it staked out, she shouldn't slip through.'

Wavre shrugged. 'What else?'

'I've had a report this morning from one of my men who has been trying to find witnesses to the accident. He went back to the Place Maubert last night with some mates and they managed to find a passer-by who had seen the thing. This person sounded perfectly sensible and said a curious thing. He claims he saw the truck hit the motorcyclist and would swear it was deliberate. He refused to make a statement, mind. Felt he couldn't get up and swear it in court. But he was sure. So we're still looking for corroboration and meanwhile I'm storing that odd fact at the back of my mind.'

Hamster-like, he looked as if he were storing it like a cache of nuts.

'I have had that man Vallat on the telephone,' Wavre said. 'On behalf of the President. Had we made any progress? I said yes, we had. Was there anything we could tell them? No, there wasn't. So when would we be able to make a report? Soon, I said. Very soon. I could feel him bristle at the other end of the line, passing on the President's extreme impatience and irritability like a semaphore. We have to keep moving, Alfred.'

'I know, I know. And this will be a day of action.'

The President's meeting was edgy and inconclusive. The Prefect of Police reported on the twenty-seven incidents to date in the capital and confirmed the view that they bore the hallmark of an extreme Left organisation of the Baader-Meinhof type. Only half a dozen incidents had been 'claimed' by underground groups and none of the groups were known to the police. There were unfortunately no leads so far. It was admittedly frustrating but he had confidence in the Bomb Squad, to which he had seconded a number of reliable inspectors and the entire resources of the *Préfecture*'s forensic department.

Asked about the explosive devices, he said that they appeared, from the fragments examined, to be artisan-made, probably in a small workshop. There was no evidence of imported products, though the possibility could not be excluded. It was known that there were suppliers of terrorist bombing equipment in Holland, Switzerland and, of course, the Middle East. It wasn't difficult to buy, though it would be costly, particularly explosives and guns. Unless, of course, they were stolen. Only there were no reports of thefts from quarries, gun shops and the like. Also, he found it curious that there had been no bank raids or major robberies associated with the bombing campaign. Usually in such campaigns, banks were robbed first to get the cash to buy the devices and maintain the gang while they were on the run. But it was not so in this case. Finance must be coming from elsewhere.

'Where?'

The Prefect shrugged. 'Libya . . . China . . .'

'Are you saying this is a matter for the DST – foreign intervention on our soil?'

The Prefect, ever jealous of the prerogatives of his department, saw his error.

'No, *Monsieur le Président*. I was speculating. You may be sure I will call on Georges Wavre if need be.'

The President said nothing and made a note on the pad before him.

Also, the Prefect of Police continued, the technical level was unusually high. In terror campaigns in other countries, such as Italy and Germany, there had always been a significant number of aborted incidents: bombs failing to go off or going off too soon. Here again, the French experience was different. Nothing of the kind had happened yet. They must have first-class explosives experts and remarkable discipline. It all smelled of Iraqi or Libyan training, the Prefect added, continuing his tour of the world's trouble spots.

The Minister of the Interior interrupted the Prefect's speculations. 'And that anarchist group? Do your people still say it comes from them?'

The Prefect shrugged. 'We had two suspects after our last raid but we had to let them go for lack of any direct evidence. *Politically*, it is my view that the anarchists or Maoists are responsible. This is evident from the nature of the bombing targets. Also, every time we mount police raids on these groups, we get peace and quiet for a couple of weeks. Furthermore, some fifteen known Left extremists have gone underground in the past three months.'

'Couldn't that be because the police keep raiding them?'

'It could, but I choose to view it in a more sinister light.'

'I cannot interest myself in these police speculations,' the President said. 'I am interested in arrests based on credible evidence. The *Préfecture* seems to specialise in arrests based on probabilities. Let us hear what steps you propose to take next.'

The Prefect moved on to outline his plan of action. It amounted to putting more men on the hunt. He had already given the necessary orders. He was certain the police would get a lucky break soon. A new appeal would be made to the citizens of Paris to be on their guard and report anything suspicious that they might see. It would go out on radio and television today and posters would be available by the end of the week. And security measures would be stepped up in all public buildings.

'A degree of energy on the part of the *Préfecture*,' the President said tartly, 'which would have done them credit three months ago but now simply testifies to their lack of resolution, coming so late and only in response to my own intervention.'

Again it was unjust and again the Prefect decided to say nothing.

The Prefect's plan of action was approved and decisions were taken in the area of public morale. They were needed: the press was now in full cry, led by the extreme Right, who saw the bombings as a useful club with which to beat the Left and Centre; and by the Communists, who felt the urgent need to distance themselves in the public mind from the antics of the splinter groups lying far to their own Left. This they found troublesome enough. But now they had lost Aristide Laborde, General Secretary of the Party, and they were mystified as to the motive for the killing.

Meeting at about the same time that morning, the party's *Bureau Politique* agreed on a valedictory statement on their dead comrade, which was immediately issued to the press, together with a political appreciation describing the assassination as a provocation by the forces of reaction who were seeking to disrupt the parliamentary majority and were hoping to weaken the party of the toiling masses. They were careful not to pin the blame on either the far Left or the Right for the sufficient reason that they had no idea from which end of the political spectrum the machine gun had been fired. 'Objectively,' a member of the *Bureau Politique* had said, 'it is the same thing, since both do the work of the imperialists.'

The meeting then made arrangements to call the party's Central Committee together on the following weekend to elect a new General Secretary and by lunchtime they had decided who that was to be.

Alfred Baum had achieved, in the past twenty-four hours, the remarkable feat of obtaining the services of no less than forty-five men and women of the DST and the police, together with a dozen assorted vehicles. These were now deployed with meticulous care and such attention to detail that Léon was heard to declare that the *chef* was slipping: he'd forgotten the flaming helicopter.

A command post was to be set up in a Posts and Telegraph van which would be parked outside the hospital and would be in radio touch with the tailing network. Two men would be on the listening tables in the van and Baum decided to take charge himself. If the girl again took a bus the essential thing was to have personnel already on the bus before she boarded it. And of course, she could take either a 73 or a 192, and in either direction. The plan, therefore, was to have an adequate number of police personnel waiting at the previous stops in either direction, in touch by radio so that they could be instructed to board any buses that came by as soon as the girl was seen to leave the hospital.

On the other hand, she might travel by car this time, and difficult as it was to follow a car successfully through the Paris traffic, Baum was confident that his men could do it. They certainly had enough vehicles to be deployed round the hospital.

All the men and women on the operation had been issued with good pictures of the girl, taken from the previous day's shoot. Baum briefed them at the end of the morning and was satisfied that nothing more could be done to ensure success. 'You will not allow a young girl to give the slip to forty-five operatives of the security services, equipped with the latest radio devices and all the vehicles it is possible to deploy,' he said. He hoped it was true.

At 1.30 p.m. he arrived at the hospital in a DST car and climbed into the Posts and Telegraph van, which had been there since the morning. Everyone else was in position.

'Everything in order?' Baum asked the men in the van.

'*Oui, chef.*'

They were testing their radio links with the cars, two of which were at the bus stops to provide liaison with those who were to get on the buses. A smaller van was outside the hospital entrance, placed to take more pictures. Inside the hospital, Léon had donned a grey work coat again and had taken his place as a temporary receptionist. Baum had made, via the hospital administrator, the necessary arrangements with the medical staff. The youth was still unconscious, linked to the life-support machines in a side ward. His possessions were in a cupboard next to his bed, the envelope safely in the leather satchel.

At twenty minutes past two a red Renault 5 driven by a young man wearing dark glasses stopped outside the hospital entrance. The blonde girl alighted, dressed as she had been the previous day. The car drove on a few yards and parked in a space that the police had contrived to keep free for just such an eventuality. The number of the Renault was noted.

The girl ran up the steps and through the glass doors of the hospital. At the desk she asked for Guido Ferri. 'I was told to come back today,' she said to the young receptionist who had been so taken with her the day before. 'I am his sister. The doctor should have given permission for me to see him.'

'A moment, please.'

The receptionist telephoned the ward. 'It's all right, Mademoiselle, you can go up to intensive care on the fourth floor.' He tried a smile but she ignored it. 'A smasher, but sullen,' he said to himself.

On the fourth, she followed the signs to intensive care and presented herself at the desk.

'I am Mr Ferri's sister. May I see him?'

'Ah, Mademoiselle Ferri,' the ward sister said. 'I'm sorry we couldn't let you see your brother yesterday. I'm afraid he is still unconscious. It was a very severe trauma to the skull. He will not know you are here, of course.'

'I know,' the girl said. 'I won't stay long with him. Where is it?'

The sister thought she didn't seem all that distressed, but then some people hid their feelings. As they walked along the corridor she said: 'The doctor knows you are here. He will come to talk to you.'

'Yes.'

The sister opened the door of the side ward. The girl went in and the sister closed it solicitously behind her. The young man was lying on his back, tubes entering his body at various points, bags of saline solution and urine suspended, flex linked to monitoring devices. His heartbeats travelled in green waves across a TV display. The girl glanced at his face and then at the complex support apparatus. Then she went to the cupboard, which was the only item of furniture in the room apart from the bed and an upright chair. Inside she found what she was looking for and quickly transferred the envelope to her handbag. As she did so, the door opened and the doctor came in.

'I was checking his things,' she said, unruffled.

The doctor explained how serious her brother's injury was and how the heart could fail at any time. She was welcome to phone for news whenever she liked. If he was to pull through, they had no idea when he might regain consciousness. The outlook was uncertain. Expecting to have to deal with distress, possibly tears, he was surprised at this girl's composure. She hardly seemed to be listening to him. A cold fish. Or perhaps she was stunned, in shock.

'I would like to stay a few moments more,' she said.

'I understand,' the doctor said. 'I will leave you. You will not touch anything, of course.'

'No.'

The doctor left the room. The girl took a small plastic bag from her handbag, approached the bed and pressed it to the youth's face, covering his mouth and nostrils and pressing it round the tube. Then she took a towel from the handbasin and put it on top of the bag. She went to the foot of the bed, where she could see the TV screen. In less than half a minute the green lines had stopped moving.

She replaced the towel by the basin, removed the plastic bag and stuffed it into her handbag and quickly left the room. As she passed the ward sister in the corridor she did not turn to thank her or say goodbye. The staff nurse at the monitoring desk was taking a coffee with a friend and did not look at the screen linked to side ward three until two minutes later. Then she rushed along the corridor, calling to the ward sister.

Meanwhile, the girl had descended in the lift, holding her shoulder bag firmly against her hip and looking straight ahead.

As she stepped out of the lift on the ground floor, Léon's left hand went up and pulled at his ear and a workman waiting in the lobby walked out of the door. As he appeared on the step, two cars parked nearby started up their engines.

'She is about to come out of the hospital,' Baum said into a chest mike. All the cars were tuned in to the van's wavelength. 'Her car is still parked with the driver at the wheel. Alert everyone, please. This is it.'

As the blonde girl appeared at the top of the steps, still holding her shoulder bag, a camera in the smaller van was taking pictures.

'She is coming down the steps, turning right in the direction of the parked car, which she has just seen. It's about ten metres away from her.'

The girl walked fast towards the car and as she approached it the driver leaned over and opened the passenger door for her. She got in and closed the door, and the car pulled away from the kerb.

'They're on their way,' Baum said. 'Travelling down the Rue Dutin. At the end they'll have to turn right to follow the one-way system, but Leopard watch out in case they get worried and make a break to the left. Beaver pull out and follow behind, keeping eighty metres distance. Over.'

'Beaver to control. I heard you, chief. Over.'

'Control to Zebra. They will be passing you about now. Give them fifty metres and fall in behind. Over.'

'Zebra to contol. They are passing me now. Will do. Over.'

At this point the red Renault 5 reached the end of the Rue Dutin, turned right in an orderly fashion and was lost to Baum's view. The steady voice of the man in Zebra came over the loudspeaker in the van.

'Zebra to control. They turned right again into the main road. The traffic's heavy and we'll keep in touch, but Fox should watch for them. Over.'

'Control to Fox. A red Renault 5, man driving, woman passenger, will be level with you at any moment. Pick them up. Over.'

'Fox to control. Can see it in my mirror, coming up pretty fast. We're ready to go . . . They're level now and we're pulling out immediately because the traffic's rotten . . . They're a couple of cars ahead, heading south. You'd better notify whoever's ahead of us. We can't carry this one on our own. Over.'

'Control to Bison. Red Renault 5, male driver, woman passenger, coming towards you. Fox is behind them. You fall in as well. Over.'

At this point the red Renault did an unexpected thing. Instead of maintaining speed, it fell in behind a 73 bus and as the bus slowed down at a stop, the car stopped behind it, deliberately blocked in. A moment later, the girl was out of the car and into the bus just before the automatic doors were closed.

'Fox to control. The woman's transferred to a 73 bus travelling south. Do we follow her or the car? Over.'

'Control to Fox. Damn! Follow the bus.'

Baum instructed Bison and three other cars parked along the route to do the same. There was no hope of picking up the red Renault, which had turned left across the oncoming traffic and was speeding down a side road. The girl seemed to be keeping to the same route as yesterday, though it didn't follow that she would get off the bus at the same spot and take the Metro. Clearly, she had some training in taking evasive action. Now the trouble was that despite their careful preparations, they had no one on the bus itself.

Baum had an idea, cursing himself for not thinking of it sooner. 'Control to Beaver. You will break off and go at once to the Metro station at the *Gare de l'Est*. I want Maurice to take up a position where you know we lost the girl yesterday: in the tunnel leading to the main line station. She may just follow the same route on the principle that we'd never expect her to. Over.'

'Beaver to Control. We're off. Over.'

The girl must surely reckon that the bus could be followed. But if the lads had worked properly she had no evidence that they were tailing her at all: everything she had done so far had been precautionary, that was all. Wasn't his imagination getting just a shade overheated? After all, as far as she knew, no one had the faintest idea of the contents of the envelope. It wasn't likely to occur to her that the thing was now a DST plant. From where she viewed the situation, the likely thing if the police were on the alert was for them to have arrested her at the hospital. At least they'd have queried the false address she'd given. And what about the courier's false identity card? They'd have asked her about that too. No, the girl was simply following routine evasive action. And the men had their instructions perfectly clear: if she gets wise to you, arrest her. Whatever you do, don't let her get away.

But it looked as if the girl wasn't keeping it up. Few people did. Even KGB-trained operatives would get sloppy in their evasive action. It happened repeatedly. Most arrests could be traced back to poor tradecraft. And now this girl was actually repeating what she had done yesterday.

'Beaver to Control. The bus has stopped opposite the *Louis Blanc* Metro station. We are in the traffic just behind . . . She's out of the bus . . . crossing the road and down the stairs of the Metro. Over.'

'Control to all cars near *Louis Blanc*. Follow the plan and be careful. Over.'

A man each from Beaver and Fox managed to reach the Metro twenty seconds after the girl had disappeared down the stairs. They were armed with tickets and they knew she was expected to take a *Porte d'Italie* train. But in case she went the other way this time, one man peeled off to the opposite platform.

The man heading for the *Porte d'Italie* platform happened to be of much the same build as Léon: on the plump side and with bad feet. He could hurry but he couldn't run down three flights of steps. He did his best, but as he arrived on the platform the tail lights of a train were receding into the tunnel and the girl was nowhere to be seen. The DST man had an immediate vision of being reduced to the ranks, in the regular police, in uniform, on the beat, and somewhere in the distant provinces. He nearly wept. Not knowing that Baum had had the foresight to send a man direct to the *Gare de l'Est*, he was convinced that the girl had got away – a bloody little blonde, outsmarting the lot of them. He couldn't believe it. He felt sick.

He signalled across the tracks to his colleague from Fox to

go back to the car to give the news. Then he waited for the next train and took it as far as the *Gare de l'Est*. He did this for no clear reason. But in these things you never knew. By some miraculous fluke he might pick her up again and rehabilitate himself, stay out of uniform, out of the provinces . . .

Meanwhile, the girl was travelling in the first carriage of the earlier train past the *Château Landon* station, then on to the *Gare de l'Est*. Here she alighted, as she had on the previous day, mounted the steps two at a time and turned left into the long tunnel towards the main line station. The tunnel was deserted. The few people who had alighted from the Metro train were going towards the exit to the street.

The girl glanced back as she approached the bend. There was no one behind her. Everything looked satisfactory. It had been an easy exercise, just as she'd told the others it would be. Not an exercise she would have entrusted to anyone else. But carrying it through successfully like this would be good for morale. Do the hard ones yourself. Constantly show them that you are better, more audacious than the others. So they had taught her at the training camp in the Harz mountains. Set an example, they'd said. Always set an example, lead from in front. We may lose some precious people that way, but every time that happens, a half dozen others are steeled for the struggle. Politically – statistically even – it was sound. So had they taught her. She knew it was good doctrine.

As she turned the bend in the tunnel she saw ahead of her a man standing against the wall. He seemed to be waiting for someone. Just at the foot of the two stairways. It did not smell right. He looked like a cop. The cheap dark suit in this sticky weather, the heavy shoes, the institutional haircut. He had the *face* of a cop. Suddenly, it struck her. She may just have shaken them off at this spot yesterday. After all, it was a likely place: getting round that bend ahead of whoever was following her, and then taking one flight of steps instead of another into the mass of people in the station concourse.

But maybe this young man was not here for her at all,

even if he was a cop. But on the other hand, what if it was for her? And what if, instead of following her into that mass of humanity up there, he had instructions to arrest her? In the fifteen yards or so separating the bend from the spot where he stood, she made up her mind. As she walked towards him she reached into her bag, opened it, seemed to be looking for something. She went up to him.

'Do you have a light?'

The DST man, Maurice, put his hand in his jacket pocket and was withdrawing it, holding a lighter, as the girl's hand came out of the bag, holding the small gun with its projecting silencer. The tunnel was still deserted. She brought it up to his head as if it were the most natural gesture in the world and fired twice, aiming between his eyes. The *phuttts* of the silenced gun were inaudible in the general noise from the station above. As a look of pure astonishment gripped Maurice's face and the holes made by the bullets began to ooze dark blood, his knees sagged and he slumped slowly to the dirty floor. The girl was up the nearest stairs and away into the crowd before his body had come to rest.

The heavy man who had followed in the next train reached the scene of the killing just as a small crowd had gathered. 'Make way, police,' he said. When he recognised the man on the ground his stomach heaved and in sheer misery and frustration he burst into tears.

Once again, the girl walked calmly down the Faubourg St Denis and into the Passage, covering the final few yards quickly.

'How did it go?' the man in the grubby white coat asked her.

'All right,' she said. 'Is Serge back?' She looked unconcerned but her knuckles were white as she clutched needlessly on her shoulder bag.

'Just got here.'

'Did he get rid of the car?'

The man nodded.

'Good. I have to change quickly and go out again to

deliver something to Command. I shall leave my gun here. I want you to lose it tonight for certain. Right?'

'If you say so.'

She went into the back room where Serge was waiting for her.

'I told you,' she said. 'No problems. But I had to deal with a fucking cop. Just in case. On reflection, I doubt whether he was there for me at all, but one has to be sure. I'll need a new gun. See to it: you know what I like.'

Then she went into the foul-smelling toilet that adjoined the hideaway and vomited repeatedly into the basin.

Chapter 7

The *Port de Javel* lies along the left bank of the Seine on the western side of Paris, linking the Garigliano, Mirabeau and Grenelle bridges. At one time it had had its importance as a port for the big barges which took merchandise off the ocean-going steamers at Rouen and laboured up the Seine to the capital. Nowadays it is nothing more significant than a series of riverside facilities for handling mainly builders' supplies – sand, aggregate, paving stones and the like. There are some modest warehouses, low-tonnage cranes and a customs shed. Few barges use the *Port de Javel* and part of the frontage has been taken up by berths for an odd assortment of craft. There is a *bateau-lavoir*, where washing is still done but is unlikely to be done much longer, and a jetty for occasional craft plying this part of the river. Maybe a couple of dozen houseboats, converted barges and similar craft are permanently moored here, some of them serving as living quarters for people who through lack of money or excess of romantic longings continue to live on the water. There is some life in the place on weekdays, when barges are being unloaded and trucks pull alongside to take the cargoes. At weekends and at night it is deserted, save for an occasional boat-dweller.

The blonde girl, now once more a smart brunette who could be anyone's favourite secretary, took the Metro at *Strasbourg-St Denis*, changed twice and alighted at *Javel*. It was just after 5.30 p.m. and the rush hour had started. Steadily growing crowds were pushing into the Metro station and she had to elbow her way up the steps onto the Place. She descended to the river level by the steps at the side of the Mirabeau bridge, walking slowly and stopping from time to time to look behind her. Workmen from the port were coming up the steps and a couple of them whistled at her and made a joke. She paid no attention. At the foot of the steps she turned left, walked fifty yards along the river's edge and turned on her heel and walked back the way she had come. Her tail was clean, she decided. Then she followed the river for a few minutes until she came to a converted barge moored a little apart from the others. It was in dire need of paint and the gangplank was splintered and rotting in several places. *Marie Louise*, barely legible in gothic script on the bows, identified it.

The girl gave a last look round and rapidly crossed on the gangplank. Then she descended the small flight of steps into the open well and knocked twice, waited and knocked twice again on the door leading to the boat's interior.

After a moment the door was opened, she went in and the door closed behind her.

The interior of the boat offered something of a contrast with the outside. The saloon was neat and reasonably clean and furnished with bunk seats, plentiful cushions, laden bookshelves and a few ceramic pieces. A long table occupied the centre of the narrow cabin. Four men were sitting round it. There were Coke cans on the table, over-full ashtrays and a couple of street maps. Two portholes were open on the river side but little enough air was getting in and what did arrive was hot, dry and dusty. The air inside was heavy with cigarette smoke. A radio was on at low volume, giving traffic news.

'Ah, our *compagne* Ingrid at last,' said the man at the head of the table. 'Did you get it?'

The girl opened her black patent leather bag, took out the envelope and tossed it onto the table. 'Of course,' she said. Then she sat down on the vacant chair, pulled a Coke can towards her, tore away the closure and drank.

'And the boy?'

'I dealt with that. There's no one to interrogate now.'

'That whole exercise was too complicated and risky,' someone said. 'There was always the chance that the accident wouldn't prove fatal and he'd break down under interrogation. It was a hell of a complicated way to plant the envelope.'

'It was what Felix ordered,' snapped the man at the head of the table. 'So let's hear no more about it. Ingrid has closed that chapter. A brilliant job.'

He picked up the envelope and examined it. 'Stupid bastards,' he said. 'Why the hell didn't they open it?' He looked closely at the edge where the flap had been sealed and at the name, so carefully copied by the DST handwriting expert. 'Any half-witted cop could see it's addressed to Seynac, and even cops know he's the big wheel at *l'Huma*. After all the trouble we went to.' He paused and looked round the table. 'What do we do now?'

'I think Felix should be consulted,' one of the others said. 'This ploy with the Defence Committee stuff is just about the best thing we have. It has more political impact than any number of bombing incidents. It's one thing to hear there was a bomb which went off six streets away, but quite another to feel that the very heart of the State machine has been penetrated.'

The girl nodded. 'After all my trouble I wouldn't like to see it spoil. I had to deal with a cop, too. You may have had it on the radio. *Gare de l'Est* a couple of hours ago.'

'We heard it. He's dead.'

'I'd be pretty surprised if he wasn't.' The girl said it with a straight face and continued drinking.

'Our *compagne* is running too many risks,' said the man who wanted to consult Felix. 'Shooting cops in the Metro in working hours is for the strong-arm boys, not for the leadership.'

'Sometimes the leadership has to *lead*,' the girl snapped. 'From in front. Not from a cosy room at base.' There was an edge of suppressed hysteria to her voice.

'I wasn't criticising,' the man said, retreating.

'You had better not,' the girl said, her voice rising. 'You are in no position to criticise. We get good political theory from you, Brunot, but we don't get much action. You'd do best to restrict your contributions to the discussions on strategy and leave the tactics to others.'

'All right,' the man at the head of the table said. 'None of this is helpful. We should now start the meeting by congratulating our *compagne* Ingrid on her successful mission. She sets an example for us all. With the document back in our possession, I think we need to re-examine the theory and *praxis* which lay behind the operation so that we can make a proposal for René to take back to Felix. *Compagne* Brunot has the floor.'

The man who had tangled with Ingrid cleared his throat and leaned forward, his elbows on the table. He was what he looked: a lecturer in political science at the *Sorbonne*, and his name was not Brunot. He had the pale, smooth skin of an adequately nourished member of the middle classes but sported an ample and heavily drooping Mexican-style moustache as a gesture in the direction of who knew what revolutionary position. His voice was cultured and surprisingly gentle. He was thirty-two.

'Let's go over it,' he said. 'Our aim is destabilisation. Felix judged that a leakage from the Defence Committee would provoke public alarm and an outcry from the press, since the Defence Committee could be regarded as the most secure body in the State. More so, of course, than the Government itself.'

He paused to light a cigarette and blew a cloud of smoke into the airless cabin.

'The task was to obtain a top-secret document and to let it be discovered under totally perplexing circumstances. Addressing it to Seynac, of course, was the extra twist designed to start a witch-hunt and reinforce our main objective: to show the nation that the Left are traitors – clever and resourceful traitors – while we, the Right, the true nation, prepare for action.' He pulled at his cigarette. 'Our position has not changed and will not change: we of the true nation have learned our lesson from the tiny handful of anarchists who terrorised Paris at the end of the last century. They let off their pathetic home-made bombs in Parliament, in a café at the Gare St Lazare, here and there. How can that kind of lunacy change the fate of a nation, people asked. They must be mad. But they weren't mad.

Anyone who has bothered to read the trials of Vaillant and Emile Henry can hear it all spelled out. A bomb could change the climate of opinion, they said. It could do what could never be done in a political campaign. And of course, they were right. In our conditions today, a bomb can be worth a million votes. There is no more effective way to wipe the democratic nonsense out of the electorate's mind and prepare it for firm government by a man of strength. The dialectic is impeccable.'

As he spoke, he seemed to become the victim of his own words – listening to himself, oblivious of his audience, transfixed by his own unanswerable logic. It was theory made flesh. The heady, passionately absorbing manipulation of history.

He stumped out his unsmoked cigarette and lit another. 'I think Felix will agree that we must try to push this under the noses of the police again. I speak as one who has been closely involved in the operation from the start, but I hope my views are not on that account subjective.' His manner and style of speaking were precise, pedantic.

'Why not tip off someone in the press?' the girl asked.

'I fear that would be useless. The police will mistrust anything they haven't actually unearthed themselves. This has to be *believed*. After all, it *is* a leakage from the Defence Committee. We have to be certain no smart policeman decides it is a forgery. They have to be convinced it was taken on behalf of the Soviets. It's the sense of helplessness that matters. The feeling that we can do whatever we decide to do whenever we choose. Certain animals mesmerise their prey. It is the image I leave with you.'

There was a brief silence, broken by the hooter of a passing barge.

'I said that thing with the motorbike and the accident was too elaborate,' the girl said, showing her irritation with Brunot's manner. 'All right, I know we had to dispose of that young man. He was expendable, sure. But there's too damn much ingenuity in this group. We're like a bunch of prissy intellectuals trying to show how clever we are, when what we need is something simple, politically relevant, practical. A little less philosophy and a little more action.'

'No one is forbidden to suggest what that action should be,' Brunot said drily through his cigarette smoke. 'I claim no monopoly in ideas.'

'We could deliver it to Seynac at *L'Huma* or somewhere else and get someone to tip off the police for a raid immediately afterwards.'

'A raid without a warrant would bounce back if the document isn't found. *With* a warrant it takes too much planning.'

There was another silence.

'Supposing,' the girl said, 'we simply posted it to the editor of the *Figaro* or the news editor at the T V Centre?'

'No good. If they approached the Ministry of the Interior it would certainly be suppressed and the paper or the T V would go along with it. And if we sent it to a more independently-minded journal, everyone would scream "forgery" and the police would be only too happy to agree. If history teaches us anything at all, it is that suppression is always preferred to the pursuit of the judicial process. They knew Dreyfus was innocent and yet, quite rightly in my view, they –'

'Yes, yes,' the man at the head of the table said, 'but what do we do now?' He turned to the younger man seated on his left, a thin, pallid youth who had said nothing so far. His delicate fingers constantly played with a signet ring which he had removed from his left hand. His head was shaven, giving him the look of a dedicated seminarist who spent too much of his time poring over devotional texts.

'René, when is your next contact with Felix?'

The youth did not look up from the ring he was playing with. 'Next Sunday,' he said, 'at the usual time.' He seemed to be taking little interest in the proceedings.

'Between now and then we have to work out some proposals. You all know how to find me if you have any ideas. Let us move on. I want to discuss the elimination of Laborde last night.'

'A neat job,' someone said. 'It was too good, though, for

that filthy swine. Those bastards don't deserve a quick end like that.'

'You will commend the team on our behalf,' the man at the head of the table said to the girl.

'I will.'

'Have the cars been disposed of?'

'They have.'

'Brunot, how do you see the political consequences of our initiative?'

'Laborde favoured working with the Socialists and staying in the Government. Now he's bound to be replaced by Froissard, who is the only other man of national stature the Communist Party has. And he's a hard-liner who has forgotten nothing of the primitive Leninism he learned in the Cominform twenty-five years ago. He hates the Socialists and favours going it alone to preserve the Marxist purity of the party. And that, of course, will reduce the Communist vote next time. And so it has been one of those rare political assassinations which actually change the course of politics. *Voilà*!'

He was a man who thought in a series of theoretical formulae, always drowning the particular in the general. A dead policeman was not an individual killed. It was a move in a political process. A bomb detonated and people torn apart was part of the dynamic, the creation of a new range of political possibilities. He was a political animal and no other kind of animal at all. His deeply cultivated sense of history had left him no room to look at what he was actually doing.

'We'll have confirmation that Froissard takes over at the weekend when the Central Committee of the PCF meets,' he said. 'It seems to me a foregone conclusion.'

'Do we have any other actions this week?' the girl asked.

'Not in Paris. There are some planned in the provinces. We will meet again next week. Right, that's all. We will leave separately.'

The political calculations of the man called Felix paralleled, but did not precisely coincide with, those of the Command. Whereas the objective of those who made up the Command

and those in the State apparatus who were involved with them, was the replacement of the present parliamentary system by something more authoritarian, more 'national', more disciplined and hierarchical – all convenient euphemisms for a dictatorship of the Right – the objectives of Felix were less ambitious. His concern was the defeat of the Left, even if the nation voted for the Left. He had no ideological objection to a violent shift Rightwards, and in this he regarded the Command as natural allies. But he was just sophisticated enough politically to recognise that the *status quo* was a better bet – safer, less prone to outside interference, possibly more stable. But a *status quo* of a different political complexion.

He knew that every bomb that went off discredited the Government almost as effectively as it discredited the extreme Left, who were held responsible. But whereas the Command regarded that fact as part of the process of getting rid both of the Left, the Government and the very system which had created it, Felix calculated that the system would hold. The activists of the Command, and the Prefect of Police, the Minister of Defence and others might wish it otherwise. He, Felix, told himself that he was playing a subtler game. He was, he knew, supping with devils. But he had confidence in the length of his spoon. Put another way, he was playing poker, but it wasn't the first time he had done so. He knew cards. He knew what he was doing. He was, indeed, an old hand at manipulation, at operations on the thin line between politics and terror.

'It has not been a good day,' Baum said to his wife later that evening. 'Not at all good. What do you have for supper?'

'Steak, *frites* and a nice salad. And I got one of those *millefeuilles* that you like from Daumier's.'

'Good. I hope I can eat. My liver is playing me up again.'

'It's because you're worried,' his wife said. 'Always when you're worried about your work, we have this trouble with your liver. Do you want to take something?'

'Maybe a pill later.' He sighed and pushed out a foot towards one of the cats. 'A lousy day.'

'Your shirt,' his wife said. 'The cuffs are frayed. I must turn them.'

'I made a fool of myself. *Hubris*. Pride. Over-confidence.' He shook his head.

His wife knew that he would talk like this about events that he had no intention of revealing, so she did not ask what he had been so foolish about. Instead, she went out to the kitchen and tossed the chips in the deep, sizzling oil, examined the steaks on the grill and finished laying the table. A fine aroma of garlic wafted through the apartment.

Baum sat slumped in his armchair, his chin on his chest, thinking about his liver. Then he thought about Georges Wavre and what he would have to say about the events of the day. Then, because he was a professional, he thought long and hard about what should be done next. His fall-back plan would have to be operated: the one which he had not revealed to Wavre, the one which he'd prepared in the absurd and improbable event that the girl got away from them.

There was nothing wrong with that plan, but he was using up goodwill and patience pretty fast, and if Georges Wavre's nerve gave way, the whole thing could be taken out of his hands. Also, a good man had died because of his miscalculation. And what was the miscalculation? That the opposite side was no match for the DST, whereas they had proved themselves competent, alert and ruthless. If their women would shoot policemen at three in the afternoon in a public place, what would their men not do? It was a sobering thought.

They ate in silence. Estelle knew when to speak and when to let him wrestle in silence with his problems. Despite his worries and his liver, he did justice to the steak and the *patissier's* feathery pastry. With his coffee he took a generous glass of cognac. It was a further sign: Alfred had certainly had a bad day.

'Can I do anything?'

He smiled and patted her hand. 'Thank you, no. You must forgive me. I'll be all right tomorrow, which is another day and full of possibilities, no doubt.'

Unusually, that night he dreamed of his work, but the dream was curious. The girl who was a killer and the puzzle of the leaked Defence Committee documents played no part in it. Instead, there rolled endlessly before him the clip of film from the Bois de Boulogne – the one which had driven him repeatedly to the archives and had made him feel so liverish last week. Only, in the dream he knew precisely what the film meant and there was no mystery at all. When he awoke he suffered the utter exasperation of recalling the dream in all save its essential: the meaning of the film. And that he could not for the life of him remember.

What Alfred Baum had not known was that while he was doing justice despite his liver to Estelle's excellent underdone steak, the President of the Republic was sharing some smoked ham and a bottle of white wine with Guy Mallard, his mistrusted and heartily disliked Minister of the Interior. A pragmatist, the President was about to carry through an exercise which, he flattered himself, met the needs of the country and the electoral needs of his party, not to mention his personal ambitions, in approximately the right proportions. And he proposed to sell it to his colleague.

'The Prefect of Police,' he said, taking a mouthful of ham and talking through the shreds of meat in his mouth, 'the Prefect of Police is either an incompetent fool or a sinister knave.' He paused and looked at Mallard. 'Which?'

'He is not a knave,' Mallard said. 'I admit he has not been successful in the matter of the bombings. He could have been more – imaginative.'

'If he were in the Army he'd be court-martialled,' the President said. 'It's as simple as that.' He did some more chewing. 'Something has to be done and I now propose to do it.'

The Minister of the Interior raised his eyebrows. With the President one always had to be cautious, and that meant saying as little as possible. He sounded like a bully, and indeed he was a bully. But more than that, he was devious. And, in the Minister's view, totally without scruples. And so he said nothing.

'I think,' the President said, 'that for the sake of the nation we have to take this entire business out of his hands.'

'But one cannot operate in such matters without the facilities of the police.'

'What have those facilities given us so far?'

'I admit, nothing.'

'Well, then, I do not see what we shall lose.'

'But who could take it on?'

The President, who was pleased with his idea, was savouring the moment and made the Minister wait for the answer. He finished his mouthful and took a draught of the wine. Then he wiped his mouth on his napkin.

'The DST,' he said. 'There's more energy there. I'd have more confidence.'

'But the law only allows them to act against external threats to security. We have no evidence that this is an external threat.'

'You heard the Prefect say in the meeting that the training and arming of the terrorists could be originating abroad.'

'That isn't evidence, *Monsieur le Président*.'

'It is the task of the DST, first of all, to find that evidence, and then in the light of it to take over the *affaire*. Will you tell Wavre or shall I?'

'I can tell him.'

'And will you tell the Prefect of Police or shall I?'

Guy Mallard winced at the thought. 'It will have repercussions, you know. He has many friends – in the press as well. Perhaps it should come direct from you.'

The President grunted. 'The man's second rate. A hopeless fool. Telling him is no problem. I will do it tomorrow.' He poured himself another glass of wine. 'Also, I have another problem looming on the political horizon.'

Guy Mallard waited. The President was taking his time over this one.

'It could be the biggest problem of all.' He paused again. 'So far, it's only a phone call. From Washington. But I smell all kinds of trouble such as only the Americans can cook up.'

'Who called you?'

'The President's Executive Secretary. Directly on behalf of that clown in the Oval Office. You know Kissinger's in Brussels at a meeting of the NATO Council. In some kind of advisory capacity: you know, power without responsibility – an ideal condition. Well, it appears that the good Doctor will be paying what they call a private visit to Paris and wants to see the President of the Republic. It appears that he has a personal message from the US President.'

'When will that pleasure be yours?'

'The Prime Minister and I will see him on Wednesday. But here's the significant part of the news. Kissinger will have Bruback with him.'

Guy Mallard's eyebrows were raised a fraction. 'What would the CIA want to see you for, and in Kissinger's company?'

'Because it is worried about the internal situation in France and is planning some kind of intervention. None of their damn business, you say? Quite right. But that will not deter Bruback. And it is because I am invariably right on such matters that something has to be achieved quickly on the bombings.'

'Naturally,' Guy Mallard said. 'Naturally.'

When he had left, the President allowed himself a private smile. He was pleased with his idea. If the DST cracked the problem, so much the better. It badly needed cracking. But if they didn't, then would it not be evident that the man politically responsible was Guy Mallard, the Minister of the Interior, to whose office the DST directly answered? Such a failure would hit him harder, more publicly, than a failure of the *Préfecture de Police*, which also headed to him, but which was a department that the public had long ago decided was either corrupt or incompetent – possibly both. But not so the DST.

And with the elections in mind, it would be no bad thing for Mallard to look useless. The man's ambitions, he reflected, outstripped his abilities . . .

During the next four days to Sunday there were explosions in two provincial towns but none in Paris. Also, during the four days Baum made his peace with Georges Wavre and convinced him that his new plan had to be viable, for the good and sufficient reason that no alternative could be thought of by either of them. Also during the four days, the process of taking the *affaire* of the terrorist explosions away from the police and placing it in the hands of the DST was completed without benefit of legal sanction, since no one believed it was a foreign plot, least of all a plot involving espionage, which was the only kind of activity that the DST had licence to concern itself with.

On the Sunday, at two in the afternoon, the young man known in the Command as René drove a closed 2CV van from Vaugirard, where he had a room at the top of a tenement, to the Bois de Boulogne on the far western side of the city. He parked the van beneath the trees in the Route de l'Etoile and climbed into the back. Fifteen minutes later a middle-aged man in grey slacks and immaculate navy blue sports jacket alighted from a taxi on the corner of the Route de l'Etoile and the Route de St Denis and walked at a leisurely pace down the Route de l'Etoile in the direction of the van. When he came within sight of it, he left the footpath and walked off into the shade of the trees, slowing his pace: a Sunday afternoon *flaneur* on his way to an assignation, or maybe on the lookout for a fresh adventure . . .

The young man René now emerged from the van, transformed. He was wearing high heels and his T-shirt had been replaced by a woman's silk blouse. What had looked like trousers now looked, in their new setting, like a woman's slacks. His pale, rather effeminate face had been carefully made up – the lips red, the eyes outlined, and over his shaven head a long blonde wig had been fitted.

He walked towards the middle-aged man among the trees, and when he reached him, the man took him by the arm and they started to walk to and fro, deep in conversation. This, then, was the assignation and no passer-by would have found it of more than momentary interest.

On this occasion, unlike the previous Sunday, there were no DST cars in the vicinity randomly playing cops and robbers with their opponents in the KGB. The conversation between René and Felix lasted for fifteen minutes and the few strollers who saw them reacted much as Luc, the young policeman from Nantes, had reacted – with a knowing smile at the sight of a prosperous businessman's Sunday tryst with his young secretary. Unless it was the waitress who served him his *café crème* somewhere in town on weekday mornings.

The conversation over, René regained his van and disappeared into the back, to reappear shortly afterwards in the driving seat as a man. The man calling himself Felix had walked briskly away towards the edge of the Bois and picked up a cruising taxi at the Porte Dauphine.

René drove the van back and forth in the Bois until he was satisfied that he had no one on his tail and then made for the Porte d'Auteuil, where he re-entered Paris. Ten minutes later the van was parked in a side street close to the Mirabeau bridge. René walked down to the *Port de Javel* and climbed aboard the *Marie Louise*.

'There's a change of plans,' he told the man who had conducted the last meeting. 'Felix wants to bring forward next week's main operation.'

'To when?'

'Tuesday.'

'Christ, forty-eight hours. It can't be done.'

'I was told to tell you that it has to be done, regardless of all difficulties. Those were his words.' The young man's eyes were glistening and he spoke with a kind of mindless fervour. He was carrying the Word incarnate.

'Did he say why?'

'He said there would be a political event on Wednesday which had to be decisively influenced. He said our action would have altogether different significance on Tuesday night as compared with a week later. "Do not become intoxicated by the action," he said to me. "Remember always the political outcome. A death on a Tuesday can mean something totally different from the same death on a Wednesday." He said that.'

'And he wants exactly the same action?'

'Exactly the same.'

The other man shook his head. 'And the Defence Committee document? What did he say about that?'

'We are to deliver it to Seynac at *l'Humanité* and the police will raid the place immediately afterwards. He agrees now with our view that the original plan was too complicated. We are to tip off the *Préfecture* but he is also taking steps. He did not say what they were.'

'And when is that to be?'

'On Wednesday at six p.m. exactly.'

'We must call the Command together this evening,' the other man said.

On that Sunday Alfred Baum had taken one of his rare days off and could be seen, Estelle by his side, wandering in slacks, open-necked white shirt and a rakish panama hat round the Versailles Cat Club's Annual Show. Here he was no longer a special kind of policeman (indeed, his friends among the cat fanciers thought he was merely an obscure civil servant), but a locally recognised expert on long-haired cats, with a respectable reputation at shows in the Paris region. On these occasions, with his cronies and the prim ladies of the Fancy, he would spend happy hours debating the points of Cameo Reds or Creams, assessing the density of a coat, the width between the ears or the purity of eye colour.

His own pair had won their share of cups in their day, including Best in Show at Gentilly, and if retirement one of these days was going to offer any compensations, it would be the chance to breed more cats, attend more shows, bask in the modest prestige of being a recognised expert, and maybe bring home a few more trophies.

Estelle, whose view of cats fell this side of idolatry but who welcomed anything that gave her Alfred relief from his work, liked these expeditions to the shows because it was very nearly the only activity that they were able to share.

But this time, though there were some splendid cats to be seen, Baum found he could not immerse himself in the show. His liver was still troubling him. His mind was still enmeshed with the events of the past week. And despite the drama of the stolen minutes, he had not yet exorcised his demon: the clip of film from the Bois de Boulogne.

'You are not enjoying yourself as you usually do,' Estelle said.

'I'm sorry. My liver again.'

'Your mind isn't on the cats. It's on your work.'

Baum smiled at her. 'Look,' he said, 'look at that Pewter over there. A fine bushy tail. And see the orange eyes. A very useful cat, that.'

Estelle shook her head. 'Alfred, you're impossible,' she said.

'I know, my dear. But I told you as much when we married.' And he chuckled and planted a kiss on her cheek.

Also on the Sunday afternoon the Central Committee of the French Communist Party met in the town hall of the suburb of Ivry and elected Jacques Froissard, a former metalworker of Valenciennes, as General Secretary. In a three-hour speech to the Committee, he paid tribute to his predecessor, whose policy of alliance with the Socialists in the Government he proceeded to demolish. 'What France needs is fundamental social change,' he announced. 'The Socialists do not favour change: they are the party of reform and capitulation. They are objectively the agents of reaction. We, on the other hand, must offer the country a radical alternative – a Communist programme directed against big capital in the interests of the toiling masses.'

When the Bourse *opened on the following day, newspapers carrying banner headlines still predicting a Left electoral victory were waved about and sixteen points were wiped off share prices by teatime. That day, also, francs were sold heavily on the international exchanges and the Bank of France was forced to intervene and buy, despite the Minister of Finance's assurances that the currency was strong enough to find and maintain its own level. After trading all day on the floor of the currency 'snake', the franc closed at its lowest-ever value against the Deutschemark. The illegal flight of francs across the Swiss frontier in suitcases and the boots of cars, which was to become such an unmanageable phenomenon in the months up to the election, began in earnest.*

'The bourgeoisie will now demonstrate its lack of patriotism,' the Communist l'Humanité *wrote primly. 'By its actions it will show that the working class, led by the Communist Party, is the only class which knows how to defend the interests of the nation.'*

A meeting in the Governor's office at the Bank of France decided on measures to protect the currency, none of which were to prove effective as the bogey of a Left victory gripped the minds of brokers, bankers, industrialists, speculators and the financial advisors of little old ladies living as best they could off the revenue from investments which were not enabling them to keep their heads above the tide of inflation.

On the following day the franc was to plunge through the floor of the 'snake' for the first time and despite the intervention of the Bank, which cost eight billion francs of the country's foreign exchange reserves.

Chapter 8

The day after the Cat Show Alfred Baum did the simple thing: he telephoned Armand Seynac, Editor in Chief of the Communist newspaper *l'Humanité* and member of the party's *Bureau Politique*, at his office.

'This is Baum, Deputy Director of the DST,' he said amiably. 'I would appreciate an opportunity of meeting you, Monsieur Seynac.'

'This is a strange idea. I have no business with the DST. Aren't you entirely concerned with foreign spies?'

'Usually, yes. And I am not suggesting for a moment that you come within that definition. Nevertheless, I would like to have a talk and I can guarantee that you will find it as interesting as I will.'

There was a silence. Then Seynac said: 'I would like to call you back in ten minutes. Where can I reach you?'

Baum gave him the number of his private line at the DST. Ten minutes later the phone rang.

'Seynac here. You must know as well as anyone that my line at *l'Huma* is listened to by who knows what services – perhaps your own. I am now on a safer phone.'

And no doubt you've consulted your colleagues too, Baum said to himself.

'Good. As I say, I would like to meet you. Today,' he added.

'Very well. Where do you suggest?'

'I suggest neutral ground. And let us make it discreet. I shall be on the *bateau mouche* travelling eastwards which stops at the Alma bridge at two seventeen this afternoon. I suggest you board it there and go to a seat aft on the upper deck. I will be there. We can have a pleasant trip on the river in this terrible heat.'

'Very well, I shall be there.'

Baum had a sandwich and a beer at his desk and got a DST car to take him to the Grenelle bridge in time to catch the boat. The sun blazed down from a relentlessly blue sky and he wished he were more appropriately dressed for a summer trip on the river. On board the river boat, he adjusted his hat to keep the sun from his eyes and turned over carefully in his mind what he had to say to the Communist leader. He couldn't fault it. The thing made sense.

At the Alma stop three people came aboard, one of them a tall man with a mane of white hair and the aquiline face of a professor. He came aft, looking carefully about him like someone who suspected a trap. When he was abreast of Baum, the latter raised his hat.

'Monsieur Seynac, I recognise you. I am Baum.'

'I'm afraid I cannot return the compliment. I think I have to ask you to identify yourself.' Seynac sat down in the next seat and looked at Baum carefully.

'That's reasonable.' Baum showed him his DST identity card with its mug shot and description. Seynac looked at it carefully.

'There are provocations . . .' he said, and left the sentence unfinished.

'Oh, I know. We may even be discussing one.'

Seynac said nothing, took out a pack of American cigarettes, offered it to Baum and lit one for himself.

'I have a strange story to tell you and you may well wonder why I take you into my confidence. The answer is simple: I have no choice. You will see what risk I run but you will also see that whatever our differences may be, here we have a community of interest.'

Seynac nodded and still did not speak.

'A photocopy of a secret document touching on the security of the State has been picked up by us purely by chance. It was addressed to you at *l'Humanité*. I have to tell you at once that if it was *not* a provocation – if it was being sent to you with your knowledge, then you have committed a grave offence under the *Code Pénal* and you and I will find ourselves on opposite sides in the matter. If, on the other hand, it *is* a provocation, you and I have a very real identity of interest.'

Seynac looked at Baum with heavily lidded eyes and slowly turned his body round to face him. For a moment he said nothing. Then he asked: 'Do you have a tape recorder on you, Monsieur?'

'You may feel my pockets,' Baum said. 'You may speak in the lowest possible voice, below the range of any portable equipment out in the open. This has to be an honest conversation between us.'

'Very well. Tell me more of this provocation, for you must realise that is what it is. Otherwise you'd be chasing me, not talking to me.'

'I am not at liberty to tell you precisely what the documents contain,' Baum said, speaking slowly and with care, 'but I have reason to believe that another attempt will be made to deliver them to you.'

'Then you have not got them at the DST?'

'Let us say that we have had them and no longer have them. Anyway, if I am right, you will be in very considerable danger since you will be in possession, however briefly, of State secrets, and I fear you would have the greatest difficulty in persuading the authorities that you neither sought them nor intended to make use of them or hand them to a third party.'

'We are a political party, not an espionage organisation,' Seynac said drily.

'You also run a newspaper which is not always scrupulous in attacking Government policy. For this reason I have to tell you that if you should be tempted to ignore my proposal, take delivery of the documents and use them in your paper, you will be made to look very foolish. I said they had been in our hands. You will naturally appreciate that we did not allow them to leave in the same condition as when they reached us. Let us say they are now *doctored* State secrets.'

Seynac smiled a thin smile. 'So the provocation becomes a counter-provocation. I believe you spy-catchers call it disinformation.'

'It does. But here is the problem. We at the DST work on our own, as you will understand. We do not tell other services what we are doing. I therefore cannot guarantee that someone else – the *Préfecture* perhaps – won't be aware of what is happening and possibly try to catch you red-handed, as it were, with the documents. That, indeed, is my major concern. And that is why I need your cooperation.'

'What do you want?'

'I want you to help my people to intercept the messenger. And this can only be safely done in the *l'Humanité* building.'

Seynac said nothing. They were passing beneath the ancient Pont Neuf and were rocking gently in the wake of another boat plying in the opposite direction.

'I will have to consult my comrades. From our point of view your proposal presents considerable dangers.'

'I know that very well. Unfortunately, this is urgent. The envelope can be delivered to you at the newspaper at any time. My guess is that it will be one evening, probably during the rush hour, when it would be virtually impossible for us to tail the messenger.'

They had reached the Nôtre Dame bridge. The cathedral glistened in the sun. American tourists in their blinding white double-knits clustered round the great doors. Seynac got up.

'I appreciated this meeting,' he said. 'I will telephone you in one hour at your office. But tell me one thing. If someone is arrested in the lobby of our newspaper, having just delivered an envelope full of State secrets addressed to me, am I not completely vulnerable at that point – vulnerable to a provocation mounted by the DST itself?'

'You are, Monsieur, you most certainly are. And what you have to decide is whether this entire meeting is a machiavellian plot or an honest attempt to take the Communist Party at its word.'

'I do not understand.'

'Well, Monsieur Seynac, you claim to be a truly national

party with no foreign allegiances. What I am saying to you is that I need your help in a matter pertaining to the security of our country. It is a matter in which any national party would feel obliged to help.'

'We have not always been honestly treated in the past. It has made us very cautious.'

'All I can say is that you must now make the best decision you can. I very much hope it will be affirmative.'

Baum got up from his seat and they shook hands.

'I don't know,' Baum said to himself as the angular figure retreated, 'I really don't know.' And he shook his head in the familiar gesture.

The man with red hair, Jean-Paul, and his fellow car expert, Berenger, were receiving their instructions from the group in the Passage St Denis during a meeting on the Monday afternoon at pretty much the same time that Baum and Seynac were making their improbable trip down the river. The two men left the meeting separately – Jean-Paul in his bomber jacket, T-shirt and jeans, Berenger wearing a crumpled suit which was loose enough to cover the bulge where he had pushed a Beretta into his belt. Both were cursing the change in the timing.

They met at 5.30 p.m. in the ironmongery department of the *Bon Marché* department store in the Rue de Sèvres, where they bought rope, a knife and some tools. They then separated, and when the store closed at 6 p.m. Jean-Paul was lying behind rolls of lino in the carpet department and Berenger was in a disused office attached to the accounts department on the top floor. They remained there until the cleaners had finished their work towards midnight. Then they found each other in the basement. A pair of security guards, doing their rounds every two hours, passed through the basement area just after 2 a.m. Jean-Paul and Berenger jumped them from behind. They were now wearing stocking masks. One of the guards put up a struggle and was smashed on the back of the skull with a hammer from the store's own stock. The other put up his hands.

They left the guards gagged and trussed like chickens

behind a pile of boxes and made their way to the security office next to the service door of the store. There they found a third guard who took one look at Berenger's gun and decided that discretion was the better part of valour. He too was trussed up with the rope they had bought earlier.

'Right, let's get to work,' Berenger said. 'Where are the stores?'

'Follow me, I cased the place last week. There shouldn't be any locked doors ahead.'

They made their way back to the basement and by the dim glow of the security lights, found their way to the stores. Stacked at one end were the kitchen items – refrigerators, stoves, cabinets.

'This will do,' Jean-Paul said. 'Give me a hand.'

They removed the cardboard outer casing from a refrigerator, taking care not to damage the casing. Then they bore the container back to street level and found their way to the bays where the store's delivery vans were loaded. Five vans, part of the fleet, were parked side by side in the bay.

'Keys for the doors?'

'They'll be hanging in the office,' Jean-Paul said.

It took them five minutes to locate the box containing the keys. Then Berenger loaded the cardboard container in the van while Jean-Paul short-circuited the ignition with wire which he took from the pocket of his jacket. The engine sprang to life, sounding dangerously noisy in the enclosed space.

'Come on, we'd better not hang around.'

Berenger thrust back the folding doors and as the van emerged slowly into the side street, he closed and locked them, pocketed the key and jumped aboard the van, which sped away in the direction of Ménilmontant to the east.

'Neat, that,' Berenger said.

'Piece of fucking cake, but I think we should have wasted those guards, just to be on the safe side. The real fun's tomorrow.'

They drove in silence through the deserted streets, getting deeper into the maze of broken-down tenements, workshops and garages in Paris's poorest quarter. The van turned off the Avenue Gambetta into a narrow street which was part waste land and part shacks and private lock-ups. When they stopped, Berenger got out, unlocked the padlock on the roll-up entrance to a garage, and stood aside as Jean-Paul drove the van inside. The door was rolled down behind them.

During the next hour they changed the van's number plates and painted out the serial number of the vehicle on the doors of the cab. Using stencils which closely resembled the style of the painted-out numbers, Berenger gave the vehicle a new number. Jean-Paul found in his collection of keys one which fitted the van's ignition. He checked water, oil, battery and tyres.

In a corner of the garage was a crate marked:

Pomodori iscatoli
Tomates en boites

It bore a canner's name in Vicenza and an addressee in a Paris suburb. The two men lifted it carefully aboard the van, rigged up a light on a long flex and set to work to open the crate. Using polypropylene packing material, they transferred the contents, which were not canned tomatoes, into the cardboard container from the store and sealed it with sticky tape. Then they wiped the van for fingerprints, let themselves out of the garage, locked up, and drove to their rooms in Berenger's car, which had been parked at the end of the street.

It was 4.30 a.m. and getting light, though Paris was not yet shaking itself awake.

Also on the Monday, in the hideaway behind the *Teinturerie* in the Passage St Denis, Ingrid spent a half hour with the Paris street telephone directory. She telephoned in turn each of the subscribers living at 88 Faubourg St Honoré, pretending each time to have a wrong number. Of the twelve listed numbers, four failed to answer, and these she called several times during the day and evening until the total not answering had been reduced to two. She noted their names.

Also during the day she went out with Serge. She was wearing a dark wig and had changed her appearance by means of heavy make-up and a pair of spectacles. They took a bus to the Faubourg St Honoré and walked down past the fashionable shops until they came to No. 88, an apartment building exactly opposite the entrance to the President of the Republic's Elysée Palace. Ingrid was carrying a clipboard and a sheaf of papers. Serge walked on past the building and turned left up the Rue de Duras a few yards further along.

Ingrid knocked at the concierge's door inside the street entrance of No. 88.

'I am doing a market survey on behalf of the gas company. We want to know what appliances people use most. May I check on your residents?'

'What do you want to know?' The concierge was Portuguese, and though she had her instructions on enquiries of this kind, her tenuous grip on the language made it difficult for her to ask for identification or turn people away.

Ingrid read off the names of some of the residents, asking which apartments they occupied and noting down the answers.

'Thank you,' she said. 'I shall go up and knock at a few doors.'

There were two apartments on each floor: one on the street, the other giving on the internal courtyard. Floor by floor, she checked the names against the doors of apartments on the street side. Both the families who appeared to be away occupied apartments at the back. She did not ring any bells.

Then she returned to the ground floor, slipped into the courtyard and entered the door leading to the service stairs. On the top floor, occupied entirely by store rooms and maids' bedrooms, she spent some time looking for ways of access to the roof. Then she returned to ground level.

'Thank you,' she said to the concierge on the way out, 'I have what I want.'

She rejoined Serge round the corner in the Rue de Duras as he emerged from a block of flats which adjoined No. 88. Then they walked quickly away, deep in conversation.

'All right, so it looks OK,' Serge was saying, 'but operations like this shouldn't be rushed. We need more time.'

'Felix's orders are perfectly clear,' the girl said. 'The operation has to be brought forward to Tuesday.'

'What's the event it's supposed to coincide with?'

'I don't know and I don't need to know. And nor do you.'

On the same Monday afternooon, shortly after 5 p.m., Alfred Baum received a telephone call on his private line.

'Following our conversation this afternoon,' Seynac's voice said, 'I can confirm that we will cooperate.'

'I am very glad to hear it.'

'But first I would like you to listen to this.'

There was a pause and what sounded like static. Then Baum heard, electronically distorted but plainly intelligible: '*I have a strange story to tell you and you may well wonder why I take you into my confidence.*' It was his own voice, his own words from the conversation on the Seine.

There was a click and Seynac's voice came over the wire. 'You would hardly expect me not to take some simple precautions in such an encounter. The French security services have a long record of provocations, as you well know. I was a little surprised that you never asked *me* about a tape recorder.'

'What, and force you to leave yourself unprotected? Surely that way, whatever *you* might think of my proposition, your colleagues would not let you cooperate with me.'

'I await your proposals.'

'I will send you two men. I want one to join your regular receptionist in the lobby at the newspaper, and the other will sit around among the messengers and people waiting to go upstairs. We will arrange rotas so that the two posts are manned throughout your office hours. There will also be some of our people outside, but you won't notice them.'

'Very well. Tell your men to report to Aygoult, our business manager. I will tell him it is a party matter.'

That same afternoon, the Prefect of Police spoke on the telephone to the man calling himself Felix, having taken certain precautions as to the security of the call.

'Our friend hasn't been able to give me any hard news on what they're up to at the DST,' the Prefect said. 'It's just bad luck, but Wavre and his number two, Baum, simply don't talk.'

'You must keep trying. We need to know what measures they are taking on the bombings.'

'Of course. And what about this man Baum? Do you want some action there?'

'Not yet. There will be a time for that. What I want to talk to you about is the Defence Committee operation. I have decided after all to have the envelope delivered to the addressee.'

'When?'

'The day after tomorrow. The timing is deliberate.'

'What do you want from the *Préfecture*?'

'You will get a tip-off which you can quote afterwards if need be. It will be perfectly open, an hour before delivery takes place, and it will be made to whoever is your duty officer at the time. You will raid the newspaper exactly ten minutes after the delivery, which will be at six p.m. precisely. We discussed how the raid should go.'

'Yes, yes.'

'Use men of the *Brigade Anti-Communiste*. That will look right and they will put their hearts into it. Use all the men you can, for a quick and very thorough search. I don't need to teach you how to be a policeman.'

'And public relations?'

'An immediate press conference at the *Préfecture*, taken by you in person. Release a couple of the least sensitive pages for facsimile reproduction in the press. Maximum noise, you understand? Only, do it before anyone at Cabinet level has the chance to tell you to keep the whole thing quiet.'

'I understand.'

'I want the whole thing in screaming headlines the day after, with *l'Humanité* yelling provocation no doubt, but still yelling.'

'Very good.'

Chapter 9

Admiral Kent Bruback had spent thirty-five years in the US Navy and with a background like that it was not surprising that he regarded Henry Kissinger with a certain distaste and a good deal of suspicion. He found it unsatisfactory that a mere university professor with an uncertain accent should contrive to remain a key figure in US foreign policy despite the fact that he was no longer in office. The Admiral was a straightforward man who called assholes assholes, spades spades and Communists Russian scum. None of this made him a fool: indeed, he was very smart, with a street smartness so heavily overlaid with service bluster that it could scarcely be detected at all. If he had once been the youngest full Admiral in the Navy and had later been chosen by the President to take over at the Central Intelligence Agency at a time when its morale lay in tatters, its direction at odds with the Senate and its results pathetic and known to be pathetic – if this had happened it was not by the grace of God or good fortune. He had schemed and elbowed his way to the top of the Navy. To him Henry Kissinger, another man who knew the career value of a sharp knee in the groin, epitomised all that was wrong with government in Washington.

Now, however, walking out to the 707 put at their disposal by the NATO Command at Brussels airport, he wound his great arm round Kissinger's shoulders and said heartily: 'Henry, you're one hell of a guy.' Dr Kissinger, in no way misled by the show of bear-like, and thus dangerous, amiability, said nothing.

After take-off, alone in the forward part of the plane, with two Secret Service men seated well away at the rear, the

Doctor and the Admiral accepted Scotches from the orderly. It was their first opportunity to talk alone about their mission to Paris.

'We have here,' Dr Kissinger was saying, 'an explosive situation which can destabilise the structure of the Western Alliance. Can anyone imagine that a significant Communist recovery of electoral strength in France will not be followed by an advance in Italy, followed later by Spain and Greece?'

'Hemminge has been keeping me posted from Paris,' the Admiral said. 'He tells me the Communists are behind this terror campaign.'

'I doubt it,' Kissinger said. 'They don't work that way. What are Hemminge's sources?'

'We don't reveal sources,' the Admiral said shortly.

'You'll probably find he sits at his desk and reads newspapers and then goes to dine with thoroughly unrepresentative people who have more money than sense. In these situations, our people develop overheated imaginations. In twenty years I haven't had a situation appreciation from the CIA which was worth the paper it was written on. And that goes back to the days when paper was cheap.' The Doctor smiled at his little joke. 'You'll find,' he added, 'after you've been in this job for a while, that everyone lies to you, Kent, but everyone. And none more than your own senior men. Dulles used to fire people who said they didn't know this or couldn't do that, and ever since then the guys have concentrated on saying what they think management wants to hear and to hell with the facts.'

The Admiral snorted. All this might be so, but he was not happy to be hearing it from Kissinger. 'So what do we do?' he said.

'Firstly, we try to shift their Government into some kind of action, and we do that by the simple expedient of issuing threats. They'll hate it and become offended and then abusive in the French manner, but they'll listen. No one in Europe is more mesmerised by our money and power than the French. That's why no one makes a bigger public fuss about it. You'll see.'

'And what about a little action there by our people?'

'The President is terrified that your people will blow it, Kent. Terrified.'

'Which shows you what a hell of a President we have.'

'It shows you that he has no confidence in the CIA, which is why he put you in there.'

The appointment, which was very recent, had been a mystery to Henry Kissinger, who regarded Admiral Bruback as an excellent man to be in charge of an aircraft carrier on mission in the Pacific, but a doubtful asset at the head of the CIA.

They drank Scotch all the way to Paris, and when they landed at the military airfield at Villacoublay, they had not dented the problem confronting them. Nor had they grown to like each other any more.

The protocol man who greeted them out on the apron was from the Prime Minister's office, not the Quai d'Orsay. A US General from the Embassy was there too. They exchanged rapid pleasantries and sped away in an Embassy car to the splendours of the Hotel Meurice.

There Dr Kissinger changed into a dinner jacket and a couple of hours later was on his way to the *Ecole Normale Supérieure*, where he was to lecture on 'the role of diplomacy in confrontation geopolitics'.

Admiral Bruback retired to his room, where he ordered some supper and put through a telephone call. A half hour later he was joined by Rolf Hemminge. The two men smoked and drank Scotch on the rocks and Hemminge talked at considerable length. The Admiral said very little and asked only a few questions. He was a man who listened carefully and didn't believe in talking a lot. People took this as sagacity, whereas it was often mere caution: having wandered out of the Navy, where he felt entirely at home, into the twilit world of intelligence, Admiral Bruback could often not see clearly ahead of him. Things were said which he barely understood. References were made to past events on the assumption that he had some background, whereas he had none. Who, for God's sake were Sorel, Pareto and Spengler that Hemminge had to quote them as the ideologists of terror? Who was Bakunin (the name was vaguely familiar)? What was the Code Napoléon? He did not know such things and did not care to betray his ignorance by asking.

On the other hand, Hemminge went on to talk long and earnestly about action rather than diplomacy, and here the Admiral felt more at home, more sure of himself. Several times he nodded and grunted his approval.

Dr Kissinger's lecture was articulate, persuasive and of an engaging cynicism which appealed to the *Normaliens*, admirers to a man of *realpolitik* and *raison d'état*. There was a satisfying logic in the proposition, elegantly expressed, that in a range of situations and in a number of historical periods, the ends did after all justify (however cautiously the thing might have to be expressed) the means.

Well enough pleased with the evening's proceedings, Dr Kissinger made his way back to the Meurice and was fast asleep by midnight. He liked to put in a good eight hours when he could. He had this difficult meeting at the Elysée on the morrow at ten. Fortunately for him, his sleep was deep. He was not awakened by the two explosions half a mile away just after 1 a.m.

The events leading up to the explosions can be chronicled as follows.

At four o'clock in the afternoon, a delivery van from the *Bon Marché* was driven down the Faubourg St Honoré, past the Ministry of the Interior on the corner of the Rue des Saussaies, and on as far as the Elysée Palace, where it slowed down, pulling up at the entrance to No. 88 opposite. Two men in white coats descended from the cab, leaving the driver at the wheel. They opened the back of the van and manhandled a large carton to the ground. The printing on the carton proclaimed: *Réfrigerateur Frigor*. As the men carried the carton across the pavement and into the building, the van drove on as far as the Rue de Duras and parked round the corner. To the police on duty across the road at the Elysée it was clear that the van was getting out of the heavy stream of traffic down the Faubourg. They wished all drivers had as much sense.

One of the men knocked at the concierge's glass door.

'Delivery from the *Bon Marché* for Madame Thierry.'

'Second floor front.'

They carried the container slowly up the stairs to the second floor and placed it against a wall. Then both men removed their white coats, beneath which they were wearing the uniform of servicemen from the gas company. One of them rang the bell of the front apartment. It was answered after a moment by a small, shuffling woman in her sixties.

'Gas company. There is a smell of gas in the building and we have to examine your appliances.'

'There's no smell in here.'

'We have to check ourselves. It's a rule when there's a leak.'

The woman still had the door open only a few inches. She looked mistrustfully at the men. Berenger gave her a smile and it seemed to settle her mind. She opened the door wider.

'Follow me.'

Jean-Paul closed the door behind them. As they followed the woman across the hall, he brought the edge of his right hand down violently on the back of her neck in a karate chop. There was a faint crack as the vertebrae dislocated and she slumped silently to the floor. Jean-Paul knelt down and pressed her nostrils together with one hand, with the other over her mouth. He kept his hands in this position for a minute, felt her pulse and then he got to his feet.

'Right, we'll get the gear.'

They retrieved the container from the landing and closed the front door. After satisfying themselves that there was no one else in the apartment, they hauled the container into the living room, which fronted onto the street, overlooking the courtyard of the Elysée beyond the far pavement.

'I'll leave you now,' Berenger said. 'Good luck.'

'A piece of fucking cake,' Jean-Paul said.

He accompanied Berenger to the front door and bolted it after him. Then he returned to the living room and got busy with the container.

Meanwhile, Berenger walked down the stairs and called out 'Thanks' to the concierge as he went by. He walked round to the Rue de Duras and boarded the van, which drove away. In the cab, he removed his false moustache and grey wig. The van was abandoned shortly afterwards in a side street in the northern part of the city and the driver telephoned the houseboat *Marie Louise* to say the merchandise had been safely delivered.

Meanwhile, Jean-Paul had torn open the container and distributed the contents on the floor of the living room. They consisted of two Armbrust 300 anti-tank guns, made under licence by Breda in Italy from designs of Messerschmitt-Bolkow-Bohm in West Germany. With them were two missiles with armour-piercing warheads capable of penetrating 300 mm of armour plate at 300 yards. The gun had been carefully chosen. It gave no firing report, no muzzle flash, no rear blast and no smoke: the ideal weapon for firing from an enclosed space, in which the rear blast of most guns of this calibre would promptly kill whoever fired them. The Armbrust would not.

Jean-Paul had practised the assembly procedure. Within minutes the barrel, sight, pistol trigger mechanism and shoulder rest of both guns were locked together, ready for firing.

Now he had time to kill. He dragged the body of Mme Thierry into a bedroom, attended to fingerprints on the front door, and went in search of the TV set. There was none, and he cursed to himself. In the kitchen he found the remains of a chicken and some fruit which would do for his supper. To his dismay there was nothing but a half bottle of sweet white wine in the apartment. It would have to do, and no one could seriously suggest that it fell within the prohibition against drinking during operations.

He settled down on a divan in the living room, smoked three cigarettes, stubbing them out carefully on the polished top of a low table, put his feet up and slept until 8 p.m., when he was awakened by the telephone. He let it ring and after a while it stopped. Then he cut the wire with a knife from the kitchen, brought the food and wine into the living room and set to with an appetite. Operations never affected his capacity to eat. 'Nerves? What the fuck are they?' It was the boast with which he always liked to show off.

When his watch showed 1 a.m. it was time to get to work. He checked that the back door was unlocked, that his pocket torch was working, that the laces of his boots were well tied. He was a man for detail. Then he opened the window and looked out. Two policemen were on duty outside the carriage entrance to the Elysée courtyard opposite. Street lights and a night lamp in the courtyard itself threw a dim glow onto the neo-classical façade of the Palace some 150 yards from the window. That was half the gun's maximum range: no problem.

Jean-Paul knelt down just inside the open window and brought one of the Armbrust 300's to his shoulder. The other lay ready to fire by his left knee. Both were loaded with shells which would prime themselves 0.8 of a second after leaving the muzzle of the gun. The guns themselves were discardable after firing one shot. The Command had insisted on two shots and therefore two guns. Accidents had been known to happen, guns to jam, ammunition to be faulty.

Jean-Paul released the safety catch, took aim at the steps of the Palace and slowly squeezed on the trigger. The kick of the gun and the *whoosh* of the projectile both told him that all systems were go. A moment later the explosion came as the HEAT missile penetrated into the dressed stone wall at the top of the steps. By then he had dropped the expended weapon and picked up the other one. A second later he had fired it. There were barely five seconds between the two explosions, both of them against the wall. Then the police started running into the courtyard, whistles blew, more police emerged from the guardhouse and the sound of shattering glass and falling blocks of masonry reached him as he ran for the back door of the flat.

He raced up the service stairs in the dark, following the layout as Ingrid had described it and not using his torch. On the top floor, he turned into a corridor, found the fourth door on the left that Ingrid had indicated, and went through it into a toilet just as a door further down the corridor opened. It must be someone awakened in one of the maids' rooms by the crack and rumble of the two explosions.

Jean-Paul found the window and was out onto the cornice at the back of the building, edging along it to the point where the building abutted a similar apartment block in the Rue de Duras. Using his torch sparingly, he found an open window and jumped through it into a bedroom in which someone was asleep. He heard a gasp from the bed as he found his way by the light of his torch to the door, and was out into the corridor and on his way down the stairs before the terrified girl in the bed could summon the courage to turn on her light.

No one saw him leave the building in the Rue de Duras and walk rapidly away from the corner with the Faubourg St Honoré. And no one saw him, later, slip into the Passage St Denis and enter the *Teinturerie*.

'A piece of fucking cake,' he said to Ingrid, Victor and Berenger.

'Well done,' Ingrid said. She was smiling at him for once.

He looked at her and said nothing. He would show the bitch that there were men who had more guts than bloody women.

The headline of the Paris edition of the *International Herald Tribune* read, in the largest type available:

ELYSÉE PALACE SHELLED
Extensive Damage, No Casualties
Crisis Cabinet Today?

Henry Kissinger had the paper propped up in front of him at the breakfast table in his suite and smiled to himself as he read. It might be fortuitous, this latest outrage just before he met the French leaders, but he could hardly have wished for better timing. No one could now say that things were under control. They were manifestly not. It would be interesting to see how the Frenchmen would explain away the short-range shelling of the Presidential Palace.

He finished his orange juice and drank his black coffee.

'I told you it was the Communists,' Admiral Bruback said when he joined him at 9.30. 'Shelling the President of the Republic! It has to be the fucking Communists.'

'It hasn't,' Kissinger said. 'It is probably the last thing they'd do.' He despaired of making the Admiral see his point, and so did not try. It did not augur well for the CIA and all its works.

At 9.45 the austere figure of Alexandre Vallat appeared. 'There has been a small change in our arrangements,' he said. 'The President and the Prime Minister will receive you in the Ministry of Marine in the Place de la Concorde.'

'I guess the Elysée is out of commission since last night,' the Admiral said with a grin.

'Not out of commission, but a certain amount of clearing up is necessary and we shall be more comfortable at the Ministry.'

Vallat's face was expressionless. He was not an admirer of the Americans.

At the Ministry of Marine they were ushered into a conference room whose lofty ceiling was bedecked with nymphs, satyrs and cupids. Beneath all the rococo exuberance, the President of the Republic and his Prime Minister were waiting. The President's well-developed sense of precedence and the respect due to his person told him that a President of France did not readily receive an advisor, even to the US President, even if that advisor was the redoubtable Dr Henry Kissinger. Nor did he normally receive, of all people, the head of the CIA. It wouldn't look good under banner headlines and he did not believe that such a meeting had anything to offer which would be to France's advantage. He therefore shook hands with the two Americans without allowing his face to crease into anything resembling a smile. The Prime Minister for comparable reasons did the same. The Americans, wanting to strike a censorious and disapproving note from the start, also did not smile. Vallat hovered in attendance, a picture of official gloom. The whole thing was dispiriting in the extreme.

When they were seated – Vallat with a notebook and ballpoint poised – the President extruded from the back of his throat a half dozen reluctant words of welcome and asked Dr Kissinger please to state his business.

He had a personal message from the President, Kissinger said. It was a verbal, not a written message. He felt the French President would have preferred it that way. What the U S President had in mind was the stability of the French Republic, for whom etc. etc. . . . The recent outrages were seen as very worrying in Washington. Some assurances that they could be brought under control would be most welcome. Also, from where they viewed things, France's American allies were even more concerned about the outcome of the elections. A Left victory, one realised, presented grave problems . . .

Dr Kissinger's voice with its rich gutturals droned on. The President of the Republic looked doggedly ahead of him. So, perforce, did the Prime Minister.

When Kissinger had finished, the President cleared his throat: 'But these are all internal matters, Dr Kissinger,' he said. 'We do not come to Washington when your Blacks riot.'

'If France is lost to the Communists, it becomes a European and therefore a world matter,' Kissinger said. 'It is something to which the United States could not remain indifferent. The eighty-one elections caused us some concern, as you know, with Communists coming into the Government. Recent polls raise the possibility of a further Communist advance this time. I repeat – the United States cannot remain indifferent.'

'Is this some kind of threat?'

'No, *Monsieur le Président*, but I am authorised to tell you that the United States will do what it can within the limits of recognised international practice to help the French Government to deal with its difficulties.'

'I am not aware that the French Government has sought any such help.'

'That is true, but it is a situation which, in our view, may well change.'

'And what if it does not change?'

'Then, naturally enough, our Government can be expected

to take certain precautionary measures of a financial and commercial nature at the very least.'

The Prime Minister intervened. 'Will you attack the franc?' he asked.

Kissinger shrugged. 'Our banks will wish to protect themselves. The US Treasury cannot restrain them if they take the view that the French situation is unstable. Similarly, the big US corporations with interests in France, and those negotiating to buy French equipment and services – what can we say to them other than "beware"?'

There was a silence. 'Tell your President,' the French President said, 'that I appreciate his interest and must necessarily reject his active participation in the measures we are taking to deal with these transient difficulties. You may rest assured that we shall overcome them. As for the forthcoming elections, they must remain strictly a French matter. Strictly.'

'Why aren't we holding this meeting at the Elysée, Mr President?' the Admiral asked suddenly. He sounded as if he were on the quarterdeck.

The President looked him squarely in his baby-blue eyes. 'Because, Admiral, my office is being redecorated.'

The Admiral made a sardonic noise which failed to become a laugh. 'You are being subverted,' he said. 'I don't see why the hell you fellows don't take steps. Everyone knows it's the Communists.'

'Thank you for your advice, Admiral,' the President said. 'It is clearly based on a deep comprehension of our complex political situation.' He rose. 'Gentlemen, I will only add this. It seems to me that you wish us to take administrative action – police action – against the Communists. I dare say that is what looks logical in the sub-tropical climate of Washington DC. And that, I imagine, is why I have the honour to be addressing, of all people, the head of the CIA. But I must tell you that I refuse to be pushed into a course of action which could well lead to civil war in our country – a civil war which I can by no means guarantee to win.' He fixed the Admiral with a stony stare. 'This is not a colony, Admiral. This is not La Paz or Santiago or even Buenos

Aires. This is Paris. And so I think we have nothing more to discuss. Please convey my respects to the President, and enjoy the rest of your stay in our country.'

They shook hands. As he released the Prime Minister's hand, Dr Kissinger said: 'Please remember, Prime Minister, we cannot control what our banking system may do. It would be regrettable . . .' He shrugged, smiled thinly and retreated behind the bulky figure of the Admiral.

'Let us see your man Hemminge this afternoon,' he said on the way down the stairs.

'I'll fix it, Henry,' the Admiral said. 'The stupid sons of bitches,' he added.

Rolf Hemminge lived in a vastly expensive apartment in the 16th, near the Bois de Boulogne. The place had been gutted and reconstructed to his exacting standards and there were six coats of lilac paint on the doors in the living area, tenderly illuminated by chandeliers of Venetian glass. His Aubussons were of the finest quality and in the dining room he had a fine pair of terracotta heads by Greuze, but spotlighted as though they were being offered for sale in the flashier kind of gallery. The deep settees and armchairs were upholstered in heavy off-white silk and some of the furniture was covered in *café au lait* suede. The entire place spelt a slightly vulgar and out-of-date aestheticism. The manservant was ebony black, from Somalia, splendidly muscled and clad in a white galabiya with gold-thread embroidery.

Dr Kissinger was perched tentatively on the edge of one of the deep armchairs. The Admiral stood with his back to the window, which was open to the oppressive heat. Rolf Hemminge, as exquisite as his apartment and somehow equally obsolete in appearance, lounged in another chair. It was 4 p.m. and bloody marys had been served.

'My informants,' Hemminge was saying in his slightly precious voice, 'tell me that it is the Communists. Their estimate is that destabilisation will favour them at the election. The population will be buying peace and quiet with their votes.'

'Rubbish,' Kissinger said. 'Even the French Communists aren't that stupid, and they're just about the stupidest in Europe.'

'I guess it isn't stupid, Dr Kissinger,' Hemminge said. 'In this country, people vote for what looks like the winning side. They've done it in the past and the calculation is that they'll do it again this time.'

'What's your evidence?'

Hemminge looked towards the Admiral. 'Well, that's a difficult one, sir. I don't know that I'm free to discuss sources.'

'You're not,' the Admiral snapped. 'I go along with Hemminge's appreciation, Henry. He and I have talked, and I buy it.'

'It's nonsense,' Kissinger repeated. 'And tell me this: why have they made no arrests? Are you telling me their police are useless?'

'Part useless, part corrupt.'

'Are *we* active in all this, Kent?'

'I wish we were,' the Admiral said quickly.

'Do you have contacts in the police or the DST?'

Hemminge nodded. If Kissinger expected a more detailed answer he was to be disappointed.

'And you don't know how near they are to cracking the problem?'

'I do know, Dr Kissinger. They are not at all near to cracking the problem.'

'Is it purely internal subversion?'

'I believe it is, but Moscow must have okayed it.'

Kissinger made an impatient gesture. These people were as firmly imprisoned in their schoolboy demonology as the Russians were in theirs. Argument was time wasted. 'Be that as it may,' he said, 'we have to find a way of internationalising the matter so that we can intervene properly. If we leave it to the French they'll foul it up. We did a little softening up this morning. I think they took my point about the banks. But we've a way to go yet.'

'Don't you have to catch your plane, Henry?' the Admiral said suddenly.

Kissinger looked at his watch. 'Yes, let's go.'

'You take the car, Henry, I'll stay on here and talk with Rolf a little. I want to brief myself. Tell the driver to call back for me.'

When Kissinger had left, Admiral Bruback turned to Rolf Hemminge: 'Now then, Rolf, let's get down to some real business. You said I should meet this guy Pellerin – their Defence Minister.'

'I've fixed that for later this evening at the apartment of a reliable colleague of his.'

Chapter 10

At exactly 6 p.m. a tall man with red hair walked purposefully through the heavy glass doors of the *l'Humanité* offices in the Faubourg Poissonière, looked around briefly and made for the reception desk to the left of the entrance. He was carrying an envelope in his left hand. His right hand was in the pocket of his bomber jacket.

'Give this to Armand Seynac right away,' he said to the receptionist. 'It's urgent. Get it straight up to him.'

'Will you wait while I check that he's in?' the receptionist said. She picked up the internal phone. The man with red hair stood at the desk but his eyes did not stay on the girl. He kept looking around the lobby and examining the people sitting there.

The man behind the desk, next to the receptionist, picked up an empty mailbag.

'I'll take this up, then,' he said, and moved from behind the desk as if he were making for the lift. But as he passed immediately behind Jean-Paul, he suddenly lurched into him, forcing him against the desk. At the same time he brought the mailbag down over Jean-Paul's head, pinning his arms inside. A burly, middle-aged man who had been sitting across the lobby, got up with surprising speed and helped his colleague to secure Jean-Paul's arms. They had seen his right hand inside his pocket and were taking no chances.

The whole thing was over in seconds. Jean-Paul was bundled through a door to the back of the building and out through a fire exit. Outside, in the narrow street, a DST car was waiting. He was hustled in, a DST inspector next to him and two in front. His hands had been handcuffed behind his back. Meanwhile, another inspector had entered the building through the front door and collected the envelope.

'Thanks, darling,' he said. 'You did it beautifully. Tell Seynac everything's OK.'

A few moments after they had driven away, there was a commotion of police sirens outside and four police cars disgorged sixteen uniformed and plain-clothes men at the entrance. They surged through the lobby as if they knew their way about the building. Most of them made for the first floor, where the editorial offices were located. Two disconnected the lobby switchboard and searched the receptionist's desk.

The search of the premises lasted for half an hour. Despite the protests of Seynac and others, the police ransacked the executive offices. The Inspector in charge refused to answer when asked if he had a search warrant, and shrugged when he was told that he was providing the paper with its lead for the following day.

The Inspector commandeered a telephone in an empty office and got through to the Prefect of Police.

'Dumail here, sir.'

'Well?'

'Nothing, sir. Absolutely nothing. We have done a thorough job.'

'I don't understand. It was delivered on time. We had a man outside who reported that the messenger had gone in.'

'But did he come out again, sir?'

There was silence on the line. 'The bloody fool!' the Prefect sighed. 'Why did no one think of telling him to wait and see?'

'Shall we search for the messenger?'

'No. Bring your men back.'

Meanwhile, the DST car was speeding towards the Rue des Saussaies. It drove into the underground garage and one of the DST men went to the phone.

'We have him downstairs,' he said to Alfred Baum. 'Shall we bring him up to your room?'

Someone had already alerted Baum to the catch.

'No. Fingerprinting first, and check the prints on the

computer. Then I'll want Inspector Allembeau to have him for a bit. I've briefed him and he's arranging for one of his men to keep the thing going for as long as we need tonight. I don't want to see him until tomorrow morning.'

Jean-Paul was led out of the garage to the lift. He walked with a swagger and would not answer when the DST men spoke to him. They were familiar with this type of bravado – common enough for the first hour or two. They shrugged.

In Inspector Allembeau's room they unlocked his handcuffs, gave him a cigarette and shrugged again when he refused a coffee. Then he was fingerprinted by a young man who came in with the equipment, while another man came in and took pictures. They had emptied his pockets. He was not carrying a gun after all. Nor did he have an identity card.

Inspector Allembeau was a quiet-spoken man in his fifties whose mild manner obscured a sharp brain with a streak of malevolence in it. He was regarded as the most unrelenting interrogator in the department and though he never raised his voice, his record of confessions was unequalled.

'Give them time and they'll contradict themselves,' he said. 'Always, their story has a flaw in it. Let 'em relax and they'll reveal it to you.'

Jean-Paul's story was simple and totally incredible, and he would not budge from it. A man he knew vaguely, name of Gilles, had paid him 100 francs to deliver the envelope to *l'Humanité*. That was all he knew about it. Where did this happen? Oh, in the street. Which street? The Boulevard de Clichy. That was where he sometimes saw Gilles. Did they frequent a café together? No, just met like that, around Clichy. How long had they known each other? A year or two, perhaps more. And what did Gilles look like? Oh, you know, a short fellow with sort of dark hair, like, just ordinary. The sort of fellow you'd meet up with in the streets around Clichy.

No, he didn't know what Gilles did for a living. Poncing, perhaps, but he couldn't be sure. Where did he live? Not the faintest. And where were the 100 francs? He'd split them to buy his Metro ticket and he'd bought a packet of fags. Where were the fags? Oh, if they weren't in his pocket he must have lost them somewhere. Unless the bloody cops had had them in the car.

Inspector Allembeau noted it all down as if he believed every word and was merely trying to get things absolutely right. He was the soul of politeness and concern. Of course, he said, they would like to let Jean-Paul go home as soon as they possibly could: just as soon as these trying formalities had been completed. And where, by the way, did he live?

'I can't remember,' Jean-Paul said.

'You can't remember where you live?'

'I can't remember. I must have amnesia as a result of the beating I got in the car.'

'You got a beating? Show me the marks.'

'There are no marks. Your men know how to avoid them.'

The Inspector sighed. 'We are not making progress,' he said. 'Let us see if the fingerprints can help us.'

The fingerprints could help. They belonged to one Jean-Paul Macé, age thirty-three, formerly of the Foreign Legion (three years), with four terms in prison, of which two were for GBH in the course of affrays and two for robbery, one with violence. It appeared that Jean-Paul Macé had spent a total of nine years under detention of one sort or another since the age of sixteen.

'All that?' Allembeau said gently. 'Tut, tut, such a waste, don't you think? And now this. The court will surely take a very serious view.'

'I don't know what all the bloody fuss is about. For Chrissakes, I only delivered a fucking envelope for a pal.'

'Ah, yes, and no doubt you did it in all inocence. But will the court take that view when one considers your background as a villain? Or will the Judge take the view that you knew what you were doing, that you were part of some sinister organisation? For that, my friend, is what you have to consider. And if he takes the less charitable view, the Penal Code provides some very, very stiff penalties.'

'Like?'

'Like fifteen years hard régime.'

Allembeau shook his head. 'Would you like a coffee, my friend?' he asked considerately.

Rolf Hemminge's reliable go-between proved to be the inquisitive Pichu, head of Ambroise Pellerin's private office, and the man who had been disappointed not to be included when his boss met Georges Wavre. He had been with the Minister for some seven years, including four in the political wilderness and three in ministerial posts. He had a first-class brain of the filing system type, infinite energy and a useful willingness to do whatever was required of him. Ambroise Pellerin regarded him as completely trustworthy – his *homme de confiance*, such as all politicians find useful. And this confidence extended beyond politics into that more private world where the Minister's whereabouts and the Minister's telephone calls would have been of more interest to his wife than to his professional associates. In all these matters, the pale, somewhat lemur-like Pichu was, in the Minister's view, a paragon. He had plucked him from a lower level of the civil service – he had an eye for a good man – and had made of him that peculiarly French product: the man who owes his career almost entirely to his sponsor. Hence the reliability. Hence the trust. Hence, in the devious and dissatisfied mind of the neurotically ambitious Pichu, the passionate hatred of Ambroise Pellerin, now embedded like a slow-release poison in his very nature. Hence, too, the miniaturised radio-microphone beneath the top of the Louis Quinze-style commode which stood against the wall in Pichu's salon where Hemminge had made the introductions and he, the Admiral and the Minister were now comfortably seated, bottles and glasses on a low table between them. Pichu himself, discreet as ever, had left them the apartment for the evening and had gone off to some haunt of his own. Not knowing who the Minister wanted to meet, and taking care not to ask, he had provided a comprehensive range of liquors: it was a touch of typical thoughtfulness, of attention to detail.

The two Americans drank Scotch. The Minister helped

himself to a small glass of port. '*Messieurs, je vous écoute*,' he said.

He had brought the Admiral to see him, Rolf Hemminge said, because he felt it must be fruitful, *mon cher ami*, for the new head of the CIA to make contacts of his own with leading politicians in France – with men of goodwill whose political philosophy led them naturally into cooperation of this sort. *Vous me comprenez bien?* It was important, he averred, that the head of the CIA should hear at firsthand what leaders of French opinion were thinking, planning, hoping in the present extremely delicate – he might say dangerous – situation. He touched on the bombings, referred briefly to the forthcoming elections, execrated in passing the Communists, and ventured to suggest that as friends of French democracy and the *status quo* in France, the Government and people of the USA were concerned, even alarmed, certainly willing to do all in their power . . .

He went on in this manner for some little time, hinting at collaboration here, waving the possibility of American intervention there, creating an atmosphere in which things could be said, ideas put forward, which by their nature needed to be cocooned in this kind of suggestive politico-conspiratorial miasma. He was an experienced organiser of the unavowable. The sensitivity of his homosexual nature, coupled with his years spent persuading the reluctant and encouraging the faint-hearted, made him good at this kind of thing.

Not that the Admiral thought so. These subtleties, if they did not escape him entirely, at any rate failed to impress him. They all faced, did they not, a tough task in a tough and ruthless world: the defeat of Communism. He was beginning to lose patience with the elliptical Hemminge. There were direct questions to be asked. This tiresome faggot was not asking them. He decided to do some asking himself.

'I want to know, Minister, what you men will do if the polls are proved right and the Communists advance at the next elections?'

'It depends, Admiral.'

'On what?'

'On many things which cannot be foreseen now. On the mood of the country, for one, and above all on the mood of what I shall call the real France – those who will have voted against Communism and Socialism and who, by and large, are the driving force of our society.'

'What if they're angry as hell? What if they're in the mood to *act*?'

'Then that is one political hypothesis and we would have to see how we should confront it.'

The Admiral grunted impatiently. He was surrounded by prevaricators and did not like it.

'Would you, personally, be willing to act, to take command?'

Ambroise Pellerin allowed his eyebrows to rise visibly in a very deliberate gesture of surprise. 'You would hardly expect me to commit myself to such a course here, in advance, just like that.' He spread his big hands deprecatingly.

'Are you saying no?'

There was a long pause.

'I am not saying no.'

'Are you willing to take steps, Minister?'

Another pause. 'It would depend on the steps. And I would be less than frank if I did not tell you, Admiral, that I cannot discuss such a matter with you in any greater detail than that.'

'Will you keep in touch with my friend Rolf here?'

'I will.'

'And can we rely on you to keep us briefed? We get nothing but garbage through our Embassy.'

The Minister made a gesture which could – and was – taken as affirmative.

'That's great,' the Admiral said.

Later, on their way back to the Hotel Meurice, the Admiral said: 'Is that the best you can do, Rolf?'

'Not necessarily, Admiral. There are others who are closer to us, but Pellerin has the muscle, the charisma, to be the front man when it comes to it.'

'Is he really such a pussy-foot as he makes out?'

'Not at all. But he's been around long enough to know you don't commit yourself, even to the CIA, ahead of the game. I said you should meet him: I didn't say he'd give you all the answers you were after. But you can take my word for it, Admiral, when the chips are down, Pellerin will play.'

When Pichu got back to his apartment later that night, he unloaded the cassette which had been recording the evening's proceedings in a cupboard of his bedroom, played it back twice and decided that it should be delivered next day. Then he went to bed.

Next morning at eight, Baum had Allembeau in his office.

'Nothing so far,' Allembeau said. 'We talked to him all night. He's got his little story and that's all he knows. I would say he's a real catch and not an innocent intermediary at all.'

'I have not been idle,' Baum said. 'Last night I talked to a friend who looks after the archives of the Foreign Legion down in Aubagne. You know, they like to keep nice fat dossiers on their members, past and present. This man Jean-Paul Macé is quite interesting.'

He pulled a crumpled sheet of paper from his pocket, smoothed it on the desk and peered at the writing on it.

'Ah, yes, what do we have? It appears that Macé was always very interested in politics of the cruder kind. A highly political fellow, in fact. At one time a member of FANE, the neo-Nazi outfit. Then it appears that what they had to offer was too mild for him, and he developed links with the Italian *Terzia Positzione* group. They argue with bombs and machine guns. In the Legion he was always trying to prove that what this country needed was a firm hand. Blood would need to be shed – that sort of stuff. In fact they regarded him as something of a nut. But there is absolutely no trace of his ever having been drawn to Left-wing causes. Right terror, yes. Left terror, not as far as one can see.'

'So what do we do with him?'

'We keep talking.'

'Rough?'

'No, not rough. Perhaps I should have a chat with him. He might appreciate a change of physiognomy. Let's have him in.'

The swagger had not abandoned Jean-Paul. Indeed, it had been reinforced by the consideration with which he had been treated. Allembeau he had found easy. The pigs in this outfit were nothing compared with what he'd encountered in the past. Now there was this plump little fart who just stared at him and shook his head. He could stare as long as he fucking well liked, it wouldn't make him talk. Sooner or later they'd have to let him go, of course. All he needed to do was keep his cool, take it easy. There was nothing to it, dealing with these assholes.

'I am sorry that you are unwilling to cooperate with us,' the plump man with the look of surprise was saying. 'You must realise that you are likely to be here for a very long time in that case. We don't mind, of course, but I think you will.'

Jean-Paul said nothing. He tried to out-stare Baum but didn't succeed. He stretched his legs and yawned.

'This is not the police, you understand,' Baum said. 'This is the DST, where we order things differently.' His voice was soft, almost apologetic. 'No one knows you are here, of course,' he murmured. 'No one at all. So that our dialogue can go on pretty well indefinitely. It seems a shame to take up so much of your time when it could all be settled in a few minutes, and then you could have the full protection of the law once more – legal representation and all that goes with it.'

'You can't hold me indefinitely,' Jean-Paul said.

'I can,' Baum said, as if he himself regretted the fact deeply. 'Oh, yes I can. You see, you have been telling us lies all night. You have wasted a lot of the Inspector's time and now you are wasting my time too. We are patient men, but we have colleagues less patient than us. You would be well advised to cooperate with me, lest you find yourself obliged to cooperate with less amiable characters whether you like it or not. Do I make myself clear?'

'Fuck off,' Jean-Paul said, and yawned again.

Baum sighed. 'Very well, then we will hold you until we make another arrest. Then we shall see. If I were you, I would pray the arrest comes soon. It gets very tedious here. And we shall continue to ask you questions.' Baum sighed again. 'Take him away,' he said.

After Jean-Paul had gone, Baum turned to Inspector Allembeau. 'I don't believe we will get anything out of that fellow. I dare say if we beat him to a pulp something would emerge, but I am not yet so desperate that we need to let the heavy mob loose on him. Also, this is a sensitive matter in all kinds of ways and it could rebound very nastily. No, I have a better idea.'

He proceeded to tell the Inspector what his better idea was.

'You like taking risks, Alfred,' Allembeau said.

'I don't like it. I just find I have to do it sometimes, that's all.'

That afternoon Jean-Paul was taken several times to a room at the end of the corridor on the first floor. There he was interrogated by a tired Sergeant who made no progress with him. From time to time, the Sergeant left the room to fetch a file or a cup of coffee. Each time he went, Jean-Paul moved to the window and weighed up the pros and cons of a getaway. He concluded that it could never be done in daylight but might work in the dark. *Ergo*: make the interrogations stretch out as far as he could.

Shortly after 10 p.m. he was brought back to the same room. The Sergeant was tired, bored and without hope of getting anywhere at all. After a half hour, he said, 'This is dry work. I'm getting some coffee. Do you want some?'

'Yes,' Jean-Paul said graciously.

The Sergeant left the room and locked the door behind him. Jean-Paul went to the window, climbed onto the sill and hoisted himself onto the outside ledge. Then he lowered himself until he was hanging from the ledge by his hands. Thrusting away from the wall, he let himself drop. The distance to the ground at full stretch was only eight feet and he had learned how to drop greater distances than that in his Legion training. He fell expertly, picked himself up and made off at a run down the Rue des Saussaies. There was no one about and the men on duty at the DST entrance further up the street did not see him.

'Fucking easy,' he said to himself.

By the time he had reached the *St Augustin* Metro station he was satisfied that they weren't tailing him. 'Must be missing me about now,' he said to himself. 'Stupid bastards.'

On the platform there were three men deep in conversation. When the train drew in, two of them got aboard in the same carriage as Jean-Paul, while the other sprinted for the exit and was soon in a phone booth at street level.

When he had finished with the call, Baum dialled a number. It was a booth at the *Gare de l'Est*. 'Listen, Léon, he's on a train which could be heading for the *Gare de l'Est*. Two of our men are with him. Is the grid in place around the station?'

'Yes, chief. I've deployed about fifteen men and we have two cars.'

'Good. I'll take odds that he's heading your way. Good luck.'

At the interchange at *Chaussée d'Antin* two more men were waiting on the platform for trains running to the *Gare de l'Est*. The two on Jean-Paul's train followed him up the stairs and along the corridor to the new platform. When a train came in, they got into a carriage at the far end of the train, while the two waiting men got into Jean-Paul's carriage.

At the *Gare de l'Est* Jean-Paul got up from his seat, pushed past the crowd around the door and alighted on the platform. The four DST men saw him and got off the train. One of them immediately hurried up the stairs to the exit and a telephone.

'We're at the *Gare de l'Est*,' he told Baum. 'Three of our men are with him. So far, so good, chief.'

'Good.'

The other three kept a fair distance behind Jean-Paul as he made his way down the long tunnel where Ingrid had decided to shoot. He was picked up again by the DST men standing at the top of the stairs into the station concourse, and they stayed close to him as he walked towards the exit. At the exit, Léon was standing reading a newspaper. He folded the paper into his pocket as Jean-Paul came abreast of him and crossed the Place by his side.

Now Jean-Paul set off down the Faubourg St Denis, and as he did so, a slim girl stepped out of the shadow of a doorway, an unlit cigarette between her lips.

'Have you a light?' she asked.

'They took my fucking lighter,' Jean-Paul said.

'They plan to follow you here,' Ingrid said. 'Keep walking. You can go to my place but shake them off first.'

As she said it, Léon came abreast of them and caught a glimpse of her face. It pressed a button somewhere in his memory. It could be the girl from the hospital. Different hair, but the features looked right. He caught the words, 'Keep walking,' and realised at once that someone had blown their plan. He had to think fast. There were at least two DST men following behind, maybe fifty yards away. Luc should be on the next corner, about a hundred yards ahead. If he tried to nab them now, one of them at least would get away. But if they separated and didn't walk on together, it was just as likely that they'd lose one of them. He decided to nab the girl.

The scuffle lasted only a few seconds. Léon grabbed the girl's arm and pulled her towards him. He aimed to pinion her arms to her sides, relying on the other men coming up to go after Jean-Paul. What he did not reckon with was what happened next. Instead of making a dash for it, Jean-Paul swung a heavy fist into Léon's face and a knee into his groin. The older man doubled up, releasing the girl, who ran off down the Faubourg. The two men saw what happened and broke into a run, but they were some thirty yards away and the girl and Jean-Paul had a head start on them. Luc, ahead, was too far away to see what had happened.

The girl ran diagonally across the road. She was in good trim and ran fast. Jean-Paul ran the few yards to the Passage St Denis, darted down it and kept running past the *Teinturerie*. He, too, was in good shape. The DST men never had a chance.

Luc saw the girl running towards him and heard one of the the DST men shouting. He decided that she had something to do with the case and darted across the road to intercept her. But cars travelling in both directions held him up and she was past him and into the main thoroughfare a little further along before he could reach her. The crowds coming out of the theatres swallowed her up.

It was another disaster . . .

POLICE PROVOCATION AT l'HUMA! had been the screaming headline on the following morning's *l'Humanité*. A sharp photographer had managed to get a shot of the men of the *Brigade Anti-Communiste* blundering about in the offices: it was spread all over the front page, next to a solemn editorial by Seynac, denouncing the police raid as a manoeuvre designed to discredit the Communists.

'*What were they looking for?*' he asked. '*There is reason to believe that a secret document had been sent to the newspaper with the aim of being "discovered" in the raid. But the trick failed. We must now be doubly vigilant.*'

The inside pages carried accounts of bomb outrages in the north and south-west. The rest of the press had led their front pages on the bombings, which had claimed six lives.

Now, at the DST, Alfred Baum received Léon's report and managed to suppress his fury, telling himself that it could have happened to him. What seemed clear was that there had been a leakage from the DST offices. He sat at his desk, which was empty of all papers, and allowed the implications of such a fact to sink into his consciousness. It accorded with his growing conviction that they were dealing with a situation which was all of a piece. He tried to marshal the facts in his mind: four months of bombings with no police success of any kind, then the leakage of defence documents handled in such a way that it was clear that whoever did the deed was more interested in the political consequences than in getting them into the hands of the Soviets or anyone else. And there was one other fact, one that would not go away: the clip of film from the Bois de Boulogne.

He decided to run it through once more, and after making a call on the intercom, shuffled unhappily down to the projection room. There he sat alone in the dark as the fifty seconds of film shot by Maurice were projected on the screen.

First, a motionless figure could be seen standing among the bushes, looking away from the camera. It was Galievich. Then the camera panned a short distance to the right, and in the background could clearly be seen a man in a dark jacket, walking across from right to left. He had his arm through the arm of a girl with long blonde hair. She was wearing slacks and a blouse and the man was talking while the girl listened. The camera moved back to Galievich, and shortly the walking pair came into the frame. The man was middle-aged, maybe fifty and his face was clearly visible. Baum knew who he was – knew it beyond a shadow of doubt.

The clip came to an end: Léon had told Maurice over the transceiver to stop wasting film. But Baum had seen enough. And what he had seen was deeply puzzling. For the middle-aged man was very well documented in the DST archives and it was his dossier that Baum had repeatedly examined in the past two weeks. And what he found there was what he already knew to be true: the middle-aged man was a confirmed and unshakable homosexual with no personal contacts with women of the kind that would lead to an affectionate and seemingly secret tryst amid the trees and shrubs of the Bois de Boulogne on a hot July afternoon.

Baum made his way back to his office, slumped into his chair and stared miserably at the wall. Why had he allowed himself to become so obsessed by the film? What was there about it which connected it indissolubly in his mind with wider events? At one level, the idea was preposterous. At another, altogether credible. But one thing was certain: he would never get anyone – perhaps not even Georges Wavre – to accept that there was a connection. And if anyone had asked him, Alfred Baum, *why* he saw such a connection, and what the connection actually was, he knew he would be totally unable to give a coherent answer. 'Sometimes,' he said to himself, 'you *know* something. You have no proof, no evidence even, but *you know it*. What you've been doing for most of a lifetime tells you it is so. And then all you can do is hope that trivial things like facts will obligingly bear you out.'

He got up and tried pacing back and forth in the small room. It was not helpful. He sat down again and forced his mind away from the film and onto the consequences of last night's disaster in the Faubourg St Denis. He would keep the area under surveillance, but after what had happened he expected that they'd keep clear of it. There was just a chance they'd come back to collect some gear or something. But he had no right any longer to expect such luck. Luck came to those who deserved it, and on present form, the DST deserved nothing at all. On Sunday there was a cat show at Ivry that he'd been looking forward to. He had good friends there and there would be some nice animals to be seen. But he would have to give it a miss. Instead, it would be a walk in the Bois de Boulogne. It would probably be quite useless – a dull and lonely way of spending a Sunday afternoon. Also, Estelle would not be happy about it, and though she did not complain, her silent, reproachful look did more damage to his peace of mind than any amount of shouting could have done. Be that as it may, he knew he wouldn't get his liver to behave itself until he had exorcised the ghost that was haunting him from the shady woods around the Route de l'Etoile.

He was sustained by the thought that almost everyone's tradecraft was faulty. Creatures of habit all, even well-trained operatives hated changing their encounter arrangements.

It was on that day, Friday 20 August, that the public mood began to veer dangerously from alarm towards hysteria. The franc closed the day 40 centimes down against the dollar and the Bank of France devoted another 5 billion of the reserves to their fruitless efforts to protect the French currency. The Bourse recorded the heaviest fall in share prices in a single day since the events of 1968. In Ministerial offices in Paris final preparations were being made for a meeting of the leaders of the EEC, due to open in London on the following Monday. Both the President of the Republic and his Prime Minister would attend, and both expected some difficult private conversations with their European colleagues about the unstable and deteriorating situation in France.

Chapter 11

The weather was working itself up for a storm. The city could do with it: perhaps it would clear the heavy, fume-laden atmosphere and make Paris more habitable. All that Alfred Baum hoped was that the storm would hold off until later. Estelle had sighed eloquently and packed him some lunch that morning, and now he had found a fallen tree trunk to sit on and was eating a roast leg of capon and other delicacies, washing it all down with draughts of red wine from a half bottle. He would have preferred a couple of sandwiches and a beer but hadn't liked to hurt Estelle's feelings and had accepted the so-called *piquenique*, which was more like a proper Sunday lunch, but taken *alfresco*.

The time was close to two o'clock and he had been hanging around the Route de l'Etoile since midday. Léon had briefed him on the right spot and he had recognised the landmarks. The only thing that was odd (and that, decidedly) about this plump man in a panama hat eating his lunch alone among the trees was the fact that he had by his side a golf bag. Whatever there was in the Bois de Boulogne, there was no golf course. Baum was aware of being faintly ridiculous – he who had never played golf or anything resembling it in his life.

His lunch finished and the paraphernalia of the picnic stored in a pocket of the golf bag, he made his way to a thicket about fifty yards from the roadway and settled down out of sight of the passing cars to open the bag and remove the contents. These proved to be a metal tube about three and a half feet long and six inches in diameter, linked to electronic recording equipment and a pair of headphones. As a long-range microphone it was the best of its kind, but as an accessory carried on a hot Sunday afternoon in the Bois, it left a lot to be desired. It was highly visible, heavy and impossible to pass off as anything other than what it actually was. The trick would have to be to stay out of sight yet near enough to remain within the range of the equipment. That, he reckoned, would be about 100 yards under these conditions.

At 2.15 a white 2CV van drew up close to the point where Baum was hiding in the bushes. The driver seemed disinclined to go for a walk. It was difficult to see, what with the intervening trees and the distance. At 2.30 Baum saw a man approaching along the Route de l'Etoile. Despite the distance, Baum knew at once who he was. So, apparently, did the occupant of the van. A blonde girl alighted, and both walked away from the footpath and came together about seventy-five yards from Baum's hideout. They started walking back and forth among the trees, the man talking, the girl occasionally adding a word. She had long blonde hair and walked looking down at the ground ahead of her. She walked with an athletic tread. It was difficult to see her face.

Baum lifted the directional mike, leaning the barrel on the low branch of a tree. He was picking up the noise of their footsteps without difficulty, and after some adjustment, their voices came over in snatches. There must be some distortion in the circuitry, Baum thought, because the girl's higher voice was coming through low, like that of a man. Their constant movement, and no doubt the interruption caused by the intervening trees, were making reception very poor. He wished he'd been able to bring a technician with him, but this quest was somehow his alone. He didn't want anyone to be in on it until he'd proved out his hunch. And then, if his hunch was sound, there would be a host of other reasons why he wouldn't want it to be known around the office. Not now that he was certain there was a leakage. Not if these secret meetings in the Bois were what he suspected. Not after the recent failures. Not at all, in fact . . .

He caught some words from the man: 'The agreed action . . . September sixth . . . the exact route . . .' The mike was picking up a lot of garbage in the background.

The girl was asking questions: '. . . if we are not ready? . . . new command post?'

Baum concentrated on keeping out of sight and keeping the directional mike trained on the couple as they moved to and fro. He hardly paid attention to what was said: he would be spending hours with the tape later on anyway. He checked that the cassette's spools were turning on their spindles. He was getting a fair amount of the dialogue now. Maybe he was getting lucky at last. About time. All the cards had been against him. Perhaps this was the ace coming his way at last.

The couple had separated. There had been no sign of affection between them, either when they met or on parting. The encounter had had all the mannerisms of a business meeting, save for the setting. They hadn't even linked arms as in the film. And that girl . . . Decidedly ungirlish. More like a youth, really. Baum smiled to himself. Like a youth because it was in fact a youth. The thing was obvious – a pretty good cover for a Sunday meeting in the Bois de Boulogne.

He stowed his equipment behind a bush and walked fast towards the road. The man had already set off in the opposite direction. As Baum reached a point ten yards or so from the footpath, the van started up. He was just in time to see its registration number. He wrote it on a slip of paper, collected his golfing gear and set off to find a taxi. He had not felt as relaxed as this for a couple of weeks. He, who dealt always with mysteries, hated mystery. This one had been solved and it was as if a weight had been lifted from his spirit. Solved but not resolved. That would be an altogether different and more complex matter. But sufficient unto the day was that particular problem.

The plump man with the incongruous golf bag, sweating profusely but looking strangely contented, caught a train at the Gare Montparnasse and was at home having black coffee in Versailles by 4.30.

It was Coincidence – that famous lady with the long arm – who dictated that another of the notorious DST stake-outs should have been ordered for that same Sunday afternoon, also in the Bois de Boulogne, but at the far side around the Porte de Madrid and well away from Alfred Baum's *piquenique*. Much the same team as before had been sitting around, sweating, in the same cars, and nerves were frayed as they had been frayed on earlier Sundays.

'If all we're going to have on these little outings of ours is a geezer getting it up at the sight of some kid's tits in the middle distance, we might as well hand the whole thing to the vice squad. It's more in their line.' Léon was not happy. His car had been parked under the trees for several hours and they weren't off duty until six. That was over an hour from now and no one believed the KGB was going to offer them some action in those sixty minutes.

'Maybe if nothing happens this time the bosses will give the whole thing up as the lousy idea it is,' Luc said.

'Why should they? They're not the ones who have to do it.'

The traffic in the Avenue du Mahatma Gandhi was heavy in both directions. The Avenue was the long side of a triangle of which the shorter sides were formed by the Boulevard Maurice Barrès and the Boulevard du Commandant Charcot. This was the area of the stake-out, and Léon's lead car was stationed to observe the flow on the Avenue in both directions as it approached or left the Porte de Madrid.

The radio crackled into life. 'Lizard to Fox. Soviet Embassy car proceeding north on the Route de Neuilly towards the meeting of the two Boulevards at the Porte de Neuilly. We got a clear look at him. It's our old friend Galievich. He has another Russki next to him.'

'Oh, Christ,' Léon said, 'Why doesn't he go to a tit and bum show in Montmartre? It'd be easier for everyone.' He pulled himself up in his seat, started the engine. 'Fox to Beaver, Fox to Beaver. Pick up the Russian car at the Porte de Neuilly. You and Lizard tail him. We'll stay here till we see what he's up to. If there's two of them perhaps it's business and not pleasure this time. Over.'

But the Russian Zis never reached the Porte de Neuilly. It

turned sharply into a narrow lane between the trees just before the Route de Neuilly joined the main thoroughfare. As Lizard reached and passed the turn-off, the DST men saw the Russians slow to a halt a hundred yards or so up the lane. They radioed the news back to Léon in Fox.

'Lizard and Beaver come in as close as possible, then it's foot surveillance. I'm joining you. But be careful, for Christ's sake, and don't rush it. Over.'

A few moments later the six men from the cars had spread out on foot around the spot where the Russian car was parked. Galievich and his companion had not budged. Léon, sweating, irritable, but now thoroughly alert, looked at his watch. It was a few minutes before five. 'If it's a drop of some kind,' he said to Luc, 'it's probably timed for five o'clock. You see, exactly at five they'll get out of the car.' They could watch the vehicle adequately through the trees from an angle which must have been blind to the men inside it.

But it did not happen in quite the way Léon had predicted. Exactly at five the second man got out of the car alone and started to walk back and forth in the lane, looking around him in what was intended to be a nonchalant style.

'Galievich's cover,' Léon said. 'It begins to look interesting. When he's satisfied the coast is clear, he'll signal Galievich. I give it another sixty seconds, then we'll see old Peeping Tomski emerge, you watch.'

This time he was proved right. The second man, apparently satisfied and unable to see the DST men among the trees, suddenly bent down and appeared to be adjusting a shoelace. A moment later Galievich got out of the car and sauntered back towards the Route de Neuilly. A few minutes earlier a blue Renault had driven into the Bois from the Porte de Neuilly and had parked at the corner of the lane. Galievich was walking towards it.

'That car!' Léon had difficulty in keeping his voice down as he spoke into his transceiver. 'If he gets into it we all rush it. And at once. At the double, all of you. If Bison can reach it within a minute, step on it, pull up alongside and beat us to it if you can. Now get going, all of you. I'm issuing no more orders.'

The car named Bison was cruising down the Boulevard du Commandant Charcot when it picked up Léon's message. The driver thrust his foot down, took the car onto the wrong side of the wide road to overtake a truck, jumped the lights at the Porte de Neuilly and raced up the Route de Neuilly.

'That's him, there on the right,' his companion said.

The Russian had climbed into the blue Renault and was talking to the driver. The second Russian was now walking back and forth in the Route de Neuilly, on the far side of the road. Before he could realise that the innocent-looking DST car was there on business, it had passed him, swerved across the road and screeched to a halt exactly level with the Renault. Each DST man took one side of the Renault and each leaned against a door as their colleagues came up, panting, from three directions. The second Russian broke into a run, heading towards the Porte de Neuilly. 'Let him go,' shouted Léon as he reached the Renault.

The standard procedures were soon completed. Léon's DST card was waved at the occupants, papers were asked for, two identical briefcases were impounded. Then, as Galievich protested that he was a Soviet diplomat with immunity, he and the other man were politely but firmly ushered into one of the DST cars and driven off to the Rue des Saussaies, while one of the teams stayed behind to search the Renault and drive it after the other car.

From sullen resentment the mood of the men had changed to elation. Jokes were exchanged on the car radio system. It looked like a real catch, congratulations from the old man, a few bottles together to celebrate later – a job beautifully done.

The man driving the Renault had looked in the glove compartment, where he found the car's papers. The owner was stated as Robert Pichu, 17 Rue Demours. Occupation: civil servant.

Léon, in the lead car, had permitted himself a glance inside the briefcases. One contained a newspaper, folded into six.

The other contained, in a small plastic bag from a grocery store, a C120 low-noise tape cassette. As they sped towards the Rue des Saussaies he called the control room on his radio and told them what to do.

It was just after 5.15 when the call from the DST duty officer came through. Alfred Baum listened to what the man had to say, grunted, sighed, grunted again, and said: 'They are not to be allowed near a telephone. Keep them apart. Don't call anyone else. Tell Léon to wait there for me. There's a train I can catch at five thirty-five. Get a car to meet it at Montparnasse.' He rang off and sighed again.

'I really am sorry,' he said to Estelle. 'I know we were to see the Monnots tonight but I have to go back to the office. You'll know what to say to them.' He tried a smile to see how it would be received and was relieved when it was returned. 'Thanks,' he said. 'And I really am sorry. Perhaps you should have married a greengrocer.'

'I think not. Hurry back.'

'I'll do my best.'

His own tape would have to wait till later. A pity: he was in the mood to tackle it now, while the bits he had heard were still fresh in his mind. But Galievich was Galievich. Not a minnow: more like a good-sized barracuda. A distraction from the matters in hand it might be, but a worthy distraction.

He made his way down to the street, hurrying for the 5.35, his mind on the events of the afternoon, scarcely interested in what he might find when he got to the office. He continued to ponder the meeting in the Bois as the DST driver took him fast through the heat and noise of the Paris evening, and only wrenched his mind back into the present when he had Léon, flushed and triumphant, before him, making his report and putting his *pièces* – his items of evidence – now neatly labelled, on his desk. Among them was an identity card. Baum picked it up. He knew the name.

'This,' he said to Léon, 'is complicated beyond belief.'

'Why –'

'Never mind. Tell your story. Then I'll play the tape and see these gentlemen.'

When Léon had finished Baum said 'Well done' in a more peremptory manner than Léon would have liked, sent for a tape recorder and having locked himself in his office, settled down to listen to the captured tape. He recognised the gruff provincial accent of Ambroise Pellerin at once and was satisfied after a while that one of the American voices was familiar. When he heard the name 'Rolf' he knew he had guessed right, and a reference to 'the Admiral' told him who the other American was. The tape ran for just under an hour, and when it was finished Baum sat in silence for a while, looking at the tape recorder as if it had something more to tell him but was deliberately holding it back. Then he unlocked the door and sent for Galievich.

That gentleman blustered in the approved diplomatic style always used by both sides in any impasse of this kind. He announced to Baum that he could not be detained, quoting the appropriate international convention, and Baum replied that he knew that already. He demanded to be allowed to leave at once and refused to answer any questions whatever. He was escorted courteously out into the Rue des Saussaies and made off in the direction of the Place Beauvau. A Soviet Embassy car was to be seen waiting quietly in the Place and he got into it and was driven away.

Robert Pichu, sallow and watchful, was another matter. He, too, refused to talk. What he wanted was access to a telephone in order to call his lawyer. It was refused. After fifteen fruitless minutes, Baum had him taken away and decided to use the phone himself. Georges Wavre listened in silence to what Baum had to say, including a carefully worded proposal which had formulated itself in his mind during the long, arid pauses of his interview with Pichu.

'Another of your complicated and dangerous ideas, Alfred.'

'Yes,' Baum said simply. 'But if we don't do it, all we'll have on our hands is a run-of-the-mill espionage case, a scandal, a tedious and time-consuming series of debates with an examining magistrate, and God knows what else. Or, more likely, we'll have no case at all once the powers above us realise that our only evidence is a tape of a very tricky conversation between the Minister of Defence and a couple of Americans. That is *not* the kind of evidence our esteemed President will want to read about in his morning newspaper. Whereas my way we may have a most elegant little scheme. *Most* elegant, though I say it myself.'

'All right, damn you, do it. Let me know how you get on.'

Baum called Pichu, sullen as ever, back to his office.

'Monsieur Pichu,' he said amiably, 'you must realise that you are in a mess – a devil of a mess. But it may be possible for me to show you a way out of it. I don't say I will: I merely say I may be able to. But it will depend on you.'

Pichu, who had been pondering his situation and had come to a similar conclusion, allowed his eyebrows to go up. These said, 'Yes, well?' but subtly, without commitment.

'I have listened to the tape you were trying to pass to the Soviets.'

'I do not admit that I was passing anything to anyone.'

'Of course you don't, but I suggest you do not waste my time with this kind of pointless denial. As I say, I have listened to your tape. It can, of course, earn you something like ten years inside, given the circumstances in which it came into our hands.'

'Unless you, or someone at a higher level, decides that what the tape contains is more reprehensible even than what I am alleged to have done.'

'I expected you to say that,' Baum said, as if it were a perfectly reasonable line of argument. 'But my men, who are going over your apartment right now in a highly professional way, may well come up with evidence which avoids the need to use the tape at all.'

Pichu blinked and the muscle beneath his jaw tightened. 'There is nothing to be found there.'

'We shall see. And if there isn't, we have other ways of bringing your career to an end and shall most certainly use them.'

There was a silence. 'What do you propose?'

Baum's voice hardened fractionally as Pichu's lost its arrogance. 'You will work for us.'

'What sort of work?'

'There are things which can interest us from time to time. They will be explained to you and you will do what we require. In entering upon this arrangement you will sign a confession of your contacts with the Soviets and that will be kept in my safe here. It will not be used so long as you behave yourself. When you have signed you will be told what we want. But first I want to know why you were working with the Soviets. Was it ideological?'

Pichu emitted a hollow laugh. 'What, that squalid system? Not me!'

'Money then?'

'Their money never amounts to much. You must know that. But I will not pretend that money of any colour is distasteful to me.'

'If not money, what?'

'Insurance.'

Baum looked at him. 'I don't think I understand you.'

'It is simple. Look around you. Do you think this ramshackle set-up of ours is going to last for ever? Look at the progress of the Communist Party and the pathetic response of the other parties. Is anyone going to tell me that that can go on much longer? Of course not! So I took out insurance.'

'And what was the price of your insurance premiums?'

'Oh, little pieces of information from time to time. Policy matters, mostly, and personal stuff which might interest them.'

'But you work in the Ministry of Defence where you have access to the most sensitive military secrets. Is that what you were passing?'

Pichu's reaction to this was remarkable. In making his piecemeal confession he had somehow shrunk and all dignity had left him. Now he pulled himself bolt upright on his chair and became once more the high official, peremptory and self-regarding.

'Monsieur, I would inform you that I am a Frenchman. I

love my country. I am no traitor. I would never give the Soviets anything damaging to France.'

Later, Baum was to say to Georges Wavre that it was the only moment of his odd interview with Robert Pichu when he had detected some kind of principle – a sort of bureaucrat's sincerity: political secrets, *bien sûr*; military secrets, *jamais*! It was ridiculous, yet he believed him.

Now he looked hard at his man, still bristling on his chair in the dismal office. 'Have you ever given them minutes of official meetings?'

'Never! Absolutely not!'

'Do you see the minutes of the Defence Committee?'

'Certainly.'

'Have you ever made illicit copies of those minutes for any outside persons?'

'Absolutely not! They are the highest State secrets.'

'And you do not betray high State secrets?'

'Never!'

'Just lesser secrets?'

Pichu remained silent, sinking back from his show of indignation.

'Right,' Alfred Baum said, 'I will now tell you what we want you to do and how we propose to keep in touch with you. And we will then draw up a little document, you and I, and you will put your signature to it, Monsieur Pichu. After which, you will be free to go home, counting yourself a very lucky man.'

It was midnight when Baum reached home. Estelle had gone to bed. He made himself some coffee, cut himself some bread and cheese, and settled down with his cassette player and tapes. He had sixteen minutes of recording from his venture in the Bois de Boulogne which he set out laboriously to transcribe into a lined notebook. There were many breaks as background noise drowned the voices, or the voices themselves dropped too low, or the couple turned away from Baum's position in the bushes. When he had transcribed all that he could understand, he went through the text, underlining in red those passages which interested him.

What he ended up with was a series of snatches of near-coherent dialogue:

MAN The agreed action . . . without fail . . . September sixth . . . the exact route . . .
GIRL . . . the Boulevards to the Opéra and then on to the Concorde and up the Champs Elysées . . .
MAN Grenades . . . can you do that? . . . policemen . . . must seem to come from within the crowd . . .
GIRL Yes.
MAN . . . in a bourgeois quarter. Say as near to the Concorde as you can or in the Champs Elysées . . . in from Italy yet?
GIRL . . . on Tuesday. Then we'll pick the stuff up and take it to the usual place.
MAN Good . . .
GIRL Jean-Paul is being difficult since his escape. We want to . . .
MAN He knows too much . . .
GIRL . . . we think it should be done. The Command is worried by his escape . . . think it could be a put-up job. It must be . . .
MAN . . . what is necessary.
GIRL All right.
MAN So we'll meet again next Sunday at the same time.
GIRL Here?
MAN . . . the other place. Goodbye.
GIRL Goodbye.

Both cats had leapt into his lap and snuggled down there, their thick fur melting them into one two-headed animal. Baum had been staring at the text he had created, but he had not been reading. His mind was ranging again over the sinister panorama of which this formed only a small part of the foreground. The cats purred noisily and occasionally one or other of them would open a sombre eye and slowly shut it again. A bushy tail waved once or twice, aimlessly. He stroked a back and tickled an ear. Then he sighed, pushed the cats gently off his lap and settled down to make notes.

The following morning he had the 2CV van from the Bois de Boulogne traced on the police computer before going in to see Georges Wavre. He sat beneath the portraits of the two Presidents of the Republic. He had with him the sheet of paper on which he had transcribed the snatches of conversation from the Route de l'Etoile. He talked quietly, persuasively for maybe fifteen minutes, while Georges Wavre sat motionless in his chair, his pudgy hands on the blotter before him, his eyes fixed on Baum, unblinking, expressionless, doubting.

When Baum had finished, his head slightly to one side, his eyes almost mischievous beneath their beetle brows, the two men sat in silence as seconds ticked away. Then Wavre grunted, pulled a pack of cigarettes almost violently from a pocket and lit one. He grunted again.

'Damn you, Alfred, you always come up with complications.'

'This one at least is not of my making. Would you have preferred me to ignore the clip of film and pretend none of this is going on?'

'Of course I would.'

Baum grinned. 'You can still pretend I never told you. I shall not go running to the newspapers.'

'You have given me a scenario that I cannot accept. I am not saying it is mistaken in any way. Indeed, I have to congratulate you on what looks like a pretty accurate outline of what is happening. But I cannot accept it because the Government will not be able to accept it, and I am not a man to offer my masters what my masters will not know how to deal with. Nevertheless, we cannot turn our backs on all this. There is no particular virtue in action as such, but it seems to me that we have to act.'

'I think so too.'

'Make me a proposal.'

Baum sat in silence for a moment, head cocked, eyes almost shut. Then he seemed to shake himself. He leaned forward.

'I think we have to separate the events in the Bois de Boulogne from the activists in the terror campaign. Let us forget for a moment what you and I know about who controls the campaign, and concentrate instead on defeating it. That means following up what clues we have. And what are they? Firstly, this van: we'll do a straightforward police job on that. Secondly, we know that somewhere in the area of the Faubourg St Denis is a base of some sort which these people used and may still be using. We can organise a raid on a major scale – every building within a two-hundred-metre diameter. It might just throw something up.'

'It isn't much.'

'And then, of course, there's the Gaullist parade on September sixth. And there we can't afford to let any bombs go off or have any policemen killed.'

'Which means that you have to crack the thing within fourteen days,' Wavre said drily.

'Not easy, when we are in fact doing the work of the police and not the DST.'

'True, but there is one aspect of all this which is strictly our job and has to be handled with tongs, and that's this man Pichu and his meetings with the Soviets. So tell me where we stand.'

When Baum had finished his account of the events of the previous evening, Wavre turned his eyes ceilingwards in a gesture of exaggerated despair. 'As if we needed that! You see where it puts us, don't you? Normally I would go in to the Minister, tell him all, and his people would then ask Foreign Affairs to declare Galievich *persona non grata* in the usual way, thus booting him out. But if I do that I have to tell the Minister *who* was on Pichu's tape. And who knows what personal or other motives may push our esteemed Minister into ordering this or that, as the case may be? No, all my instincts tell me that the one thing we cannot do here is tell the Minister – *any* Minister – what we are up to with friend Pichu.'

'How hard it is,' Baum mused quietly, his eyes twinkling, 'to be constitutional, democratic and even law-abiding in this job.'

'And yet the constitution, democracy and the law are

exactly the things we try to defend. I suppose it's dangerous to flout your own cause, eh?'

'A fine point. We need a resident philosopher at the DST. I've always thought so. A professor of Moral Philosophy. He would be a great help to me. Perhaps he could define a few simple words like ends, means, expediency – stuff like that.'

'That's as may be. For the moment I propose not to say anything to the Minister, whatever the moral implications.'

At the door, Baum turned. 'I hear the *Préfecture* has grabbed the shelling incident for themselves, which means that absolutely nothing will happen. In a way, I don't mind. We have more than enough to do without all the forensic work that place opposite the Elysée must be throwing up.'

The computer had offered Jacob, Henri, 166 Avenue du Maine as the owner of the white 2CV Renault van. Mr Jacob proved to be a small *menuisier* conducting a carpentry and odd-job business from a yard behind his ground-floor apartment. Here, according to the DST men who paid him a call, he lived with a wife and three youngish children, and on the face of things he seemed much like any other Parisian of the artisan class. The arrival of the DST posse caused Mr Jacob considerable alarm, trading as he did largely outside the "official" market where Value Added Tax and suchlike had to be attended to. He was surprised to find that his visitors were more interested in his van than his books, and as his fears subsided his willingness to cooperate grew.

Where had he been yesterday afternoon? At home with the wife and kids. Any witnesses? Yes, the wife and kids. Come now, something a bit more credible. Well, a neighbour, one Frescati, called at about two to borrow a tool. He gave the men Frescati's address nearby.

Had he lent his van to anyone during the day? No, he had not.

What about the van, then – how long had he had it? About six years. Matter of fact, it was getting to be more trouble than it was worth and he'd had it on the market for three months. Hadn't got his price yet and was in no hurry to sell.

Evidence? He rummaged along a shelf and found a back copy of a local paper, pointed to the ad with a battered and grubby finger and handed it to his visitors. So, had many people been to see the van? No, not many. One or two. But the offers were no good.

Anyone show particular interest in it? Mr Jacob frowned in recollection.

'What about those two who looked as if they were going to buy it?' his wife asked. 'You know, the ones who came right after the ad appeared. They went over it like a couple of real experts. Had the bonnet open, digging around in there. Came twice. You remember, Henri.'

'That's right, we thought we had it sold. Then we heard nothing more.'

'Describe the men.'

Henri shrugged and screwed up his face. 'Christ, that's a tall order, that far back. Marie you've a better memory.'

'Oh, I remember them all right,' his wife said. 'After all the trouble we went to with them. Especially the tall one. A big fellow, good looking, too. And he had red hair, you know, real red.'

'Age?'

'Maybe thirty.'

'And the other one?'

'Shorter. Not so noticeable. I remember he sounded as if he came from the south somewhere. A dark fellow, thickset. That's about all I remember about him.'

'Anything else on either of them? Any distinguishing marks, anything special they said?'

The Jacobs were silent, shaking their heads.

'Did you hear either of them call the other by name?'

Head-shaking again.

'One thing,' Mme Jacob said. 'It struck me as funny. It comes to me now. The shorter one, he had a scrap of paper and a pencil and he made notes. God knows what there is about a clapped-out 2CV to make notes about, but I remember, he was jotting things down. You remember, don't you, Henri?'

'Think I do,' Henri said. His mental faculties were still

numbed by the thought that these officials might be about to start in on his books. But they appeared to be satisfied with what they had heard.

'All right, we'll check now with your friend Frescati and if you've been telling the truth you won't be bothered any more.'

One of the DST men stayed with the Jacobs while the other went down the road to find Frescati, who proved to be an insurance salesman, working from home. Asked about his movements on Sunday afternoon, he confirmed his call on the Jacobs. It all sounded authentic to the DST man, who went back and collected his colleague.

'Thank you, messieurs-dames, we shall not be bothering you.'

'I know the trick,' Baum said when he heard the story that afternoon. 'Object: to put an untraceable car on the road. Method: first, find a used car for sale, of the type that you can easily steal somewhere. Inspect it, making a note of the engine and chassis numbers, the year, colour and so on. That isn't too hard if you are really familiar with motor cars. In this case, the detailed inspection and the note-taking are sure signs. Then you steal your car – same make and colour and the same year. Then you forge your log book, using the details from the car you didn't buy, and apply for a set of replacement number plates, submitting the log book, of course, as evidence of ownership. You get the plates, put them on your stolen vehicle, and now you're running around with a car virtually identical to the other one with the same number plates. But if the police try to trace you, where do they end up? Where we did, with one Jacob, *menuisier*, in the Avenue du Maine – a totally innocent party.'

'It's neat,' said the DST man who had been on the job.

'Very. The regular police are wise to it, but now you've learned something, my friend. Anyway, thanks for trying.'

To the DST man it was a dead end. To Baum it was a small piece of the jigsaw, for it confirmed what he already knew by induction: the red-headed man who was tall and good looking had to be Jean-Paul Macé, and that tied the man in the Bois de Boulogne to the incident of the envelope delivered to Seynac at *l'Humanité*. It was all police detective stuff, of very little interest to Baum, but the official mind, one day, somewhere, was liable to attach extreme importance to it.

'If it ever gets that far,' he murmured to himself as he added the facts to the dossier he was laboriously building. Then he called Commander Roisset at the *Préfecture* and asked him to put out a police watch for a white Renault 2CV van. He gave Roisset the details.

'But not a van with H. Jacob, Menuisier, stencilled on the sides. A van with the same registration number but plain white. A particularly good place and time would be the Bois de Boulogne on Sundays, but it could turn up anywhere. If any of your men spot it I want an arrest, on any pretext you like, and then Georges Wavre would like whoever you detain to be sent to me here at the DST. Day or night, you understand.'

'No problem. Tell me, how are you getting on with that little matter of the leak, you know . . .'

'This is part of it,' Baum said darkly. 'A very important part. Your cooperation will be decisive.'

'Quite, you may depend on us.'

'Thank you, Commander.'

'If we at the DST are leaking like a sieve,' Baum reflected as he rang off, 'over at the *Préfecture* it will be more like a colander. I have very modest hopes of our friend Roisset.'

That evening he arrived home late and tired. He did justice to the plate of cold cuts and *crudités* that Estelle had prepared. It was followed by a *coeur-à-la-crème*, onto which he heaped a small Alp of sugar.

'Delicious, this cheese,' he said between mouthfuls. 'It's a long time since we had it.'

'It isn't good for you, that's why. All that cream and sugar – no wonder you put on weight.'

'You like me chubby. It's my charm.'

She smiled indulgently. 'It isn't good for you,' she repeated.

The Baums spent the rest of the evening watching an amateur talent contest on television, enjoying every minute of it. By eleven they were in bed and asleep.

The President of the Republic and the Prime Minister at the EEC meeting in London had the hard time that they had expected. The Americans must have been at work: colleagues were talking of the dangers of a shift to the left in France and its repercussions in the rest of Europe. But the Italian Premier was concerned about another aspect of the matter.

'You will forgive me, cher collègue,*' he said to the French Prime Minister, whom he had known for twenty years, 'but what worries me about your situation at the moment is not the Left, but the Right. It seems to me that we have here many of the elements which could make the situation propitious for a Right-wing coup. In the name of law and order, the defence of France, and so on, you understand.'*

'I understand.'

'You will forgive my comment on an internal matter, but you appreciate that our own Fascists in Italy would be immeasurably strengthened by a move to the Right in France. May I ask, entre vieux collègues, *are you sufficiently alerted to such a danger? Can I rely on your ability to avert it?*

'You can,' the French Prime Minister said briefly. Old colleagues or not, he was a Frenchman and he was not interested in what an Italian had to say.

In the discussion on EEC budgetary policy for the following year, he noted the marked lack of confidence in the franc that seemed to have gripped the other European leaders. The British, feeling less 'European' than the rest of them, bluntly questioned France's ability to meet her obligations if the situation was not rapidly normalised. This sally was met with stony silence from the French delegates and the meeting petered out unhappily.

Chapter 12

The oppressive weather continued and Paris sweltered under skies which turned from heavy blue to gunmetal. But the storms came to nothing. The humidity did not lessen. The city gasped for air amid the dust and petrol fumes. The streets were full of girls in shorts.

The Command was in session aboard the *Marie Louise*. Coke cans were on the table amid laden ashtrays and a street map of Paris.

'We will now take a report from *compagne* Ingrid,' said the man who led the debates.

Ingrid, her formerly blonded hair now returned to a deep auburn, was brisk and businesslike. 'My task was to find a suitable place from which to mount our action on September sixth. My proposal is a building site at the bottom of the Champs Elysées, next to the Rond Point: here.' She pulled the map towards her and placed her finger on a place already marked with a small cross.

'The hoarding is exceptionally high – about five metres, and it completely obscures the new building behind, which has only reached first-floor level. Our operative would be concealed on the site some time on the Saturday morning when it is open. That should not be difficult: suppliers and workmen are constantly going in and out. The operative would remain concealed on the site through Saturday in readiness for the passage of the parade on the Sunday morning. The parade starts at the top of the Champs Elysées and should pass that point at about ten fifteen.'

'You would be shooting blind,' the chairman said.

'That's right. It presents no technical problems, and it has the advantage of obscuring the origin of the missile, which I understand has a high trajectory. That will give our operative time to get away. There is a way out of the site into Avenue Roosevelt.'

'It's a long wait for whoever does the job,' Brunot said.

'There are worse fates,' Ingrid said shortly. 'The weather is good. It would be a chance to read a good book.' If it was a joke, she did not indicate as much with a smile.

'Does anyone have an alternative proposal?'

There was silence.

'Very well, we adopt the proposal. Now, who will be assigned to the job?'

'I have a good man,' Ingrid said. 'Serge. He was on the Laborde operation.'

'Any other proposals?'

'There's a good man in Group Four over in Montmartre,' Brunot said.

'What has he done?'

'The Place de la Concorde bombing and the American Express job in June.'

'How would he stand up to interrogation?' Ingrid asked.

'I can't vouch for him.'

'In my opinion, Serge will hold out. He is ideologically sound.'

'We will use Ingrid's man,' the chairman said. '*Compagne* Ingrid will be responsible for the details. I will see to the getaway. I'll talk to our friends.'

'I think it would be best if Serge had someone with him,' Ingrid said. 'Will you leave it to me to nominate his companion?'

It was agreed. 'What else?' the chairman said.

'I have a matter to raise,' Ingrid said. Her face was expressionless, her slender hands immobile on the table. 'It is the question of the car expert, Jean-Paul. I recommend that he be liquidated. In my view he is an unreliable element and he knows too much to be retired. Also he has been in the hands of the DST for over twenty-four hours.'

'A useful man,' the chairman said.

'That has nothing to do with it. Reliability is more important and he is arrogant, politically shallow and lacking in self-control. An adventurer. We have no room for such people. And how, exactly, does one escape from the DST?'

'Where is he?'

'At my place. I have hidden him there since he escaped. We reckoned his face was too well known for him to be wandering about, especially in the area where he lives.' The colour had mounted slightly in her cheeks.

'Does anyone object to our *compagne*'s proposal?'

The youth calling himself René had said nothing so far. Now he shook his head. 'People aren't that expendable,' he said. 'Jean-Paul has done good work for us.'

'I am not proposing to eliminate him because his work isn't good but because his defects of character place our whole project in jeopardy. You are being sentimental.' Ingrid's voice was sharp, devoid of emotion.

'I think we must have more respect for people,' René said.

'We must have more respect for our cause,' Ingrid snapped. 'There is no room here for sloppy sentiment.'

'Ingrid is right,' the chairman said. 'I accept her proposal and request her to do what is necessary. Is that the decision you wanted?'

'It is. I have already made the necessary arrangements. I expected your agreement.'

Their meeting finished and they left the houseboat one by one and made their separate ways along the quayside and up to the bridges over the river. The girl took the Metro, alighted at *Strasbourg-St Denis* and made her way on foot into the Sentier district, along ancient streets given over to wholesale clothing establishments, makers of trimmings, belts and handbags, and shops converted into fabric warehouses. She entered a doorway next to such a shop selling linings and climbed the narrow stairs. The prevailing smell was of camphor, hot glue and Eastern cooking. All the floors save the top one were occupied by artisans who pursued obscure, dying trades. On the top landing she paused, took out a key and opened one of three doors.

'It's me,' she called as she shut the door behind her.

Jean-Paul did not move from the bed at the far side of the room. He wore Y-fronts and a blue string vest. He was smoking and he had a racing paper open across his chest. He did not look up. He had grown the ragged beginnings of a beard.

'The Command has agreed that you can move out today but they want you taken by car to the new place they've allocated for you.'

'Where's that?' Jean-Paul still did not look at her.

'Out at Montigny. They have a small house there. It's discreet and you'll be able to take some exercise without being seen. It's all fitted up and they've had your things collected from your old place. Berenger saw to it.'

'I don't want to wallow in cow shit out in the sticks. I want to stay in Paris.'

'They say they'll get you a place in Paris in a week or two, when things have quietened down. For now, you'll go to Montigny.'

He looked up at her for the first time and pushed the newspaper aside. 'Come here,' he said.

She ignored him, went to a stove in the corner and put on a saucepan of water. Then she busied herself with a coffee pot.

'I said come here.'

'Oh, fuck off. You don't talk to me like that. In any case, Serge will be here with the car in twenty minutes and you have to get ready.'

'There's time. Come here, damn you.'

'I'm not interested.' She was reaching for mugs. 'Do you want coffee?'

'No. You know what I want.'

'I said I'm not interested.'

Jean-Paul hauled himself off the bed and started to pull his vest over his head. 'You'll come here, *now*, or I'll knock the shit out of you. You're keen enough to get it most times, so what's so pure about you suddenly?'

'I make love when I feel like it, and since you've been around you're as good as anyone else. Nothing special, but OK for when I need it. Right now I don't need it, so get dressed.'

She had put the mugs on the table and was putting coffee

into the pot. The gas roared insistently and a hiss came from the saucepan as the water heated up. Jean-Paul walked over to her and grasping a handful of her short hair, pulled her head back sharply so that she was forced to look into his face.

'Do you want that pretty face of yours all smashed up? I can do it, you know, in three seconds with one blow. It would be all you deserve, you bloody little cow. Now get your clothes off – fast.'

He let her go. She turned round and without a word pulled off her blouse, stepped out of her jeans and pulled her pants down to her ankles and kicked them off. She walked over to the bed, stretched herself on her back and turned her face away from him.

'Get on with it,' she said. 'I want a coffee before we go.'

Afterwards she said: 'That's your last time. I hope you enjoyed it,' and moved over to the wash basin on the other side of the room, sickened that she had responded.

As they drank coffee, Serge knocked and was admitted.

'The Command has agreed to the plan for Jean-Paul,' the girl said. She looked at Serge, her eyes expressionless.

'Montigny?'

She nodded. Then they went down the stairs to the car parked on the pavement round the next turning.

'I'll drive,' the girl said. 'You two sit in the back. You'll be less noticeable.'

She got into the driving seat and took the keys from Serge. As they drove away, Jean-Paul said, 'I'll need a gun.'

'There's one in your bag. It's in the boot with your things from your room.'

They drove in silence out of the Sentier and eastwards, leaving Paris by the Porte de Vincennes and heading for the forest of Fontainebleau. Soon the urban landscape gave way to fields and then to the dense forest where kings had hunted in their splendour, slaughtering great herds of deer and wild boar. The car left the main road, taking a left fork into the deep part of the forest.

'Where the fuck are we heading for?' Jean-Paul asked. He had been dozing and awoke as they moved along a narrow secondary road, the forest enclosing them on either side.

'I'm not driving along the *Route Nationale* with you in the back,' the girl said. 'They're likely as not to have road blocks up. This way we can get to Montigny without going back onto the main road at all.'

They drove on in silence for twenty minutes. They were in the densest part of the forest and there were no cars in sight. As they passed a crossroads, the girl said: 'The Command approved our plan this afternoon and I am responsible for your safety.'

Serge leaned forward as she spoke. 'I could do with a piss.'

She brought the car to a halt off the road on a rough layby. 'Will this do?'

'It's fine. What about you, Jean-Paul?'

'I might as well,' he said.

The two men got out of the car and Serge fell back, allowing Jean-Paul to go ahead of him into the bushes. When Jean-Paul had installed himself, Serge drew a Firebird from his pocket, fixed the silencer and advanced towards the other man, whose back was towards him. As he came on Jean-Paul shouted, 'Hey, find your own spot, can't you?' By then Serge had reached him, and lifting the gun carefully to the back of Jean-Paul's skull, he fired twice at point-blank range. The silenced gun scarcely made a sound.

The girl walked over. 'Good,' she said. 'He was filth. Scum!' She looked down at the crumpled body. Jean-Paul had fallen among the bushes. He would not be visible from the road.

'Do we need to pull him further into the wood?' Serge asked as he put the gun back in his pocket.

'It doesn't matter. The sooner the pigs find him and understand what we do when we have doubts about our people, the better.'

They went back to the car and Serge took the wheel, turned and made back to Paris, driving fast.

The technique of the *rafle* – the police raid on a building, a group of buildings or an entire block – was developed to an acceptable pitch of efficiency by the Gestapo and their French confederates during the Occupation, and though the French police had had little occasion to use it since the end of the war, the procedures had become a kind of folk wisdom, handed down by successive generations of policemen during the forty or so years since the Germans were thrown out of France. It was this technique that Alfred Baum now set in motion in collaboration with Commander Roisset.

The area was a large one for such an operation: the block of some seventeen streets and alleys lying within the triangle formed by the Boulevards Magenta, Strasbourg and St Martin, through which ran the Faubourg St Denis where Léon had failed so spectacularly to make his arrest. Essentially, the technique consists of blocking the exits to a given area and then working through the area, building by building, in as rapid a style as possible and deploying as many men as can be prised loose from other duties. Speed is of the essence if anyone is to be caught at all: speed, and thorough briefing. For in using maybe one hundred men, it is certain that more than one of them will be a prize bloody fool who ought instead to be sweeping a floor somewhere and whose incompetence cannot be remedied by the fact that he is wearing a police uniform. This man (or men), certainly present somewhere in the raiding party, may be the one to miss the quarry or miss a clue which points to the quarry. The only way to minimise the chance that he will touch his cap and pass on is to drive into his skull all that can be driven as to the appearance and likely behaviour of whoever is being sought, plus the details of the kind of physical set-up which could give reasonable cause for suspicion.

Alfred Baum was a master of the mass briefing, where he deployed the clarity of intention, the authority and the almost mystical persuasiveness of the greatest type of orchestral conductor. He now brought these natural skills into play in the big underground garage of the Rue des Saussaies, where he had assembled by prodigious effort 114 men, some in uniform, some not.

All had been issued with photographs of the blonde girl

from the *Hôpital Beaujon* and of Jean-Paul Macé, ex-Legionnaire, ex-jailbird and recent escapee from an interrogation room of the DST. Baum lectured them for ten minutes on how to recognise the originals of the two photographs if, as was probable, their hair and much else about them had been changed. Then he turned to a large map of the district, pinned to a board, and using a walking stick as a pointer, allocated the various groups to their duties in each of the seventeen streets that interested him in the triangle. Some of the men were to set up road blocks around the perimeter of the triangle, with instructions to examine the identity cards of all passers-by and to hold those who could not give an account of themselves. Most were allocated to the house-to-house search.

Baum spent some time on how they were to combine a measure of necessary courtesy towards innocent citizens with a greater measure of firmness in getting into apartments, shops, offices and workshops whether their occupants wanted to be invaded or not.

'We can always apologise afterwards,' he said. 'But what we cannot do is explain away unnecessary force or destruction of property. I want an orderly operation, is that understood?'

There was a ritual murmur of assent. No one thought the thing could be done without plenty of rough stuff and no once cared overmuch about splintered doors and the odd citizen with a bruise.

'I expect very little,' Baum said to Georges Wavre after the briefing had been completed. 'No doubt we shall have a number of spinoffs – illegals of one sort or another unearthed. But these people we are dealing with strike me as far too smart to have stayed on in an area where our men have tried to arrest them. And in any case, I have no firm evidence that this lair of theirs is in fact within my triangle, except that if it isn't they'd have been using another Metro station.'

'I think we have to do it, though,' Wavre said. 'If there is ever an enquiry they'll want to know why we didn't do the spectacular thing. What, no searches? No "hard" interrogations? It would look incomprehensible to the lay mind.'

The interest of the *rafle*, which was mounted between the hours of 1 p.m. and 3 p.m. on Thursday 26 August, lies only in what happened when the group of men responsible for covering the Passage St Denis reached the *Teinturerie* which was four shops along on the left-hand side. Three men – an Inspector and two Sergeants – pushed their way through the glass door of the shop while two of their colleagues went through the separate street door and raced up the stairs leading to the workshops and dingy offices above.

'Police!' the Inspector said to the man in the white coat who was checking the labels of garments which had been cleaned in the rumbling machine at the back of the shop.

A police card was waved at him, and in defiance of Baum's instructions, the three invaders made their way to the rear of the shop, shoving the white-coated man aside and paying no attention to his enquiry as to what the devil was going on.

One of the policemen rummaged around in the shop, pulling garments aside on the rails, looking under the counter, and glaring dubiously at the German cleaning machine as it rotated and splashed its load behind its glass panel. The other two made their way to the back, one to each door. The door on the left led to the evil-smelling toilet. The man who had chosen it did not let it detain him for more time than it took to look around the stained and peeling walls. The right-hand door was locked.

'Hey, you, open up here.' It was the Inspector who had chosen this door.

'I haven't got the key,' the man in the white coat said. 'The owner has it, and he's away for five weeks. In the south. Holiday.'

'What does he keep in it?'

'Nothing much.'

'What does that mean?'

The man in the white coat winked broadly. 'You know, just what he needs – a divan. He doesn't use the rest of the furniture in there.'

'Bring his birds here, then?'

'It's none of my business what he does on his own premises. But he certainly doesn't entertain his wife in there.' He laughed, and the policeman laughed with him.

'Still, we have to see inside.'

'I tell you, I haven't got the key. Honest.'

The Inspector hesitated. He had already broken down several doors to no useful purpose and was beginning to feel that there would be some kind of inquest about all this mayhem after it was over. He took out a notebook and made a note: '*Teinturerie*, 7 Passage St Denis. Not suspicious. One locked room, owner absent, employee without key.' Then he put the notebook back in his pocket.

'All right, we won't smash your door.'

The man shrugged: 'I don't mind what you do. It isn't my door. But if you broke in, he'd need another lock, quick. He's got a hell of a redhead just now . . .' He finished with another wink and a laugh which tried to be dirty.

The policeman laughed too. Then he called his two colleagues and they left the shop. The bell of the door clanged noisily behind them. None of them knew that they had added another failure to the DST's growing list of disasters.

After they had left, the man in the white coat continued with his labelling for twenty minutes. Then he took a look outside, satisfied himself that the policemen were no longer in the Passage, and went back inside. He unlocked the back room, went in and locked the door behind him. The room looked much as it had done when Ingrid and the others had been using it. They had not been there since the encounter with Léon out in the Faubourg, and the contents of the cupboards had been taken away.

The man picked up the phone and dialled a number. When the handset was taken off the cradle at the other end, he replaced his own handset and immediately dialled again. A man's voice answered.

'Yes?'

'*Teinturerie* here.'

'Yes.'

'The expected event occurred and is over. Things are exactly as they were.'

'Good.'

They rang off and the man returned to the shop, locking the back room after him.

Chapter 13

Rolf Hemminge lunched frugally off a plate of smoked salmon with a little potato salad, washed down with half a bottle of a good Chablis. With no newspapers worth reading on a Sunday, he had open next to his plate Emilio Lussu's *Théorie de l'Insurrection*, which he found sufficiently interesting to keep a pencil ready to mark the occasional passage. He finished his meal with a peach which he first washed carefully in a finger bowl. The black servant was off for the day. He would make the coffee himself. He enjoyed these modest Sunday forays into the kitchen, though he was not sufficiently interested to bother with cooking. But he liked to make Turkish coffee, and occasionally he would heat up something.

He brought the coffee back to the small *salon* where he had eaten, and lit a half-Corona. He put his book aside and looked at his watch. It was 1.30. He would leave in ten minutes. While he smoked he ran over in his mind the points which would need to be discussed. Then he took the coffee cup back to the kitchen, replaced the book on his desk, and let himself out of the apartment, double-locking the front door behind him.

Once out in the street, he followed his regular routine. He walked to the Avenue Charles de Gaulle and took a taxi as far as the Air France terminal at the Porte Maillot. The meter read fourteen francs. He gave the driver twenty francs. 'Wait for me here until your meter reaches sixteen francs,' he said. 'I'm not absolutely sure that I'll come back. If I do, I'll want you to take me to the airport, which will be a nice run for you. If I don't, it's because I've made other arrangements. In which case you can keep the change.'

The DST men who had been following the taxi saw it waiting and assumed that Rolf Hemminge would return to it, which was what they were intended to assume. Meanwhile, and as they waited, he walked fast through the terminal and out of the side exit in the street which ran along its flank. There he looked round carefully, satisfied himself that there was no one on his tail, and took another taxi to the Parc Monceau. The DST man who had been detailed to follow him into the building had lost him in the multi-layered labyrinth of corridors.

It was some time before the men from the DST realised that their bird had flown, and even longer before their colleagues spread out in one of the famous DST grids in the Bois de Boulogne concluded that there would be no action today.

In the Parc Monceau he walked to a prearranged spot which the young matrons with their children usually avoided because it had become a parking place for a group of winos who favoured the benches there for their afternoon naps. Now there were two old men and a very ancient bundle containing a woman stretched out and fast asleep. René, in his habitual Sunday disguise, was already there. Rolf Hemminge walked up and down with him on the gravel path between the dusty bushes, talking carefully, covering the points that needed to be covered, repeating what was important and posing questions. The conversation lasted close to twenty minutes and then the two parted. René drove away in his 2CV van and Rolf Hemminge took a taxi back to a spot within ten minutes of his home. He walked the remaining distance, let himself into the flat and settled down once more with Lussu's somewhat pedantic but comprehensive study.

Meanwhile, René was driving his van across Paris, westwards towards the *Port de Javel*, where he parked and made his way on foot to the *Marie Louise*. There he reported on his meeting and an hour later, close to 5 p.m., he walked back along the quayside to the steps at the side of the Mirabeau bridge and regained the van, parked in a side street on the other side of the main road. He nosed the van forward into the fast-moving traffic travelling eastwards along the Avenue Emile Zola, waiting for a chance to cross the stream. Intent on the tricky traffic situation, he did not see the two motorcycle police parked by the kerb immediately to his right. That they were there at all was something of a dereliction of duty: they had been detailed to keep an eye on the monstrous driving misdemeanours of the motorists returning to the city from their search for fresh air in the neighbouring countryside. The two motorcycle cops were taking a short break and a smoke before returning to the fray. It was not provided for in their briefing. They had no business whatever in the Avenue Emile Zola.

One of them had a good memory. 'Look, that van,' he said to his mate, 'that's the one with a special lookout on it. Look, the number's right.'

'Forget it. If we turn him in they'll want to know what the hell we were doing in the Avenue when we were supposed to be out on the bridge.'

'Yes, but with a special call on it, it's bound to be important. It'll do us more good than harm. Come on!'

The van had just turned left across the oncoming traffic. The two bikes were revved up, but it was a moment before they could get across the traffic flow. They kept their sirens and flashing lights switched off and used their superior speed. They caught up with the van as it finished crossing the bridge and was turning right along the main traffic artery which followed the river bank. The two cops rode side by side a hundred yards behind.

The memory man signalled to his mate: 'Shall we take him?' He received a nod.

They accelerated with a throaty roar, came level with the van in a few seconds and started their sirens and flashers as they did so. One stayed alongside while the other pulled ahead and started to slow down. The underpowered van was no match for the 1,000-cc bikes,but René had steady nerves. He swerved sharply towards the motorcyclist immediately to his left and if the rider had not been trained for just such a manoeuvre he would have been sent flying across the road. In the event, he swerved outwards with the van, braking hard, and narrowly missed the kerb of the central reservation.

The rider just ahead caught a glimpse of what had happened in his mirror and concluded that the van would not obey an instruction to halt and would certainly run him down if it could. He speeded up accordingly. There were no turnings off the freeway along which they were travelling. The second bike fell behind the van, while the man in front called for help on his radio, giving their position and direction.

'Do you want a police car?' the girl on duty asked.

'Yes, dear.'

'Where do you want it?'

'I don't know—maybe up near the Alma bridge, and I'll try to keep you in touch with our route. Over.' It was not promising.

The van, doing sixty and straining at it, followed the river, the motorcycle cops riding fore and aft. A few minutes later, at the approach to the underpass at the Alma bridge, the two policemen had their second stroke of luck: ahead they could see the rear of a tailback. It was the early weekenders on their way back into the city centre. The van would either be forced to stop or would try a U-turn. The leading motorcyclist was a quick thinker. If the driver of the van had tried to ride his mate down he must be desperate to get away. Dangerous, therefore. Possibly armed. And one could not ride a 1,000-cc monster and draw and fire a gun effectively, all at the same time. He therefore opened the choke violently, gripping the machine between his knees like an ungovernable horse, and covered the distance to the end of the tailback in seconds. He screamed his machine to a halt and was loosening his gun from its holster as he jumped clear, letting the bike crash to the ground. He turned, crouching, to face the oncoming van, now slowing down as it approached the solid mass of cars. The policeman had his gun in both hands, trained on the van's driver and ready to shoot if he tried to move from the driving seat once he had come to a stop. But once his speed had fallen to the necessary extent, René suddenly wrenched the wheel to the left. He was trying a U-turn across the grass of the central reservation and into the stream of traffic travelling westwards.

The policeman fired two shots at the van's nearside front tyre and two more at the windscreen. The second shot punctured the tyre and the third smashed into a corner of the windscreen, causing it to shatter in the immediate area of impact and to craze over the rest of its surface. The van came to a halt half way over the grass. René jumped out and raced for the parapet along the river. He was carrying a gun.

The second cop was off his bike and had his gun out. Now he crouched carefully, the gun held two-handed, level with his eyes, and fired at the running figure. Within grasp of the parapet, René heeled over. A bullet had struck him behind the right knee, smashing its way through the kneecap and out at the front. His leg buckled beneath him and as he fell his gun skidded across the pavement. Seconds later the two policemen had his arms behind his back in a full nelson.

'Have made arrest,' the first cop said into his mike. He gave his position. 'Now you can send a car, darling, and make it quick, will you? This is thirsty work. Over.'

An hour later news of the arrest reached Commander Roisset from the Inspector in charge at the *Préfecture de Police* of the 9th *arrondissement*. Five minutes beyond that, Alfred Baum's telephone rang at home.

'That van that interested you so much,' Roisset said. 'Well, my men have found it. And they're holding the driver.' He gave the details.

'Good, Commander. That's most helpful. Where is he?'

'At the *Préfecture* of the ninth.'

'Can we have him?'

'Yes, I've already told my man there to release him to you.'

'And the vehicle, please.'

'I'm told that's being brought in on a police transporter. You can have it too.'

'Thank you. I'll get some of my men over there as soon as I can.'

'We'll hold 'em till the morning for you if you like.'

'We'll see. I may be able to pick up the prisoner before then.'

Baum called the duty officer at the Rue des Saussaies.

'I want a detail to get over to the ninth *Préfecture* right away. You understand, within minutes. They're to pick up a prisoner who was arrested this afternoon. I'm told he's injured. There was a shoot-out with the police somewhere along the Quai de New York. Now listen, it's extremely important that we get this man before the police change their minds. So put a couple of men onto it right away.'

'Yes, chief.'

'And call me when you've got him.'

'Yes, chief.'

'Also, I want you to get someone else over to the police garage of the ninth to pick up the vehicle which was involved. It's a white Renault 2CV van, and if it can't be driven, get it transported. I leave the details to you.'

'Yes, chief.'

'Right, off you go.'

The duty officer had a car and two men at his disposal. Within minutes they were on their way to the *Préfecture* of the 9th. There, René was carried up from a cell by two burly policemen, his injured leg dangling uselessly. He was pale and in obvious pain. They carried him to the DST car and put him on the back seat without devoting overmuch attention to his injury. He had tried to run down a colleague and they were reserving their human sympathy for a worthier cause.

As the DST car drove away from the *Préfecture*, a police van with siren screaming came to a sharp halt and two men in uniform and two in plain clothes ran up the steps and into the duty officer's office.

'We're from headquarters,' their leader said. 'Instructions to pick up a motorist who was arrested this afternoon after a shooting incident near the river.'

'Whose instructions?'

'They come from the Prefect himself, via Inspector Vanne.'

'Christ, everyone seems to want this fellow. Who is he, for God's sake?'

'I don't know. I'm just obeying orders. Now let's have him.'

The man behind the desk shook his head. 'Sorry, can't do.'

'Why?'

'He's gone.'

'What do you mean, gone?'

'Taken. I told you he was a popular guy.'

'Who took him?'

'The DST. He must be well on the way to the Rue des Saussaies by now. Talk about inter-service rivalry!' He laughed drily.

The visitor shrugged. 'Well, I did what I was told. Can't do more than that. So long.'

'So long.'

As the posse trouped out the duty officer shook his head. It had been a pretty quiet Sunday till now. All it needed was for the Army to send a patrol. This fellow must be a real *caïd* – a big Mafioso. But he certainly didn't look it. He shook his head again and got on with writing out his report on the events of the day.

When the DST men reached the Rue des Saussaies with their captive, one of them called Baum.

'We're back with him, chief. I reckon he needs a doctor. A nasty bullet wound in the knee. He won't play football again.'

'See to it. Make him comfortable but see he's well locked up. And if anyone turns up to take him away – even if it's the President of the Republic himself – don't let him go. Do I make myself clear?'

'You do, chief.'

'Fingerprint him and get the prints through the computer. I'll want the results on my desk when I get in at eight tomorrow morning. And make sure you get hold of that van, too.'

But when a DST man reached the police garage of the 9th, he was told that the transporter had been redirected.

'Where?'

There were expressive shrugs. 'How should we know? The driver was called to the phone here and told to keep going. Sounded like the big boys down at the *Préfecture*. He could have gone anywhere.'

'Shit!' the DST man said.

'What's so fancy about a van?'

'I don't know. I just have my orders. Anyway, thanks.'

René, according to the computer printout, was in fact one Lucien Haan, twenty-two, from Colmar in Alsace, student of International Law at the *Université Libre* in Paris. His presence in the computer was to be accounted for by the fact that he had been for two years a member of FANE, the extreme Right-wing political organisation. His prints had gone on file following an incident in which a FANE mob had irrupted into the headquarters of the Franco-Israeli Society, daubed the walls with excrement which they had brought for the purpose, terrorised the office staff and smashed whatever could be easily smashed. Lucien Haan had been one of the four young men arrested as they left the building. He had subsequently been let off with a caution by a magistrate who had referred to regrettable youthful exuberance and understandable patriotic fervour.

As Alfred Baum considered these meagre facts, sipping his first office coffee of the morning, he chuckled and looked up at Inspector Allembeau. 'And they said Red Brigades. It shows you how careful you have to be not to go for the obvious answer. The Red Brigades attacked what you might call establishment targets. These people attacked them too. *Ergo*, they are from the Left. But it would seem that our friend Lucien Haan, just like Jean-Paul Macé of the Foreign Legion, was a Rightist from the maniac Right. It brings a little political clarity into all this.'

'What shall we do with him?' Allembeau asked.

'This time,' Baum said slowly, as if he was allowing the words to be dragged painfully out of him, 'this time, we cannot afford to play clever games. Nor can we afford to be gentlemen. We have exactly six days in which to wrap all this up before the Gaullist parade. If we fail to do so, more lives will most certainly be lost and people will be mutilated in various disgusting ways. I do not see how we can be scrupulous with this young man. I simply do not see it.'

'Who is to do it?'

Baum shrugged and looked miserable. 'That pig Assar, I suppose. Who else?'

Allembeau nodded. 'Will you brief him or shall I?'

'You brief him. I have enough unpleasant tasks to perform without adding that one. Now listen carefully. These are my orders. First, you will interrogate this young man yourself, starting as soon as we have finished in here. I leave the technique to you, but you have until tonight to get him to tell us what he knows. If you fail, you will warn him of what he is bringing down on his unfortunate young head, and then you will hand him on to Assar. As to that individual and his methods, my instructions are absolutely clear. Under no circumstances is the prisoner to be killed. But, on the other hand, he is to talk. And we haven't got long. I want him broken down by tomorrow.'

'He may be tough. It may not be possible to get results that fast.'

'I am told Assar always gets results fast. So let him get them this time. He isn't likely to have a worthier task.'

Allembeau got up. 'I know how you feel. Let's hope this man Haan has some sense.'

'Fanaticism,' Baum said gloomily. 'We live in an age of reviving fanaticism. Ideology makes people crazy. Then it forces those of us who like to be thought civilised to act in an uncivilised fashion. It is not a happy thought when your patriotic duty – your duty as a human being responsible for innocent lives – forces you down to the level of the vermin that you are trying to exterminate.'

Lucien Haan, alias René, did not have any sense, however. He sat sullenly on the far side of Inspector Allembeau's desk, his damaged leg extended on another chair, and refused to answer any questions whatever.

Confronted by a mug shot from the police archives, he had admitted by lunchtime that he was Lucien Haan. He had not agreed that he had been involved in the attack on the Franco-Israeli Society. Nor would he accept that he had tried to run a motorcycle policeman down yesterday afternoon on the Quai de New York.

Where did he live? He was not prepared to say. How had he come by the white van? No comment. Where had he been in the *Port de Javel* area and where was he driving to when the police had picked him up? No comment. Was he a member of FANE? No comment. Had he ever been a member? Silence.

'You are a very unwise young man,' Inspector Allembeau said wearily as sounds from the corridor announced the end of the working day for the rank-and-file DST staff. 'I told you before we started what would happen to you if you refused to cooperate with me. Now I must tell you again, in some detail. You see, it goes like this at the DST. Our task is the security of the State. There is no higher task, since the wellbeing of all its citizens depends upon the State's integrity. It follows that we cannot allow secondary considerations, however desirable, to deflect us from our duty. And those considerations include the humane virtues. You see, young man, we have reason to believe that you and your associates are responsible for a number of killings and maimings and are planning more. Your victims are in the main completely innocent citizens standing well outside the political arena in which you fancy you are operating. We have to bring this slaughter to an end. More important, we have to ensure that the State does not fall into the hands of persons like yourself and your associates who cannot distinguish between ends and means. I am old enough to recall the Gestapo and the Milice and I want no part of such institutions again. If you force us to use their methods on you, that is the risk you run. But we will not hesitate to use them in order to prevent them becoming once again the norm in this country as they were during the Nazi occupation, rather than the rare exception, as they are here at the DST.'

After his speech, the Inspector mopped his brow. 'Now,' he said, 'it is my unpleasant duty to give you a little more insight into the methods of the man into whose hands you will be delivered immediately upon leaving this office.'

He made it as horrifying as he could, much like an Inquisitor showing the instruments. He still hoped this sulky young man with the fanatic's mental blockage would see sense in time and talk voluntarily. But René was increasingly possessed by a kind of self-sacrificing fervour. He would not talk, no matter what they did to him. He would never talk. He would be the first martyr of the great patriotic cause, the cause of anti-Communism, the cause of cleansing France of alien infestation – the Jews, the North Africans – the cause of reviving the clean, decent North-European virtues that the National Socialists had understood, that had nearly given Germany her rightful place as the leader of Europe by reason of her superior genetic stock, her purer culture, her will to lead . . .

As the Inspector spoke, René increasingly distanced himself from what was being said, lost in his dream of martyrdom. Perhaps they'd kill him. Very well, he would die a martyr and one day the details would be known and he would take his place on France's roll of honour. They said the Left were the ones to throw up heroes. He would show them that the Right had its heroes too.

Inspector Allembeau's grisly catalogue of torments drew to an end. 'So you see, my friend,' he said sadly, 'there is no hope for you unless you come to your senses now. No hope at all. And what is more, no one will ever know what happened to you. So that you are being brave, or whatever you think you are being, for nothing – absolutely nothing.'

He paused for a reply. René said nothing. Then he spat on the floor.

The Inspector sighed and picked up the intercom. 'Take this man down to Room Six and tell Assar he's there. The interrogation is to start at once. Assar has his brief.'

Many victims of torture have described the point at which they discovered that they could after all withstand the worst that their torturers could do to them – the point at which they knew that come what may they would not talk. This point comes for different people at different times, depending on a complex of factors among which the effectiveness of the torture method and, above all, the moral fibre of the victim are dominant. In the present case, Assar's methods were perhaps the most effective known to any of the world's security forces. They were not based on any complex psychological manipulations, for the effectiveness of which time was invariably required. They were rather the juxtaposition of extreme violence, scientifically applied, and the effects of well-established 'truth' drugs which diminished the victim's will and created sufficient mental confusion to lead him to make revelations of what he had intended to conceal.

As the enormity of what was being done to him, and the indefinite extension of it into the future, at last embedded itself in René's consciousness, he struggled to find a formula which would somehow—anyhow—reduce the agony, delay it, offer respite however brief, while avoiding the need to tell them what they wanted to know. He could gain time with lies. But his mental confusion made the truth easier to recall than the lies he had prepared for such an eventuality. Each time he said he would talk, and the agony subsided, he found that he could not formulate the false names and addresses, the invented activities, with which he had hoped to hold them at bay.

His torturer was perfectly well aware of such mental struggles and subterfuges, and the respite from agony became each time shorter, until eventually René realised that he could no longer play for time: no time was being offered any more.

'The names of your associates.'

'Who are you seeing?'

'Who is the leader?'

'Who gives you your orders?'

'Where do you meet him?'

'Where do you all meet?'

'The names of your associates.'

'Who are you seeing?'

By 3 a.m. he had given some of the cover names: Brunot, Ingrid, Felix. He found, in his confusion, that the true cover names came out. The false ones he had prepared would not come into his mind at all.

Yes, he got his orders from Felix. Where? In the park. Which park? He couldn't remember. Always the same park? Not always. Sometimes the Bois de Boulogne. And who was Felix? He didn't know. They could break him in pieces, he still wouldn't know. He didn't know anyone's real name. They could break him in pieces . . .

They worked on the meeting place. Where did they meet? No answer. Where did they meet? A place . . . somewhere . . . a place . . . didn't know. Where did they meet? A place . . . Marie Louise . . . Marie Louise . . .

At 4 a.m. he lost consciousness again. 'Obstinate little sod,' Assar said to the man working with him. 'Better ease up a bit. We're to preserve him intact, they say. Let's break for an hour and get a quick kip.'

They left him lying on his back, breathing heavily. During the ensuing hour he vomited and inhaled the vomit, unable to move from his position. He died asphyxiated ten minutes before Assar and the other man returned.

Chapter 14

'There is very little here,' Baum said. 'Very little. A few cover names which may not even be authentic, an admission that he was meeting Hemminge, whom he allegedly knew as Felix, in some park or other as well as the Bois de Boulogne – which we knew already – and nothing else.'

He shook his head over the notes that Assar had provided. He had not been called during the night, despite his instructions. Assar had decided that the row which was bound to break out when they found that the prisoner was dead might as well keep until the morning. And so he had called the DST doctor instead and had awaited Baum's arrival at the office just after eight. Then he had told him, putting the most favourable construction on it that he could.

'Get out!' Baum had shouted at him. 'Incompetent! Get out of my sight!'

And he had got out and away for a sleep, leaving his notes on the interrogation.

'We have these four cover names,' Baum said to Inspector Allembeau. 'Felix, Brunot, Ingrid and Marie Louise. Felix we know, and I suppose we can take Ingrid or Marie Louise to be the girl who visited the hospital. I don't see that it gets us very far.'

Allembeau grunted. 'There's one thing,' he said, 'and it's not much, but we ought to consider it. When he was giving names he didn't give Marie Louise. That came later when they were questioning him about the meeting place. That's when he said "Marie Louise". Can we make anything of that?'

'Perhaps that the meeting was at this Marie Louise's place. But how do you find a Marie Louise, for God's sake?'

Allembeau grunted again, took out a cigarette and lit it. 'Let's build with what we've got. This fellow has a meeting with Hemminge in some park or other on the Sunday afternoon. It's a fair assumption that the meeting was between two and three, and if your experience the previous week is anything to go by, it lasted maybe half an hour. Now, Paris isn't all that big and we know to our cost that it hasn't all that many parks. Even if it was the Buttes Chaumont, which I suppose is about the furthest park from where the police first saw him, he would have reached the Javel area by four or thereabouts.

'He was first sighted just after five, so we can reasonably assume that he used the hour to report to his associates on the outcome of his talk with Felix/Hemminge. Now, if you look on the map at the street from which the van was emerging when the police first saw it, you'll see that it made very little sense for the van to be there unless it had been parked. It isn't a cul-de-sac, but it leads to a labyrinth of narrow lanes and no one would choose that route if they were merely passing through the area. So that we can assume that Marie Louise lives somewhere nearby and that the group has its meeting place there.'

'Perhaps they moved there from the Faubourg St Denis area once we had made that too hot for them.'

'Perhaps.'

They sat in silence for a while, each struggling in his own way with the meagre facts.

'It seems to me,' Baum said at last, 'that we have one hope and one only. And it's a slender one at that. We must assume that the others know this man is in our hands. Judging by the goings-on with the redirecting of the van, it was known almost at once. And if that much is known we must assume that whoever is playing their game within the *Préfecture* has also told them by now exactly where the van was first sighted. So that if this Marie Louise lives nearby and if that was where they meet, then they should take immediate steps to change their meeting place and keep clear of that area.'

'Except for Marie Louise, who presumably lives there.'

'Unless, of course, these people are about to make a classic mistake,' Baum continued, ignoring Allembeau and speaking almost to himself. 'The blunder would be exactly what you'd expect from an underground group which had been as brilliantly successful as this one has been. Four months or so of intense activity without an arrest or a failure, save for the Jean-Paul Macé incident – and that turned in their favour – and now this. They might just be confident enough – arrogant enough – to reckon we won't find their hideout. That we won't mount another house-to-house raid after the failure of the last one.'

'Nor we will,' Allembeau said.

'Precisely. They will have guessed correctly. That's why I think they may not move away from the district. And I think it with just enough conviction to devote some DST resources to the proposition.'

He pulled a street map from a drawer of his desk and spread it before him. With a pencil he drew a rough circle with its centre at the point where the Mirabeau bridge abuts onto the Left Bank. The point where the van had first been sighted was some seventy-five yards away from the bridge.

'Somewhere in there,' Baum said, 'our Marie Louise has an apartment or something. All we can do, my friend, is to stake out the area, provide our men with whatever information we have, and hope for the best. It isn't much, but it's better than sitting here wondering.'

'Slightly better,' Allembeau said. 'We have our pictures of the girl at the hospital, and we can try our mug shots of the dead man and the Macé fellow and our description of the van on local shopkeepers, and that's about it.'

When pushed, the DST is capable of mounting highly sophisticated surveillance operations. Pushed now almost beyond endurance, Alfred Baum achieved what he liked to describe in later years as the most beautiful, the most elegant surveillance in the DST's history. 'And we mounted the whole thing in under fourteen hours,' he would tell whoever had the inclination to listen to him. 'We threw budgetary considerations out of the window, grabbed men and women from vital duties of all kinds, broke up existing marriages and maybe created new ones in the department. We acted with *complete singleness of purpose*, which is the only way to act when you are desperate.' He would pause and produce his most impish grin. 'And on that Tuesday morning, with five days left to me before the parade, I was desperate.'

Item: the keepers of the three newspaper kiosks in the area suddenly found themselves offered a free one-week holiday with bonus attached in return for letting DST men and women take over their newspaper and magazine concessions. The one who refused was offered a tax investigation instead and changed his mind.

Item: a conversation with the personnel manager of the Metro system led to the replacement of the ladies in the ticket office at the Javel station by two girls from the DST office. Two DST men were added to the platform staff as cleaners, fitted out by the Metro in their regulation work fatigues.

Item: the area became, suddenly, a magnet for lovers. They sauntered on the Mirabeau bridge. They cuddled in cars parked nearby. They strolled along the quayside past the moored boats.

Item: two DST men became temporary dustmen, unpaid, for the rest of the week, collecting local garbage and cursing their fate amid the heat and stink.

Item: dressed in a variety of gear, DST men and women walked about the area reading newspapers or deep in conversation or carrying shopping bags.

Item: a motherly type who had spent close to thirty years in the archives at the Rue des Saussaies suddenly metamorphosed into a flower-seller complete with massive basket and a daily stock of flowers collected at dawn from the market by a furious sergeant who had never thought that the service would come to this. Delighted with her job, she had installed herself at the entrance to the Metro, her transceiver snuggling in her voluminous skirts.

A radio van was parked nearby and two cars with their crews were kept on permanent rota in side streets.

'We can do no more,' Baum said when it had all been fixed up. He was reporting to a worried Georges Wavre. 'If there is anything else anyone can think of, I am not proud, I will do it. But the area is already somewhat overcrowded with our people.'

Wavre shrugged. 'Just let us hope you have a little more luck this time,' he said. 'No work of our type can succeed without a modicum of luck. You are surely due for some about now.'

'The only other thing we could do,' Baum said carefully, 'relates to the man Hemminge, alias Felix. We could bring him in.'

'And have the Embassy spring him within hours if not minutes? What would you have achieved? A diplomatic scandal. Newspaper headlines. A row with Washington and one hell of a row here. No thanks!'

'I thought you'd say that. Though you realise, of course, that we have enough to hang the man twice over.'

'It isn't the point. The point is that the thing's not politically expedient. So forget it, Alfred.'

'Nevertheless, don't you feel it would be wise from our own point of view to let the President know about Hemminge and his little meetings?'

'You can't prove anything.'

'Of course not. But I can link Hemminge to the young man René and René to our friend Jean-Paul Macé who deposited the Defence Committee documents at *l'Humanité*. The links are solid, even if more than that would be needed in a court of law. But we aren't talking of courts.'

'I'll think about it, Alfred, but I don't like it. Do you have anything on Hemminge that I can look at? If it comes to a *persona non grata* situation I need to be briefed.'

'I'll send it up to you. I extracted a *résumé* from his dossier, which is reasonably comprehensive. Then perhaps we can talk again.'

At the door he stopped and turned towards Wavre. 'Wish me luck,' he said.

'Good luck!'

Very Secret

SUMMARY OF INFORMATION IN THE DST ARCHIVES RELATING TO ROLF WALDO HEMMINGE

Born Montreal, Canada, 9.8.25 of a Canadian mother, American father. A US citizen.

Educated in state schools in Montreal and Boston. Studied Constitutional Law at Harvard, passed out *summa cum laude*, class of '49. One year in chambers of Supreme Court Justice Vanderkuyser.

Career: US Attorney General's office 1950–1. Believed to have joined the Central Intelligence Agency at end '51. Became protégé of James Angleton, specialising in covert operations. First overseas posting Teheran 1953–4, leaving one month after putsch which displaced Left Government and installed Shah Pahlevi in power. In Beyrouth 1955–62, believed involved in Ba'athist politics in Syria and Iraq. In Congo 1962–5 until seizure of power by General Mobutu.

Movements between 1966 and 1975 are obscure. Known to have been in Washington for part of time and believed active at various times in Latin America (Nicaragua and San Salvador mentioned). In 1975 appointed Cultural Counsellor to US Embassy, Paris. Since that time has been in active touch with Congress for Cultural Freedom and Radio Free Europe. Believed to be chief CIA liaison with those bodies.

Political views: Described as a hawk, favouring firm posture towards USSR and particularly promoting idea of far stronger opposition to Communism in Western Europe. As part of this philosophy he believes Socialist parties are equal menace as routes into a Communist-dominated situation. Favours extreme-Right parties and groups. All this from conversation and reports of informants close to him. No organic contact traced with organisations of extreme Right.

Personal characteristics: Subject is life-long homosexual with no long-term relationship. Favours handsome men/youths in the known age range 18–28, but possibly also outside these ages. Seen from time to time with such companions at luxury hotels: Villa d'Este, Como; Gritti Palace, Venice; Hassler, Rome. Has private income enabling him to indulge such tastes.

Speaks English, French, Italian, Arabic, some Spanish.

Known contacts include present Ministers of Defence and Overseas Territories, Prefect of Police, Commandant of Paris, Chairman of the *Banque Parisienne de Commerce*, some commercial and financial contacts plus wide contacts in the cultural field and the media.

General appreciation: It is considered possible that Hemminge's own policy may go beyond that of the CIA itself. Some of his activities may be unknown or only incompletely known to CIA leadership. As one of the few senior men who survived the collapse of the CIA's covert network during and after the Nixon Presidency (including the sacking of James Angleton himself), Hemminge may well be benefitting from some special protection or immunity. If so, its nature is unknown to the department. Whatever the facts may be, it must be assumed that in the event of a request by us for his removal, the US authorities (both CIA and State Department) would deny any misdemeanours and refuse on grounds of principle to withdraw him. If we insisted, retaliation against French personnel in Washington would undoubtedly ensue, and wider sanctions against French interests could be taken.

(Signed) A. Baum

See Dossier U/H/8101877: Hemminge, R. W.
Photo: Yes
Fingerprints: Right hand only
Voiceprint: Yes
Informants: Listed in dossier
Quality of information: Since arrival in France: Good.
Previous: Poor in detail, satisfactory on basic facts.

Later on the Tuesday Baum was back in Georges Wavre's office. Wavre had the report on Rolf Hemminge on his desk. He fingered it with distaste.

'We will see the President tomorrow morning at ten.'

'You arranged it?'

'No, we are summoned.'

Baum nodded in the direction of the report: 'What about that?'

'I agree. We have to let him know. As much in self-defence as anything else.'

'What are we to say about the enquiries into the Defence Committee leakage?'

'As little as possible, my friend. You must let me sleep on it and we will concoct a scenario before we leave tomorrow morning. In general, I do not favour telling politicians a single word more than they absolutely have to know. Even Presidents. So it needs careful thought.'

'The probabilities,' Baum said, 'point to the Minister of Defence.'

'Of course.'

'But we will never prove it without a major public scandal.'

'It would be politically credible.'

'Yes.'

'And we know how close he is to Hemminge.'

'Yes again.'

'And he was as well placed – better placed than anyone else – to carry it through since the minutes are typed in his Ministry.'

Wavre nodded unhappily. 'Does his dossier downstairs tell you anything?'

'Not really.'

'What are you getting from your man Pichu?'

'He will be meeting one of my inspectors each evening to give us a rundown on the Minister's movements, contacts – anything which might tell us something. At the first meeting we got what can best be described as venomous gossip. He does not love his boss. And so we know things about our friend Ambroise Pellerin's, er, private tastes which are not really any of our business. Also that he has asked the *2e Bureau* to give him something up-to-date on both of us.'

Wavre laughed briefly. 'Much good may it do them, unless you're keeping a pair of blondes in St Germain.'

'Of course,' Baum said, 'you realise that Pichu himself has a perfectly good motive for copying the Defence Committee minutes and passing them on.'

'Explain, please.'

'Insurance. He's a man who insured against a Left victory. Why should such a cautious fellow not also insure against a coup by the Right? It's just as plausible politically, and it might stand an ambitious civil servant in very good stead to have given them a leg up when they needed it.'

'Do you think he did?'

'I don't know. But he has to be on our list.'

'Who else?'

Baum looked at Wavre from beneath his eyebrows, head cocked, the trace of a smile on his lips. 'I think we must add one Guy Mallard, Minister of the Interior and political chief of the DST.'

'Do you know something I don't know?'

'Nothing that would stand up as evidence. Just a bit of history. I got it from reading and rereading *his* dossier. I've been doing a lot of reading of dossiers lately, and mostly it's very unrewarding stuff. But I did notice one item – perhaps totally meaningless – in our friend's file. You know he was once in the Foreign Service, before he went into politics. Well, as an ambitious young Second Secretary he was posted in 1957 to Beyrouth and stayed there for two years. Now, Beyrouth isn't a big place and the diplomatic community there is just as incestuous socially as it is in similar capitals around the world. When Mallard arrived, one Rolf Hemminge had been at the US Embassy for two years, and being the sort of man he is, must have known everyone – been a prominent local character. And it is inconceivable that a man like Hemminge, a collector of potentially useful contacts, never cultivated our Guy Mallard, another gregarious type who knew the value of knowing everyone. Yet you'll have observed that Mallard does not figure in Hemminge's dossier as a friend or even a contact. I simply do not believe they don't know each other here in Paris, and if we have nothing on it, that could be because Hemminge regards Mallard as his most important "friend" and has taken exceptional care to keep the fact secret.'

'The purest speculation.'

'Absolutely.'

'But not without a certain appeal.'

'Thank you.'

'On the other hand, it could be said that the fact that the leaked version of the minutes carried Mallard's initials and not Pellerin's points to the latter if you assume a simple manoeuvre on Pellerin's part to throw suspicion onto someone else.'

'Unless we have a double bluff here. Mallard leaving his own initials on because everyone would know that he'd do no such thing.'

'Unless as you say, we have a double bluff. And either of our men is capable of it.'

'I suppose,' Baum said gloomily, 'it doesn't really matter one way or the other. Still, it would be nice to know.'

'Tell me,' Georges Wavre said, 'how do you feel about your race against time, Alfred? You only have five days and as far as I know you are still working on very thin leads.'

Baum did his best to smile. 'How do I feel? Terrible, of course. But I am hopeful. I am active. I am in good shape. I will try not to let you down.'

'I am a spy-catcher – a political innocent,' Georges Wavre said. 'I do not pretend to understand complex political processes. And so I want you, Alfred, in five short minutes and in simple phrases, to explain to me precisely what this man Hemminge thinks he is doing.'

Baum smiled broadly and shook his head. They were together in Wavre's office once more. It was the following morning, Wednesday, 2 September at 9 a.m.

'*I* am the political innocent in here,' he said. 'In fact, you should be telling *me* what is going on.'

'Nevertheless, I want your view, if only to test it against mine.'

Baum settled himself uncomfortably in the chair and gazed past Georges Wavre, through the open window, at the curtained windows of the building opposite, as if that was where he would find his inspiration. 'I see it like this,' he said, 'and you must, I think, consider first the background of our man.

'What is he? A bright lad, no doubt – done well at university and all that, but provincial and therefore narrow in his view of the world, of society, of what is desirable as opposed to what is possible in life. A typical provincial American, you might say, for whom the excesses of the Third World and the cunning sophistications of poor old Europe are eternal mysteries, not really to be tolerated.

'Put such a man into the steamy, conspiratorial setting of Iran, the Lebanon, Black Africa, Latin America, and leave him there long enough, and what do you get? A professional conspirator. A plotter. An anti-democrat because he has never seen democracy at work, and comes to hate its compromises and small, dirty deeds when he is eventually moved to Europe and comes to live with it. A man, also, who is drunk from the power and the money of the organisation for which he works. That, I believe, is Rolf Hemminge when he arrives here at the end of 1975. A provincial who has acquired some of the glitter of the sophisticate everywhere save in his mind.'

'So far, so good.'

'And here he is, suddenly, in the most cynical and compromising of all the old Western democracies. And what he sees appals him. A large, aggressive Communist Party. A Socialist Party whose ideology and tactics he doesn't understand, seemingly playing footsy with the Communists. An advance of the Left year by year. Confusion and squabbling on the Right. Political expediency and lack of clear moral purpose. And of course, it is moral purpose that this man understands. Like Dulles, he believes the USA has a moral purpose: the destruction of Communism, the anti-Christ. And he believes from what he has seen in the Third World that it is to be done covertly, by conspiracy to match the conspiracy of Communism; by counter-terror against the terror of Communism; by ruthlessness against the ruthlessness on the other side. He is confused utterly on the philosophical problem of how to pursue noble ends by ignoble means.'

'Your political theory is good.'

'Thank you. I do my best, but I am an amateur. However, confronted with our usual messy French compromises, what does this man decide? That we lack singleness of purpose in combating the Communist menace. That the Left needs to be discredited. And since, inconveniently, it is not currently discrediting itself, it must perforce be discredited by covert means. And so he decides that action is required.

'It was easy enough for him. He already had these contacts with the lunatic Right. All they needed in order to move from sporadic action against synagogues to an effective and sustained terror campaign was money and consistent leadership. Also the belief that they were supported by the great United States. And all this was provided.

'I think the tactic was simple, even quite elegant. There would be attacks on what we have called establishment targets. They would be assumed to come from the Left, and he believed the public was politically stupid enough to equate anything on the Left with the Communists and Socialists. To avoid the danger of their being revealed as the action of the Right, he enlisted the support of those elements which are always present in our top cadres and leadership who favour Right extremism – dictatorship, in short. Our friend the Prefect of Police has been something of a key figure in all this, of course. And so, no doubt, has Ambroise Pellerin. There are others but it isn't what I'm supposed to be talking about just now.

'As for all this scum – these Renés and Ingrids and Jean-Pauls with their bombs and automatic pistols – they no doubt believe they are preparing the counter-revolution, the advent to power of French Fascism, which as you know, has a long and pathetic history of coups, failed putsches and the like. So that while Hemminge thought no doubt that he was using these people to bring the present régime to its senses, the bombers (and no doubt the Prefect and his friends) thought they were bringing back the France of Marshal Pétain and Pierre Laval.'

Baum took a deep breath and shrugged. '*Voilà* – that is my view for what it may be worth.'

'Very good, my friend. It has credibility. And do you also have a view on whether the CIA itself and the White House knew any of this?'

'I have no view whatever on that. As I said, I am an amateur.'

Wavre looked at his watch. 'Let us go to see the President and tell him as little as we dare.'

At the Elysée, beneath the chandeliers and the painted ceiling, the President listened to what Wavre had to say, while Alfred Baum sat alongside. Vallat, gaunt and inscrutable, had withdrawn after showing them in to the presence and seemed glad to go. The President's fingers tapped impatiently on his blotter and he managed to convey impatience and irritation in his glance. It was calculated to put anyone off his stride, but Georges Wavre had a stolidity of temperament which matched nicely with his stolid and immovable appearance. He talked quietly, confidently and with the conviction of a man to whom it had never occurred to tell less than the truth. Yet less – and on occasions more – than the truth was precisely what Wavre was presently telling his President.

'We are planning arrests in the next forty-eight hours,' he said blandly. 'It should bring to an end the current bombing campaign. In nice time for the election,' he added.

The President said nothing.

'We have already made a key arrest and the man has talked. Not as much as we would have liked, but usefully even so. Also, we have traced the leadership of this conspiracy back to an individual whom I think you should know about. Before I identify him I hasten to say that we have made no move in the matter and would not recommend any action. You will see why, *Monsieur le Président*.'

He proceeded to give a brief and (in some parts) accurate account of the activities of Rolf Hemminge. 'I do not imagine,' he added, 'that you would wish to take any action there. In any case, it is a political question and certainly beyond our competence.'

If he was in any way surprised the President did not show it. There was a long pause.

'Needless to say,' Georges Wavre added quietly, 'no mention of the man Hemminge's role has been made anywhere outside this room. Our own Minister is unaware of it and so are the police.'

'Forty-eight hours, you said?' the President snapped.

'Fifty-six at the outside,' Wavre replied without blinking.

'I hope we are not to have trouble at the parade on Sunday.'

'I see no reason why we should, Mr President.'

'All right. Thank you. Keep me informed via Vallat.'

And that was that.

'Dangerous, Georges,' Baum said, panting his way down the stairs.

'I have confidence in you, my friend. Otherwise I would not have made my promise.'

A coded telex was received during the evening by the French Prime Minister. It was from the US President's Security Adviser, asking amiably whether Paris had been able to achieve anything yet along the lines discussed with Dr Kissinger, and if so, what? Also, what was the latest feeling in Government circles on the probable outcome of the forthcoming elections, given that an opinion poll was being quoted in the US press, giving 55 per cent of the votes to the Socialists and Communists on the first ballot, with an increased percentage going to the Communists. The fact that this came direct from the US President's office by telex rather than through the normal diplomatic channels was not lost on the French Prime Minister. He spent ten minutes on the telephone with the President of the Republic. That irascible man then got Vallat to summon the US Ambassador to an immediate meeting.

The Ambassador, who had been copied in by the White House, knew what to expect. He left a dinner party at the Embassy and had himself driven round to the Elysée, a block away. The President pushed a copy of the telex across the desk to him.

'I am aware of it, Mr President,' the Ambassador said.

'And this.' It was the latest teleprinter sheet on the New York money market, appositely supplied by Vallat.

The Ambassador read it and said nothing.

'*Monsieur l'Ambassadeur*,' the President said in his most uninviting manner, 'you will be so good as to inform your State Department, if not your President himself, that France is still a sovereign country, that whilst we appreciate the friendly interest of our associates we do not appreciate direct interference in our affairs, and that if someone in Washington is sufficiently ill-informed about European politics to be advising the President that the French Government should take administrative action against the Left, then we can only hope that such foolish advice will be ignored. Furthermore, I am disappointed, Monsieur, that as Ambassador accredited to our Government you have not succeeded in explaining adequately to your people the nature of French politics.

'That was what I wish to say to you.'

He rose to his feet as a signal that the meeting was at an end, and the Ambassador, thoroughly out of his depth and slowed down in his mental processes by the liberal quantity of Mercurey 1er Grand Cru Classé he had taken at dinner, not to mention the bourbon he had drunk before, made his escape.

When the New York banking system opened up on that Wednesday morning (at 5 p.m. French time) a pattern developed almost at once. There was further heavy selling of French francs and the chairman of the Chase was quoted as saying that banking circles in the US were deeply worried by the deteriorating situation in France and were advising their customers who had commercial or financial dealings with that country to exercise extreme caution. The franc lost ground steadily through the day in the New York money market and was expected to do the same when London, Zurich and Paris itself opened on the following morning. The very expectation would help the prophecy to fulfil itself.

Chapter 15

Very little happened in the Javel area on the Wednesday. By lunchtime the various DST arrangements were complete, flowers were being offered at the top of the Metro steps, a pair of lovers lounged in the sun on the bridge, DST personnel became familiar with the titles of obscure magazines in the kiosks. Plain-clothes men started their discreet round of local shops, showing pictures of Ingrid, René and Jean-Paul, asking if anyone had seen them. They also carried a picture of a white 2CV Renault van of the correct vintage. They met with no success.

Someone thought of the fact that they should have tried all this on the ticket sellers at the Metro and the three kiosk holders, but all were inaccessible now and the Inspector in charge on the spot shrugged and wished he had thought of it earlier. He had set up his foot patrols, arranged rotas, checked clothing, fixed precise routes. He could do no more.

At 7 p.m. the wireless operator in the DST van signalled Rue des Saussaies that shifts were being changed and there was nothing to report. The message was conveyed to Alfred Baum, who had arranged to sleep at the office until the weekend and was wondering what to buy Estelle by way of propitiatory offering when he finally got back to Versailles. Perhaps the copper fish kettle she had been pining for since her friend acquired one last year? Expensive, no doubt, but a good idea!

On the Thursday the man calling himself Brunot, who owned the *Marie Louise* and usually slept on board, went to his nearest kiosk to buy the morning paper and found himself served by an unfamiliar woman who seemed to have difficulty with the change.

'What's happened to Madame, then?' he asked.

'A week off to see an aunt in Normandy. I believe the aunt's ill.' The woman from the DST had been rehearsed in her story and produced it with confidence. It seemed to satisfy Brunot, who walked back to the boat without noticing the couple strolling arm in arm along the quayside and seemingly much taken with each other. This was Luc, the young man who had been in the grid in the Bois de Boulogne the previous month, and in the unsuccessful tailing operations around the hospital, and was now enjoying himself getting to know a bewitching typist from the pool whose name was Chantal and whose dimples and vivid green eyes had been the subject of comment and much longing among the men at the Saussaies.

Also along the waterside and unnoticed by Brunot as he regained the boat was a DST Inspector moving cautiously among the dockers with the three photographs. And here the DST had its first small success. For three men recognised Ingrid.

'That smashing bit with the legs,' one of them said. 'The one who looks as if she has a bad smell under her nose.'

The Inspector tried to get them to recall exactly when they had last seen her, but none of them got closer than 'about a week ago'.

Where had she been going? Well, she came down the steps and walked along the riverside, eastwards. Or maybe it was westwards. Did she come back from there? Perhaps, but she hadn't been seen coming up the steps again.

This information went into the Inspector's notebook at 5.15 p.m. and was relayed to Alfred Baum a half hour later.

'It helps to narrow down the interesting area,' he said to Allembeau. 'There are disused buildings along the waterfront there, and boats of various kinds. Also, she could be coming up the steps further along at the Grenelle bridge.'

'Do you plan a raid?'

'Not yet. I'm still hoping for an arrest rather than a blind raid. I think a *rafle* can wait at least until tomorrow. Maybe even Saturday.'

At 6 p.m., in the midst of the rush hour, the flower-seller

at the entrance to the Javel Metro saw a slim, attractive girl with good legs and auburn hair cross the road from the bridge and swing round the stone balustrade and down the Metro steps. Although this was no blonde and the make-up was heavier, she was sure it was the girl from the hospital. She notified the radio van accordingly. In the crowd there had been no hope of picking her up and the DST men working on the platform never spotted her.

'It confirms at least that Marie Louise still lives there,' Baum said when he had been told. 'I must assume that is the girl's name.'

'But it doesn't tell us whether they are still meeting in their usual place,' Allembeau said.

'It doesn't.'

Shifts were changed and the night shift had a dull time of it, with nothing happening. The next morning, Friday, appeared equally hot, equally blank. Life in the Javel district went on as usual and the lengthy vigil was already grating on everyone's nerves – everyone, that is, except Luc and his Chantal. They were getting on famously – too famously.

'You mustn't keep looking at me like that,' Chantal said. 'If your Mireille knew she'd be upset.'

'She doesn't know, and in any case I'm only following orders. We're supposed to look like lovers, aren't we?'

She giggled. 'Yes, but you've been pushing it a bit.'

They were walking along the Avenue Emile Zola beneath the plane trees. Luc had decided that he fancied this sexy creature and if, in every marriage, there was an infidelity sooner or later, this was to be his. Chantal, for her part, was not uninterested.

They lunched together off a hamburger and a coffee in a plastic and chromium *Self* in the Avenue and sat afterwards on a bench in the sun, watching the traffic, the passers-by, each other, in the pleasant haze of a burgeoning affair. In mid-afternoon they were strolling hand in hand along the quayside of the *Port de Javel*, watching the men at work on the barges, keeping a lookout, but with their minds on each other. Soon the working barges came to an end and they came abreast of the long row of houseboats. Luc was searching in his mind for ways of developing this new and promising relationship.

'Chantal,' he said.

'Yes?'

'Nothing, I was just trying your name. Nice name. I like it. Chantal.' He tried to put some meaning into it. 'Chantal!'

She laughed happily. 'There's a nice name.' She pointed to a houseboat. 'Noémie. A nice old-fashioned name, that.'

'Mireille says if we have a girl she wants to call her Joanne. Sounds American.'

They were approaching the Grenelle bridge and were walking past the last of the boats.

'That's another nice old-fashioned name – Marie Louise,' the girl said. 'I like double-barrelled names – Marie Louise, Anne Marie . . .'

They reached the bridge and climbed the steps to the upper level. At the top of the steps Luc kissed her, a little awkwardly, and she did not resist.

As they did so, the man calling himself Brunot walked down the steps and along the quayside to the boat, letting himself in with a key to the heavy padlock and another to the door itself. Ten minutes later, Ingrid emerged from the Javel Metro. She was wearing a wig and sunglasses and the flower-seller failed to recognise her in the brief moment before she had turned away towards the river. A few minutes later two men, walking separately, came up from the Metro and made their way across the road to the steps by the Mirabeau bridge. All were aboard the *Marie Louise* shortly afterwards without having been noticed by anyone in the DST network.

The meeting of the Command lasted close to an hour. Plans for the parade were reviewed, arrangements made for future liaison with Felix, and future action debated.

'I shall accompany Serge for the Sunday operation,' Ingrid said. 'I am not satisfied that it should be left to anyone else. We have checked, and the building site in the Champs Elysées will be working tomorrow morning, so that's when we shall get in and instal ourselves.'

'Do you have the weapons?'

'I get them from Berenger tonight.'

'What will it be?'

'A Hotchkiss-Brandt Commando mortar and there's a small automatic weapon of some kind.'

'Do you see any problem in getting the mortar onto the site?'

'I don't think so. It only weighs about eighteen pounds and Serge is fixing up a way of carrying it as part of a load of poles or something. I leave that side to him.'

'Ammunition?'

'They're 60-mm bombs with charges for minimum range – that's about one hundred metres. There will be two HE's and a smoke bomb which may come in useful to create a diversion.'

'Any questions?'

No one had questions.

'Right,' the chairman said, 'we wish our *compagne* good luck. That is all. We will meet again at the same time on Monday.'

They made their way onto the quayside separately. None of Alfred Baum's army of DST agents recognised Ingrid or found anything noteworthy in the others, walking among the rush-hour crowds towards a relaxed and sunny weekend.

At midnight Baum decided to try to get some sleep on the narrow and uncomfortable bed that had been put up for him in a room near his own office. It didn't work. An hour later he was back in his office, listlessly turning over papers, dipping into files, sitting for long stretches with his head in his hands – puzzling, puzzling . . . And his liver was playing him up again.

It looked now as if he were heading for disaster. He was half way through Friday night and the parade was less than thirty-six hours away – thirty-six hours during which he had to rely entirely on something turning up. The initiative had passed completely out of his hands. Lady Luck, that fickle whore, was now running the game. If something unforeseen did not happen, then disaster would ensue at the parade on Sunday morning. He held no hopes from the routine police checks along the route: all that was strictly for the record. Anyone wanting to conceal himself in order to attack the parade could most certainly do so. And even knowing the approximate area they were aiming at was no real help. The target was too big.

He drank some cold coffee, pulling a face, and swallowed one of his pills. Then he wandered down to the duty officer's room and spent a half hour chatting. The duty officer had been dozing, and wanting to sleep rather than talk, was not forthcoming. Baum prowled down the deserted corridors, looked into the listening room where the radio equipment lay unattended. Then he went to archives but the door was locked. At last, close to 3 a.m. he went back to bed, not bothering to undress save for his shoes. He spent the next three hours analysing where he had gone wrong, at what point a different course of action would have produced a different outcome. He did not entertain the possibility that he had not gone wrong at all. No, there were mistakes all along the line, most of them his. Of that he was certain.

At six he got up, splashed his face with cold water, then shaved as carefully as he could. He felt depressed, drained of energy, disconsolate. He told himself it was the physical reaction to an utterly sleepless night. He'd been all right after a strong coffee. He would be able to face what bid fair to be the most unpleasant day of his life.

The canteen didn't open until 8 a.m., so he went out into the deserted street, past dustmen banging dustbins needlessly and past the endless rows of parked cars to a café he knew would be open a couple of streets away. There, among the always inexplicable mix of early-morning customers, he ordered a large black coffee. Piling sugar into it, he sipped the acrid, steaming liquid and began, slowly, to feel better – first physically and, in small tentative stages, mentally. After all, not everything was lost yet. He still had nearly thirty hours in hand. Not a lifetime, but still time enough to change a situation, to think something through, to take advantage of a lucky break.

Dear God, why had there been no lucky break? Or

rather, why had the breaks turned sour – the girl getting away at the hospital, the man Jean-Paul Macé getting away in the Faubourg, the courier René dying on them as a result of Assar's crude violence and lack of common sense? Why, why, why? Because Chance did not favour the DST, being deeply unaware of the role of that important organism. But above all because when, briefly, things had gone their way, they had fouled them up. No excuses would do. They – he – had made a mess. And now here he was, whining for mercy, for help, for luck he didn't deserve.

Pull yourself together, Alfred, he said to himself as the waiter brought a second coffee and a hot croissant, newly delivered. Stop snivelling and start to *think*, man! There's work to be done. For instance, exactly what are you going to do today?

He took a slip of paper from one pocket and a ballpoint from another and made brief, indecipherable notes: 1, 2, 3 . . . Then he summoned the waiter with a wave, paid his bill, and set off back to the Rue des Saussaies. He was feeling better, more combative, more himself.

Soon after eight, with the offices coming to life, he summoned Inspector Allembeau and got a car to take them to the radio van discreetly parked near the Mirabeau bridge. Inside the van the radio technician sat at his controls, bored and fed up because no messages were coming in and he was not allowed to use the frequency for gossip.

'We will talk to some of the operatives,' Baum said. 'Please call in Inspector Charcot.'

The Inspector, who had been making a round of the morning shift, presented himself and a desultory exchange of questions and answers ensued. 'I think,' Baum said, 'I had better talk to some of the others. Send them in to me in any order you like, at twenty-minute intervals. At least it may be good for morale.'

'Very good, chief.'

The morning was taken up with brief and fruitless interviews. At 11 a.m. Baum finished talking to one of the sergeants who was on foot patrol. Waiting for the next man, he turned to Allembeau.

'This is getting us nowhere, you know.'

Allembeau shrugged. He had never seen the old man like this before – pessimistic, unsure of himself, willing to waste time and effort.

'Perhaps it needs a fresh mind – someone who hasn't been as close to it as we are.'

'I doubt it, chief.'

As they spoke, Luc and Chantal, summoned by the Inspector, came through the door of the van and stood waiting respectfully while the great men finished their conversation. Baum seemed unaware of their presence.

'Maybe we're on the wrong track altogether in thinking that they meet at Marie Louise's place. If the blonde girl *is* Marie Louise, maybe she just lives around here and the group operates somewhere at the other end of Paris.'

'Even so, she's the only link we have.'

Baum grunted. 'I wonder who Ingrid is.' He seemed to become aware of Luc and Chantal. 'Oh, yes, you two. What can you tell me?'

'Not much, I'm afraid, chief. It's been very quiet.'

'Any theories?'

'No, chief.'

'What about you, young lady? What about a little feminine intuition here?'

Chantal smiled, displaying her famous dimples. 'Excuse me, chief, but did you say you were interested in a girl called Marie Louise?'

'I am.'

'Well, I don't know about a girl, and I'm sure I don't know if this makes any sense at all, but there's a boat down by the quayside there called the *Marie Louise*.' She looked at him as if she expected to be told to stop talking rubbish and mind her own business. Instead of which Baum looked hard at her in silence for a moment. Then she saw his face break slowly into an enormous grin. He brought one pudgy fist hard down into the palm of the other hand.

'Allembeau,' he shouted. 'Did you hear that? Did you hear what this lovely young lady said to us? She said she didn't know about girls, but there was a boat – a *boat* – called the *Marie Louise*! Allembeau, my dear fellow, *this is our break*!'

He jumped from his seat, advanced to Chantal, and taking her small frame in his arms, planted a smacking kiss on her forehead. 'You are not only a very pretty girl,' he said, 'you are also very perceptive.' He turned to Luc. 'Did you see this boat, young man?'

'Yes, sir.'

'Then learn a lesson from this young lady here, just as I have learned a lesson: that you should watch for *connections* – always connections. That is what you should learn. And what I should learn is that conclusions should not be jumped to. Now, of course, it's obvious: we are here at a port, among boats. And plenty of boats bear women's names. By hindsight the thing is obvious.' He turned to Allembeau. 'You hit on the crucial point, my friend, but unfortunately neither of us took it far enough. You asked if it was not significant that the man gave various names, but it was only when they questioned him about the meeting place that he mentioned Marie Louise. That was deeply significant. You sensed it, I did not.'

He shook his head. 'Lessons, lessons. There are always lessons.' He turned to Luc and Chantal. '*Merci, mes enfants*. Now off you go. We shall talk more about all this when we've finished the job.'

After the two had gone, Baum said to Allembeau: 'Here is what we do. This time we don't wait for them to walk into traps. There's no time for such nonsense any more, and in any case, we've proved ourselves pretty incompetent in that department. No, we prepare most carefully to raid this boat, and having prepared, we raid it. If we catch some of the birds, fine. If not, we make what we can of the boat itself. I'm no longer in a mood for taking risks.'

They spent an hour in detailed preparations. Allembeau contacted a friend in the customs department and got the loan for the afternoon of an unmarked customs launch. Inspector Charcot was called back and told how to dispose his men around the quayside and the *Marie Louise*. Allembeau went for a stroll along the waterfront past the

Marie Louise and decided how the boat was to be approached by the raiding party and how many men and what equipment would be needed.

Meanwhile, a man had been despatched to the Town Hall of the 15th *arrondissement* and thence to the home of the manager of the registry department, who was persuaded to come grumbling to his office to open up, search the files and provide details of the ownership of the *Marie Louise*. These the DST man brought back to Baum shortly after 12.45 p.m., feeling pleased with his achievement. But Baum, usually punctilious in such matters, did not on this occasion even nod his thanks. For as he took the paper he caught immediate sight of the name written on it.

He produced a long and very low whistle. 'This boat of ours belongs to one Bernard Pellerin,' he said to Allembeau. 'And you know who that is.'

'Afraid not, though Pellerin is familiar, of course.'

'Precisely. Bernard is the son, no less, of Ambroise Pellerin, our esteemed Minister of Defence. And that means, my dear Allembeau, that whatever we do to his boat, there is absolutely nothing that we can do to him. This Bernard seems to have chosen his father with some care. It seems that Assar will not after all have a victim today.'

Shortly after 11 a.m. two workmen walked slowly through the open gates of the big building site next to the Rond Point des Champs Elysées. The site was alive with building workers and no one questioned them. They were carrying between them a bundle of plastic guttering and anyone who had been at all perceptive might have wondered why guttering was being delivered at this early stage in the construction, when the tower crane had only recently been erected and the structure had barely reached the first-floor level. However, the men on the site were thinking of the midday siren and what the weekend had to offer. The two passed unnoticed into the forest of props supporting the newly laid floor of the first storey and deposited their burden behind a large pile of aggregate. Rapidly, they pulled a tarpaulin over it and scattered sand on top.

Ingrid had transformed herself. A loose donkey jacket hid the contour of her breasts and trousers a size too large masked the curve of her hips. She wore a beret into which she had crammed all her hair, and her rather severe features looked masculine enough framed in this way.

They both hid themselves in the dank cavern which was to be the new building's underground car park and waited for the site to close down at midday.

'What I want above all else is two sets of fishing tackle,' Baum said. It was 1 p.m. and he had Allembeau and Charcot with him in the radio van. Between them they were drawing their plans.

Charcot grinned. 'I have some at home but I live out at Juvisy.'

'Then find me someone who lives closer in and get him to fetch his tackle and whatever he can borrow from a neighbour. Good God, everyone in the department fishes except me. It shouldn't be difficult.'

A Sergeant posted at the door of the van was sent off on the strange quest and instructed never to come back if he failed to find the required items within an hour.

'What about the picture of Bernard Pellerin?' Baum had already radioed the Rue des Saussaies to send over the mug shot from Bernard Pellerin's dossier. He knew from his intimacy with the archives that Bernard Pellerin was in there, alongside his distinguished father. This was so because he had been briefly, back in his student days, a member of a Trotskyist group at the university at Besançon. It was a sure way of getting into the DST files, though the files said nothing about any dramatic shift in his political views.

'A despatch rider should be on his way by now.'

'I hope so. Now for our arrangements.'

Allembeau had drawn a sketch map of the quayside and the boats. It lay on a trestle table before them. 'What I intend,' Baum said, 'is that the customs launch with four of our men aboard should pull alongside the *Marie Louise* at precisely three p.m. At that time I want two of our men to be walking along the quayside from opposite directions and drawing level with the target. Also, there will be two men fishing as close to the *Marie Louise* as they can get. That is why I need fishing tackle. Any questions?'

'Reserves?' Charcot said. 'In case we run into opposition.'

'You'll have to keep your reserves back on street level and hope they can be summoned in time if you need them. I can't risk crowding the quay with people since I am told it is usually deserted on Saturday afternoons.'

'Use of arms?'

'All the men will carry side arms and will use them if they have to. I repeat: if they have to. I will also allow one automatic weapon. If we are to capture anyone, I want them alive. On the other hand, I do not want the deaths of any of our people on my conscience. Is that clear?'

The others nodded. They went on to discuss what was to be done once they had gained possession of the boat.

The photograph of Bernard Pellerin, *alias* Brunot, was passed round among the men who were to make up the raiding party and as many as possible of the other DST men and women in the area. Just after 2 p.m. two sets of fishing tackle arrived and the Sergeant who had conjured them up went away with a broad smile, as if he had conjured up the devil himself. By 2.30 the fishermen were in place, their lines in the water. No bait had been delivered. There wasn't even any sport in it. Shortly afterwards the customs launch came in sight round the eastward bend in the river and cruised slowly past. It was in radio contact with the control van.

At 2.55 Inspector Charcot, who was dressed for a lazy Saturday afternoon by the riverside, walked down the steps by the Mirabeau bridge and started to walk eastwards towards the berth of the *Marie Louise*. One minute later another DST man descended the steps by the Grenelle bridge and stood looking at the river. He carried a canvas holdall. As he watched the trim launch working back upstream from his left he gripped the holdall, glanced at his watch, and resumed his stroll past the houseboats. Ahead and walking towards him was Charcot. As the launch slowed down in midstream and turned slightly to starboard, the two men were some twenty yards apart. The two fishermen had propped their rods on the quayside and also seemed to be watching the launch. They too glanced at their watches. The time was one minute to 3 p.m.

Charcot and his opposite number came abreast of the *Marie Louise*. As they did so, one of the fishermen pulled a transceiver from his pocket and spoke briefly into it. Then he and his fellow-sportsman got to their feet. The launch had come round in a gentle curve and was now lying alongside the *Marie Louise*, some ten yards out.

Now there were four men grouped together a few feet from the boat's gangplank. The man from the Grenelle bridge opened his holdall and took out a MAT 49, allowing the holdall to fall to the ground. The four then dashed across the gangplank, the man with the automatic in the lead, followed by Charcot. Each of the fishermen had taken a crowbar from among their gear. Moments later all four DST men were in the well of the boat, confronted by the closed door with its heavy padlock.

'No one at home,' Charcot said into his transceiver. 'Door padlocked. We are about to break in. See that our rear is watched. I shall keep this frequency open. Over.'

'We hear you. Good luck.'

The two crowbars, wielded as one, prised the padlock from its moorings with a loud crack, and more heavy work on the door itself took it off its hinges. In ninety seconds the men were inside the saloon of the boat.

'We're in. Had to smash the door down so there's no hope of trapping anyone returning here. It means our people outside will have to pounce if they see anyone about to come on board.'

'We hear you. Now get to work. A thorough job. I don't mind if you have to rip the thing to bits. Over.'

The work of searching the boat went on for forty minutes. In under half that time it looked like a disaster area. Every book on the shelves had been searched and flung aside, every drawer and cupboard emptied, upholstery ripped, carpets lifted, food shaken out of packets and jars.

Floorboards were taken up and the men searched down in the bilges in the dirty river water. Cisterns and tanks were opened up and searched and improvised probes pushed down pipes.

Half way through the work, Alfred Baum and Allembeau arrived and took charge. 'We are looking for very simple things,' Baum said. 'Notes or lists, perhaps. Or maps. Or identity cards. Forget about hardware: if you find any, it will be a bonus. I want information here, not guns and bombs.'

'Well, there's a street map of Paris, chief,' one of the men said. 'It was on the table all along.' He handed it to Baum.

A few minutes later Charcot called out: 'Hey, what's this then?' He was holding two sheets of paper. 'I shook them out of a shirt at the back of this drawer. Might be interesting.' He handed them to Baum.

Looking through a porthole, Baum saw that a DST man aboard the launch was signalling. 'There are ropes fixed to hooks just below two of the portholes,' he shouted. 'They run down below the waterline. There may be containers on the ends.'

They hauled the ropes up from inside. Both were attached to heavy watertight metal containers which they had been suspending several feet below the surface of the river. Opened on the floor, they gave up automatic pistols, ammunition and six hand grenades.

Baum was not interested. 'I said it would be a bonus – good stuff for the newspapers, that's all.' He was poring short-sightedly over the two sheets of paper. They contained in abbreviated form lists of buildings in the capital. There were no notes. But against several entries ticks had been made in different ink.

'A bombing target list if ever I saw one,' Baum said to Allembeau. 'See, the TV Centre is on here, ticked. So is the American Express office. I see the Bank of France is down, but no tick yet. We have that pleasure to come, no doubt.'

He turned to the map, opened it out on the table, and oblivious to the racket and bustle around him as the men continued to take the boat apart, he pored over it. Then he held it up so that the inadequate light in the saloon fell across it at an angle. He grunted, moving the map about, trying to catch more light on it, adjusting the angle.

'I think pencil marks have been made on this map and then rubbed out,' he said to Allembeau. 'But we'll need the new equipment they've got in forensic. Is anyone in this afternoon?'

'I'll find out, chief.'

Radio communication told them there was no one in, but a technician was being summoned from his garden or his siesta and would be available as soon as he could be found and could make it to the Rue des Saussaies.

Forty minutes after Baum and Allembeau had left the *Marie Louise*, Brunot walked along the quayside and was on the gangplank before he noticed a man standing in the well of the boat – behind him the smashed door. Brunot did not have a gun with him, and as the man advanced towards him on the gangplank, he turned to run for it. Advancing from both directions along the quayside were groups of men. He hesitated, then he plunged into the dank and polluted water and started to swim strongly round the houseboat, heading downstream. Within a minute the launch had got under way and had closed in. He was hauled aboard, wet and stinking from the scum of the river.

On the Friday a situation report from the CIA Resident in Paris had reached CIA headquarters at Langley, Virginia, where it was immediately routed to Admiral Bruback. Suitably edited to strengthen its basic message, extracts were forwarded on the teleprinter to the White House National Security Adviser, the French desk at the State Department, and the US Treasury. The tone of the report had been gloomy. Filleted and chopped about, it was gloomier still. It saw disaster looming in the coming election and forecast a continuation of the terror campaign. It even ventured to predict an incident at the Gaullist parade on Sunday.

The various departments of the US Government had all day on the Friday in which to work themselves up into a state of indignation at the supine attitude of the French authorities.

Via the Treasury, the money market sensed it all and a further 20 centimes were knocked off the franc's value against the dollar. The franc had now lost 18 per cent of its value in under three weeks. The Secretary of State, presented with the latest CIA appreciation, suggested it might be wise to do a little feet-dragging in the negotiations for the purchase of new trainer aircraft from Dassault Breguet. The President summoned the Admiral to a cocktail-hour meeting and the two men managed to frighten each other thoroughly. Dr Kissinger was sought, but being on vacation somewhere in New England, could not immediately be traced.

Chapter 16

The night security man on the building site in the Champs Elysées had complained about being left alone to guard construction works of such a size but his demand for a mate had been turned down by the contractors as unnecessary. There was plenty of theft from the site, as there was from any building job, but it all took place during working hours, when wood, cement, even whole loads of bricks could be taken out on false documents, or loads could be delivered light and incomplete. At night and at weekends, the site was protected by its solid twenty-foot wooden hoarding, plastered with sixty-four sheet posters. Floodlights mounted on poles were left burning all night.

The security man, who was sixty-seven and had a gammy leg, was required to tour the site three times during the night and four times in daylight on Sundays. What with his leg and the loneliness, he had cut his night-time tours of inspection to two: one at 10 p.m., as night was falling, and another shortly after midnight. That gave him a nice run-through of seven hours for a good sleep. He needed it: he was moonlighting. By day he sold National Lottery tickets at a busy *tabac* in town.

He made a quick tour of the site on the Saturday afternoon and another just before 10 p.m., when he switched on the overhead lights. Serge and Ingrid heard him stumping about above their heads: the old man's thoroughness did not extend to the bowels of the place since access was by ladder and his leg wouldn't stand it.

'You'd better deal with him,' Ingrid said. 'Otherwise we'll be stuck down here until tomorrow afternoon, and when we get to work he could see us.'

'Lose him?'

She nodded.

'Leave it to me,' Serge said.

He mounted to ground level. The old man was still hobbling round. Now Serge could see him walking away at the far end of what would one day be the building's forecourt.

'Hi!' he called. The security man stopped and looked round as Serge advanced towards him.

'What the hell are you doing in here?'

'It's all right, grandad, I got locked in, that's all, and then I fell asleep. Care to let me out?'

The old man looked suspiciously at him as he came alongside. 'How do I know you've any right to be in here?'

'Simple. We'll go to the site office and I'll show you my card. Come on.'

The old man shrugged and growled something and they started walking. As they passed a pile of bricks, Serge fell slightly behind and picked one up, holding it behind him. Then they were walking beneath the newly-laid first floor of the building, shielded from the strong overhead lights. Serge brought the brick down with all his force on the back of the old man's head. With a groan he crumpled and as he lay on the ground the brick was smashed into his skull twice more.

He had fallen near a pit into which foundations were still being poured. It was some forty feet deep. Serge dragged the old man to the edge and heaved his body over. It hit the hardening concrete at the bottom with a thud.

'We're OK now,' he called to Ingrid. 'Christ, he had a soft skull!'

They ate sandwiches and drank Cokes, and spent the rest of the night in the security man's hut.

'I feel,' Alfred Baum was saying, 'like a small child who is holding an enormous, overcharged ice cream cornet. The ice cream is melting in the hot sun and running down his fingers, but if he takes it to his mouth the whole thing may collapse, while if he just holds it, it can only end up on the ground. That is how I feel in respect of our distinguished prisoner.'

He was back in Georges Wavre's gloomy office. It was 7 p.m. on that same Saturday evening and he had finished reporting on the events of the afternoon. Wavre, a look of misery on his face, scratched his head and then shook it sadly. 'Throughout this affair, my dear Alfred, you have presented me with one overcharged ice cream cone after another. Or, to change the metaphor and bring it nearer home, you have persistently tossed me problems of which I do not want to take delivery. You hand me stolen documents from the Defence Committee and compromising tape recordings. You show me links between terror and the US Embassy. And now you offer me, down below in this very building, the son of the Minister of Defence. Good God, man, are you trying to bring me to an early grave?'

'I bring you what I find,' Baum said simply. 'If our Republic creates messes of this kind, someone is bound in the end to stumble on them. I just happen to be the man who stumbled.' He allowed an innocent smile to appear on his face. 'I wish it were otherwise.'

'What mood is our Bernard in at present?'

'He's certainly his father's son. He exudes self-righteousness. He refuses to answer a single question, and to everything we say he replies: "I demand to see my lawyer". That's as far as we've got with him.'

'It is probably as far as you'll ever get. Have you told our Minister who it is we're holding?'

'I was reserving that pleasure for you.'

Wavre grunted and reached for a cigarette. 'I see it like this. Questioning him will be a waste of valuable time, since he knows we can't lean too heavily on him. As soon as the arrest is known, his old man will be on to everyone in sight – the President, the Prime Minister, Mallard, the lot. And for the sake of peace and quiet within the Government they'll give us their instructions: let him go – forget it – don't stir things up in that quarter. Furthermore, the longer we hold him before that inevitable point is reached, the more trouble we'll have when we reach it. Therefore, we must call our esteemed Minister now and pass this particular ice cream cone to him.'

Two calls brought the Minister of the Interior to the phone. Wavre explained carefully that in the course of a raid that afternoon in which bombs and arms had been found, the son of the Minister of Defence had been arrested while trying to run, or rather swim, away. What should they do with him?

'Give me fifteen minutes,' the Minister said. He did not sound pleased.

'I have work to do,' Baum said. 'I'll be in my room when Mallard calls back.'

The call came almost exactly fifteen minutes later.

'You have my authority to release Bernard Pellerin on the understanding that he holds himself available for questioning later. His father seemed to know about the events of the afternoon, though I have no idea how. He says there will certainly be a complaint against your department for the unnecessary damage done to his son's boat. I would say the sooner you let him go, the better for all of us. And be sure he's treated with proper courtesy.'

'You'd better do it,' Wavre said to Baum on the intercom. 'I believe the Americans have an expression: Go fight City Hall! Well, this is City Hall.'

When he was told that he would be released and was required to attend at the Rue des Saussaies on Monday at ten, Bernard Pellerin simply asked for a taxi to be called for him. Ten minutes later he was being driven away.

It was close to 11 p.m. before the technician from forensic could be found and brought back to the Rue des Saussaies. He came in apologising, as if he had no right to be visiting his aunt out at Enghien in his free time.

'That's all right, my lad,' Baum said. They were assembled in forensic around the new machine.

'It's only a specialised light source, really,' the technician said. 'Very powerful polarised light, accurately beamed. If you switch it this way and that it will pick up the faintest indentation in paper, where something has been erased or where there's been writing on a sheet of paper lying above the one you're looking at.'

He was adjusting knobs and manipulating an instrument shaped like a thick pencil on the end of a cable, holding the map at various angles and making a thin line of light bounce off it.

'The likeliest areas in which to find marks are these,' Baum said, pointing a stubby finger at the Rue Royale and the Champs Elysées.

The man worked in silence for a while. 'A pencil line was drawn along the Rue Royale,' he said, 'and then across the Concorde and up the Champs Elysées.'

'I'm not surprised. That would be the route of the parade. Any other marks?'

The technician was shaking his head. He had started at the Madeleine church and was working his light probe slowly back along the Rue Royale. He had passed the Place de la Concorde and was moving it up now towards the Rond Point des Champs Elysées, half way up that magnificent triumphal way and marking the intersection where the formal gardens end and the buildings begin – the point at which the tourists turn and walk back towards the Arc de Triomphe and the tarts do the same.

'Pay particular attention to the Champs Elysées,' Baum was saying. 'It is our last hope.'

The light continued to travel along the face of the map. The technician was working his way up the southern side of the Avenue. He reached the top. 'Nothing here,' he said. 'Now we go back down the other side.'

The point of light moved slowly, wavering in a shallow zigzag as he widened the area being examined. The men in the room were absolutely still, as if their very lives were being probed and, it could be, found wanting. For some reason the technician continued to shake his head slowly. He didn't believe in the exercise. He was missing a family dinner at home. He had been pulled back to the department during off-duty hours four times now in the past three weeks. Enough was enough, especially if the answer was going to be a lemon.

The light hovered over the Rue du Colisée and started to move down along the last block of buildings before the Rond Point. Suddenly the technician whistled. The light stopped and he tilted the map away from him. He shook his head again, tilting the map and the light source at each other at different angles. 'I think there's something there,' he said. 'Faint, but definitely there.' He was proud of his machine now, anxious to find the mark, to justify the operation.

'What is it?' Baum, leaning over his shoulder, could see nothing.

'A small cross – definitely a small cross. Look, move a little this way. Now hold the light and tilt it to suit your angle of vision. Do you see anything?'

Baum manipulated the thing. There was silence. Suddenly, he could see the tiny valleys where a pencil had marked a cross and a rubber had been used later.

'I've got it,' he said. 'It's just about the last building on that side of the street before you come to the intersection. And that, I recall very distinctly, is a large construction site. Which, from their point of view, would make very good sense.'

He turned to Inspector Allembeau and his eyes were twinkling. 'Our luck has turned, my friend. Most definitely. And now we have some real work to do at last and not much time in which to do it. First, I want a man over at the Rond Point right away. He's to let us know immediately if he sees any movement at all.'

Allembeau issued some orders on the intercom.

'Also, I want you to get the number of the site office from the telephone company and put in a call. If the night watchman answers it will be one thing. If not, it will very probably be another.'

Allembeau went off to wrestle with the phone company's bureaucracy. At the end of fifteen minutes he had a phone number. He dialled it and waited while the number rang. After two minutes the handset was lifted and replaced. He dialled again, and this time the number was unobtainable.

'It looks,' he said, 'as if the instrument has been disconnected.'

'Good. It is the first half-way hard evidence that that little cross was in the right place.'

It was after midnight. They spent the rest of the night making preparations, recalling men to duty for the following morning, working with street maps. At 2 a.m. Baum announced that he was going for a walk, and in the warm night made his way to the Champs Elysées and up through the tree-lined walk to the Rond Point. There were still plenty of people about – nearly all tourists.

Extra police had already been drafted into the area in readiness for the parade. They stood in groups under the trees at the Rond Point, and nearby he could see the dark outlines of police buses. Foot patrols were in the Champs Elysées itself. The Prefect was pretending to take his security responsibilities more seriously these days.

Baum stood looking up at the tall hoardings surrounding the building site, imagining ways in which an attack could be mounted from there against the parade, which would come down the Champs Elysées, past this spot and on towards the Place de la Concorde. In preparation for the crowds on the morrow, wooden barriers painted in red and white stripes had been piled on the pavements on either side of the Avenue. Temporary signs redirecting the traffic were ready to be erected in the morning. Under the vivid street lighting, the crowds sauntered. Mostly, at this hour of the night, it was men, alone or in small groups, hunting the immaculately artificial whores strolling alone or in pairs. In the middle of the wide pavement negotiations started up, deals were struck or heads shaken and the protagonists moved on, seeking a better deal, a special requirement.

Baum walked slowly past the hoarding, ignoring the girls, then walked back again and round to the other side of the site, along the Avenue Roosevelt. The access gates were locked. There was a light in what appeared to be a watchman's hut on the far side of the gates. Nothing stirred.

The DST Sergeant on duty came over.

'Anything, François?'

'Nothing much, chief. I haven't seen any movement in there.'

'We'll get you relieved soon.'

'Thanks, chief.'

Baum walked slowly back to the Rue des Saussaies, clear in his mind on the action to be taken tomorrow morning and certain that any move with his inadequate forces against the building site during the night would have been unwise: there was too big a chance of whoever might be there escaping in the dark.

Back in his office with Inspector Allembeau and three of his key men, he laid down timing, manning levels, the provision and possible use of firearms, and communication and control. The action in the Champs Elysées was timed for 8.30 a.m., an hour and three quarters before the parade was due to pass the spot. At four he announced that he was going to get some sleep and expected everyone else to do the same.

On the narrow bed in the next room, he found to his surprise that he could sleep despite the tension of the night, and did not wake until his alarm sounded at 6.30. By seven the DST building was alive with the sounds of hurrying footsteps, shouted greetings and, from the armoury, the metallic clatter of firearms being distributed and firing mechanisms being checked. Down in the garage beneath the building, the cars had been made ready. The equipment in the radio van had been checked and radio technicians were at work.

At 7.15 Baum called Georges Wavre at home, waking him from sleep with a brief apology.

'It's for eight thirty this morning.' He gave him the exact location.

'Do you need me?'

'No, thanks. I suggest you stay away. You never know what this sort of operation will throw up.'

'Everything organised?'

'Sure.'

'Are you going to succeed, Alfred – that's what I want to know?'

'I am, *patron*.'

'You like close-run things, don't you?'

'No.'

'Good luck, then.'

'Thanks.' He rang off and swallowed some of the coffee that someone had put on his desk.

'We set out at eight twenty then,' he said to Allembeau on the intercom. 'You come with me and we'll direct things from the radio van. We can join it when we get there. Is everything else timed?'

'Yes, chief. I've just had a report from our man on the spot. He says the crowd-control barriers are already in place and there's a devil of a lot of police in the area.'

'That's to be expected.'

'Do you think we should warn the *Préfecture* that we have this exercise?'

'Not the way things are. We don't want them blocking us. Let them stick to the routine stuff along the route of the parade.'

The DST car carrying Baum and Allembeau had difficulty getting to its destination, however. The approaches to the Champs Elysées had already been closed off with wooden barriers and cordons of police. The first spectators were straggling up from the Metro stations and walking in groups through the barriers to take up their positions along the route of the procession. The pavements where they began to line the route were separated from the roadway by further barriers and police were beginning already to place themselves along the route of the parade at intervals of a few yards.

'We'll walk,' Baum said at last. The car had become stuck in a side street for the third time. 'Come on, it's only a few hundred yards.'

At the approaches to the Rond Point des Champs Elysées there were large police buses with reinforced windows parked bumper to bumper and the pavements were black with policemen and the heavyset slow-moving men of the CRS riot squads in their knee boots, black uniforms and black steel helmets. They were gathered in double lines along the pavements leading to the Champs Elysées itself and a group of their officers was conferring with braided policemen in the middle of the Avenue Roosevelt.

'Well, well, the CRS,' Baum said to Allembeau. 'To what do we owe this pleasure, I wonder?' They were level with the building site now, and in the crowd of uniformed men Baum recognised his own people, all in plain clothes, hesitating around the entrance to the site but unable to reach it through the lines of CRS and police. They were hoping for help and guidance in this unexpected situation.

Baum made his way to the group of officers, his small, portly frame in its crumpled suit contrasting absurdly with the physique of the troops, and even with the police officers.

'Who is in charge here?'

A burly, middle-aged Colonel looked up without moving. 'Who are you?'

Baum took his identity card out of his pocket and offered it. 'Baum, Deputy Director, the DST. To whom am I speaking?'

'Colonel Roque of the CRS. What do you want, Monsieur Baum?'

Baum signalled to the Colonel to leave the knot of officers and impelled by the little man's natural authority, the Colonel took a few steps towards him.

'We need to operate in this immediate area between now and the arrival of the parade at ten fifteen,' Baum said. 'A security matter.'

'What security matter? I have no instructions about you.'

'I am not at liberty to discuss State security and in any case, you don't need instructions on our account – only identification, and that you have just had, Colonel.'

'Sorry, I'm not interested in identification. My orders are to control the area. You have no authority to move your men in here.'

'You are as much subject to the Ministry of the Interior as I am. None of this has anything to do with you or for that matter, the *Préfecture*. So kindly instruct your men to let my people pass.'

The Colonel looked down on Baum from his superior height, glad of the difference. His instructions had been exceptionally specific and he'd wondered at the time what the fuss was about. No one, no other service, to be allowed through in this area. No matter who turned up and whose authority was quoted. And he knew that the police Inspector in the sector had the same instructions. This little man could therefore be safely ignored.

'Sorry,' he said. 'I obey orders. The orders are that no one passes. And that includes you, Monsieur, and your men.'

'Where did you get your orders?'

'That is my affair and not yours.'

Baum eyed this bovine and self-important type and contemplated briefly telling him why he had to get through. But the risk then would be that the CRS or the police would insist on taking over the search themselves. And some search that would be! He turned away and rejoined Allembeau.

'They're wise to us. They've orders not to let our people through. The place is like an armed camp despite the fact that everyone knows there will be no hostile demonstrations today. They pretend it's security against the bombers, but the Prefect must have laid all this on. It's security *for* the bombers.'

'What about the CRS?'

'The Prefect must have asked for them and they're following his orders. That's how it works for street actions.' He paused and scratched his head. 'Come on. It's no use hanging about here. Where's our radio van?'

The van was parked two streets away and had not yet been interfered with by the police. Baum called the Saussaies. 'Link me up with Commander Roisset at the *Préfecture*,' he said. 'I'll hold.' A few moments later the voice of the Saussaies operator came through the mike. 'Commander Roisset is at the parade. He's inspecting the arrangements. They don't know where exactly.'

'All right. Tell them if he contacts his office to call you at once and then radio us here.'

Baum looked at his watch. It was five minutes short of nine o'clock. There were seventy-five minutes left before the parade came by. 'We have to find Roisset,' he said. 'It's the only way of loosening up this situation. He wants to make a bit of history and now's his chance.'

'What about the Minister?'

'In the parade. And Deputy Ministers are useless. It has to be Roisset. Get men from our lot here and from the Saussaies to all the key points on the route. Everything between the Arc de Triomphe and the Town Hall. Tell 'em to find him. He's to contact me on our radio frequency. Better still, he's to come here himself. And it must be by ten. Understood?'

'Understood.'

The crowds now were growing thicker in the Champs Elysées. From time to time a police despatch rider roared down the empty roadway, enjoying his own performance, cutting a figure, embodying authority – armed, mechanised and leather-clad. Further up the road the police had allowed vendors of soft drinks and ice creams to pass through the barriers. Trade was starting slowly but would warm up later. The crowd was good humoured and raised an ironic cheer each time a despatch rider rode by. Although the parade was Gaullist, it commemorated de Gaulle's entry into liberated Paris on 25 August, 1944, and that was an event which the other parties felt belonged to them too. The date had been shifted to a weekend when some at least of the Paris population had returned from holiday. The crowds, then, were made up from Left and Right and none of the main parties had any interest in causing trouble. The Left had long felt that the Gaullists were capturing the flag, as it were, but even the Communists enjoyed a good march-past, and that is what it would be.

Along the streets, party militants were selling *l'Humanité Dimanche* and doing good business. *When Will The Terror End?* enquired the banner headline on page one. Beneath it, Armand Seynac's rather ponderous prose proclaimed the party's republican principles and made some well-judged jibes at the Government's failure to arrest any bombers.

On page six, among the snippets of police news, was an item referring to the corpse of a man, so far unidentified, found near a roadside in the forest of Fontainebleau. The police said he appeared to have been dead for two weeks. It had all the signs, according to a police spokesman, of a gangland execution. Probably a contract job.

Listening to the eight o'clock news on the radio in the watchman's hut, Serge and Ingrid heard of the police discovery in the forest.

'About time,' Serge said. 'He can't be in very good condition.'

'Scum!' Ingrid said, switching off the radio. 'He didn't wash. An animal.' There was a curiously intense disgust in her voice.

'I'm going to see what it looks like outside,' Serge said. 'Then we'll have some of the old boy's coffee.'

He went down the steps from the hut and made his way to the hoarding on the Avenue Roosevelt flank of the site. He looked through a crack between the planks. Before him, lined along the pavement, were the backs of policemen and CRS troops. His heart thumped uncontrollably and he found that his knees were weak. He moved along some thirty yards to the corner of the building site and found another crack. The scene outside was the same. The place was surrounded. Was this what she called a well-planned operation? Was the girl so fanatically devoted to the cause that her only interest now was the explosion and to hell with the escape afterwards? He'd made it clear when they had selected him for the job that he would do whatever was asked of him. That was his side of the bargain. But they'd promised him the getaway was properly laid out, and that, surely, was their side. Yet now it was scarcely a few minutes after eight and the place was already crawling with cops. And there were two hours to go. He ran back to the hut.

'We're surrounded! There's fuzz shoulder to shoulder along the pavements. It's obvious: we've been shopped.'

'Calm down,' Ingrid said. 'No one has shopped us. I told you the getaway was fixed and so it is.'

'By kind permission of the police and the CRS?'

'I'm not discussing the details. When the job has been done we open the gate and go out. That's all I have to say.'

'I don't believe it.'

'You can believe what you like.'

Serge was silent for a moment. Was the woman mad? Or had they really fixed things with the police? But how could they simply walk out, watched by a hundred or so policemen? They couldn't all have been reached. The thing was preposterous. She must be lying. And yet . . . and yet . . . hadn't the planning always been meticulous? Hadn't the police always managed to fail? Preposterous as it might seem, wasn't she likely to be telling the truth?

Suddenly, he made up his mind. 'You can count me out,' he said. 'The cause is all very well, but I'm not ready for suicide just yet. Don't you see: if we come out of here after the explosion, they'll simply shoot us down. It would be just the opportunity your average fuzz would be waiting for. After all, we've disposed of a few of their mates. You may have got to the top men, but the rank and file would dearly love to shoot first and ask what we're up to afterwards.'

He got up from the bench he was sitting on, not too sure of his next move. Ingrid was sitting opposite him, a rickety card table between them. He found himself looking down the barrel of an automatic. His eyes travelled to her face. It was impassive, expressionless. He could read nothing at all in her eyes and he knew that shooting him would present her with no problems at all. He stood there, his hands on the table.

'I was wrong about you.' Her voice was steady, matter of fact. 'I told Command you were a reliable element; would go through with the assignment; wouldn't crack. But I see you're yellow. You've cracked before anything's happened.'

'I'm not yellow, I'm human. I'll play the odds but I don't play against dead certs, and this is a dead cert for the other side.'

'I tell you the police will let us through.'

'You're either lying or you're kidding yourself. Either way I think you're crazy. You're crazy to risk walking into a shoot-out we're bound to lose and you're even crazier to risk our being captured.' He tried to look into her eyes but found it difficult. 'I've no appetite for a session underground with their heavy mob. You know their methods as well as I do.'

'You're yellow, but you're going to go through with this.'

'I'm not yellow. I'm human, but that isn't something you'd understand.'

'Every coward pleads he's merely being human.'

Serge felt anger welling up within him like a kind of nausea, giving him courage and even, for once, eloquence. She wouldn't shoot him, not yet. Alone she couldn't fire the mortar. Shooting him now would abort the mission. And the mission was still her obsession.

'I'm not another Jean-Paul, you know. If you offered it to me on a silver plate I wouldn't take it. I know why you had him killed, and it hadn't much to do with reliability. You did it out of shame – self-disgust. You let him have you and you couldn't forgive yourself for it. I don't know what it is or why, but there's something wrong with you as a woman. You hate yourself and so you hate everyone else. Oh, yes, you love the cause all right. You love it hysterically. But the world's full of people who fall in love with causes and hate the people those causes are meant to defend. And that's because causes have no feelings and no needs. They don't answer back the way real people do. They don't call for compassion or understanding, like people.'

'I shall not forgive that, you filthy swine. It's all lies . . . lies . . . lies!' Her eyes were blazing and her voice shook, yet the gun remained curiously steady in her hand. He could see that the trigger finger was in place, her knuckle was white, bloodless. He found he was not afraid of the gun. And he no longer cared about the effect of what he had to say. His need was to say it.

'Jean-Paul was just a poor bastard without our advantages in life. Sure, he was crude and violent. And he didn't have the education or the politics. But he was on our side and he took on some tough assignments for us. As for his motives, who the hell are you to talk about motives?'

'Shut up, you filthy little swine!' She was almost screaming in her fury, the calm poise utterly lost, the habit of lofty command abandoned. Now her eyes were clouded, the muscles of her face taut, a vein standing out in her slender neck.

'You can yell as much as you like, though it isn't too wise. You won't pull the trigger because if you do, two things will happen. The mission will fail and, later, they'll find my body and Command will know you shot me. You'll tell them you had to, but my guess is they won't believe you. Someone will ask a small, nagging question: why did *you* survive? In whose interest was it for Serge to die and Ingrid to escape? It won't be an easy question to answer, either, after all the other narrow escapes you've had. No, they'll all begin to look odd, and then someone at Command – maybe Felix, whoever he is – will say there's been enough odd coincidences around here and perhaps we'd better dispense with our Ingrid, effective as she may have been. And they'll take you to a quiet spot and put a couple of bullets through the back of that lovely neck of yours. Just on the off-chance that you may be a police spy after all.'

He paused, breathless and astonished at his own loquacity. 'So you won't shoot me – now. Though I dare say you'll try later, after we've fired the mortar. Only I don't think I'm going to give you the chance.'

She had regained her self-control and her voice had returned to its normal, measured tone. 'If you move an inch towards that door, I shall shoot you. And take your hands off the table.'

The gun moved slightly, signalling her command. 'Sit down.'

He drew his hands back across the surface of the table, but instead of lifting them free, he slipped his fingers under the edge and in a rapid movement, hoisted the table up and towards her. As he did so, he flung himself down and sideways and the bullet went crashing through the wooden wall behind him. Ingrid had risen to her feet as she fired, but before she could train the gun on him and fire again Serge had lunged forward and knocked the gun up as he grappled with her. In a moment he had her arms pinned to her sides, the gun twisted out of her grip and lying at her feet. He picked it up and pointed it at her.

'You find it altogether too easy to shoot when you can't win an argument. Now you'll kindly calm down. And don't worry, I'm not going to put a bullet into you.'

She looked at him sullenly, saying nothing.

'Sit down.'

She sat, her fine back arched away from the chair, her head defiantly poised. Her eyes travelled from the gun to the table still lying on the floor at her feet.

'No tricks! I shan't hesitate to shoot if I have to. Keep your feet away from that table.'

She moved her feet back and tucked them beneath the chair. Then she looked him steadily in the eyes.

'I didn't know you were jealous of Jean-Paul. If that's all it is, no doubt we could arrange something, you and I. You're quite an attractive fellow, now I come to look at you in that light. And all this aggression isn't distasteful to me.'

'Sorry, Ingrid, but you've misunderstood. I'm not one of those spiders who gets the hots for the female who's going to eat him for breakfast when it's all over. I don't actually fancy you at all, but thanks anyway.'

She said nothing. Her gaze travelled round the room and he knew she was looking for ways to regain the initiative.

'I'll tell you what I'm going to do,' he said. 'I'm going to get out of here. Now. And I'm going to leave you behind to fire the mortar in a couple of hours' time. That is, if you still want to and if you can manage the thing on its own. But I warn you, it's designed to be held steady by one person while the other drops the missile down the muzzle, and I've no idea how you'll manage single-handed. But that's your problem and I wish you luck with it. Then, if you succeed and manage to get away from the fuzz, I dare say you'll tell Command all about this little squabble of ours, and no doubt they'll pass the required death sentence on me. But finding me, that'll be the snag.'

'We'll find you all right. The police will do it for us. And when they do . . .'

'Spare me the threats, Ingrid.'

He had seen a rope lying in a corner of the hut. Now he took it and quickly tied her hands behind her back, threading the rope through the bars of the chair.

'It shouldn't take you more than a half hour or so to get out of that. Plenty of time to set up the mortar and fire it – if you can. I wish you luck with the operation: I'd have willingly taken part if I thought we could get away afterwards. As it is, you're on your own.'

He put the gun in his pocket, turned on his heel and slammed the door of the hut after him. Then he ran down the steps to the ground.

By 9.30 none of the DST men along the route of the parade had reported progress in the hunt for Commander Roisset. At two intersections he had been seen earlier and had moved on, but there seemed to be no pattern to his movements. Baum wondered whether he wasn't making a private call somewhere in town.

He sat miserably with Allembeau in the radio van, trying to decide the point at which he would have no option but to tell the police and CRS at the Rond Point that there were terrorists on the building site and demand that they go in after them. The thing was finely balanced. If they went in he had no doubt that the terrorists would be allowed to get away. If they were not told by him to go in, however, it would be claimed in the inevitable enquiry that he had wilfully prevented an arrest by withholding information. Either way, he was a loser. And so, timing was all.

The radio operator had his headphones on and was listening in turn to the DST and – out of boredom – tuning in from time to time to the police frequency. Suddenly he grabbed a pad and pencil and started scribbling. Then he gestured to Baum to come over, handing him a twin set of headphones. Someone out at the Rond Point was talking to the *Préfecture*.

'. . . What's that, you want their radio post shut down? Yes, sir, I'll tell the Inspector here . . . Yes, probably in a neighbouring street . . . No, we haven't searched . . . I am instructed to tell you they've made no move, though some of their men have left the area. We don't know where they've been sent . . . Yes, sir . . . Over.'

Baum took off the headphones. 'They'll be here in a minute,' he told Allembeau. 'To shut us down. We shall let that happen: it will look splendid afterwards, of course. You and I will carry on from the car.' He turned to the operator. 'You and the driver will protest and maybe resist a little when the police arrive, and if any of our equipment is broken . . .' he smiled broadly and winked. 'I shall not hold you responsible,' he said, prodding the man's chest with a stubby forefinger. 'Only, don't get hurt, right?'

'Right, chief.'

By 9.45 Baum had failed to get a radio link via the Saussaies with the Commander of the CRS, with the Deputy Minister of the Interior or the General Inspector of Police. He thought of the Mayor of Paris but that worthy was marching in the parade.

There was no one else with sufficient muscle to get the situation at the Rond Point changed in any way. He had thought of the Prime Minister and rejected the idea. There simply wasn't time to explain to that cautious and wily politician all he would want to know before taking action. And who, in any case, would know where he could be found on a fine Sunday morning?

There were now less than thirty minutes to go before the police outriders would appear, followed by the leading line of political worthies, Companions of the Liberation and veterans of the Paris street battles of July and August '44. The crowd along the Champs Elysées and round the Rond Point was dense and noisy but the pavement round the building site had been kept clear and was deep in black CRS men and police. The sound of the band of the Garde Républicaine, stationed further up the Avenue, floated above the steady hubbub of the holiday crowd. There were a lot of children about, many of them already perched on their fathers' shoulders for a better view. Periscopes were on sale and so were the flags of France and the Gaullist Cross of Lorraine. Someone was offering British and American flags and there were few takers. It was going to be a hot day.

Baum had retained two sharpshooters and two other men nearby. All the rest were out searching for the elusive Roisset. 'If only he knew he had a chance to make a little history at last,' Baum mused, 'he'd be here like a shot.'

The DST car was parked two streets away from the Rond Point. At 9.53 the operator at the Saussaies reported that he had had a signal from Léon at the Place de la Concorde. Commander Roisset had been found and had agreed to come right away to the Rond Point. He should be there at any time now.

'Go and fetch him,' Baum said to Allembeau. 'Bring him here. Tell him I must have a private word with him on behalf of the President of the Republic.'

'Is he that naïve?'

'He is. We must use the man's extreme self-importance. It's what motivates him.'

Allembeau reached the Rond Point as Roisset was alighting from his car. He had Léon with him. Allembeau explained his business as the senior policemen at the command post caught sight of Roisset and instinctively pulled at their jackets and straightened their backs. Two of them put their gloves back on. Roisset acknowledged the group with a wave and set off with Allembeau. Léon was experiencing pleasant sensations of importance, success, professional snobbery. Rubbing shoulders with the big boys was very much to his taste.

'How can I possibly do what you ask?' Roisset said. He was installed in Baum's car. The driver was listening to the police frequency on the radio. Baum had made his explanations.

'Excuse me, sir, they're on about us again. I'm sorry to interrupt.'

'Listen,' Baum said. 'I think it may convince you.'

It was the command post at the Rond Point again. 'Roisset is here . . . With the DST men . . . What do we do if he issues counter-orders? . . . Yes, yes, but only the

Prefect can do that . . . In the parade? So you can't reach him? . . . All right, we'll try to refuse, but it isn't easy. You know what a pompous prick he is.'

'I'll have that man's stripes when this is over.' Roisset had gone red in the face, reached in his dignity and self-regard. 'Come on, we'll soon settle the hash of these people.'

It had taken Ingrid close to an hour to free herself. The rope was damp and Serge's knots had tightened as she struggled, biting and rubbing into the delicate skin of her wrists. By the time she was free, the skin had broken in two places and there was blood on the rope. She was sobbing quietly, but in desperation. She scarcely felt the pain.

While Baum and Allembeau had been transferring from the command van to their car, Ingrid was uncovering the bundle of guttering, untying it and releasing the mortar and its ammunition. The mortar, designed for commando use, weighed less than eighteen pounds and they had carried it fully assembled. The two red HE bombs and the smoke bomb were in their containers. It was all easy and convenient to move about. Then she remembered the gate, which Serge must have left unbolted. She crossed the site and slid the bolts back into place.

Next she searched for a spot where the mortar could be set up. She settled on an area between the building and the tall hoardings where the ground had already been concreted over and was level. She checked the weapon, recalling what she had read two days before in the instruction manual. She removed the bombs from their containers and laid them out alongside. It took her ten minutes to work out a way of loading and steadying the mortar single-handed, and then she set to work. Using bricks and planks which were readily to hand, she fixed up a length of the plastic guttering in such a way that it could feed a bomb down into the muzzle of the mortar, adjusting the angle so that the bomb would slide down slowly enough for her to put it in place and then grasp the base of the mortar before the bomb had slid down the length of the gutter and into the muzzle.

She practised the manoeuvre several times, catching the

bomb each time in her hands. When she was satisfied that the arrangement would work, she looked at her watch. It was 9.50: about twenty-five minutes to go before the procession reached the Rond Point.

She wondered what had happened to Serge. She knew enough to know that he would be able to talk his way out if the police questioned him. And what would he do then? Where would he go? Command knew all about his friends and family. It wouldn't be hard to track him down. And they would have to do it fast. He knew far too much to be left on the loose. And if they didn't find him, the DST might get to him first and make him talk. She didn't doubt their ability to do so: that much was clear from his attitude this morning. She had been wrong about him. He had no guts.

And what about her? Was this to be the end of the road? Command had made the arrangements for the getaway but she somehow no longer believed in it. Serge had been right: it was one thing to fix matters on high but quite another to stop the rank-and-file cops shooting first. Thoughts of death or failure usually never crossed her mind during an operation. They all said she had no nerves, and although that was nonsense, it had always been true that she knew how to control them. She'd always had that iron self-control ever since she was a child. She had needed it then as she had needed it since, in the movement. Beatings either broke you or toughened you, and long before she could reason the thing out she had decided that she would not break. And so the beatings and the unutterable harshness at home had come to mean, for her, the price the weak had to pay for not being strong. If that was how life was, then she would be among the strong. And strength came to be, in her mind, the cardinal virtue. The strength of the individual, leading to the strength of the community, the nation. From that to admiring the strong men of history was an easy step. When had there been glory, rectitude, discipline? When had there been a proper respect for order? Under Napoleon. Under Hitler. Very nearly under de Gaulle. When she lay sobbing in her bed as a child she dreamed of a fairy princess who would spirit her away to a place where all was peace and love. In her adult fantasies there was a strong ruler who had swept away the rottenness and squalor of society and rewarded the cardinal virtues: obedience, fortitude, courage. And this was the dream of virtue which sustained her as she played her deadly games with bombs and automatic weapons. Nietzsche had understood. And in France, Daudet and Pétain.

The minimum range of the mortar was 100 yards. The problem was preventing an overshoot. But using the high trajectory, the weapon could be fired almost vertically over the hoarding, pointing up the Avenue towards the advance of the parade. That would mean the bombs would explode opposite some other building and it would take them a while to decide where they had been fired from. Her thoughts wandered between the practicalities of the operation and the distant memories stirred up in her mind by Serge's outburst.

She realised that she was weeping again. It was a long time since she had wept, and now she made an attempt to suppress her tears. Why was she crying? 'I am crying for my own life,' she told herself. 'I am crying because I am about to die and I have never been in love.'

Chapter 17

Commander Roisset, with Baum trotting beside him and Allembeau close behind, reached the group of police and CRS officers at 10.04. By now the roar of the crowd further up the Champs Elysées was rolling down the broad Avenue towards them swelling steadily as the head of the procession advanced down the middle of the road. It was clearly visible, coming towards them at a good walking pace, led by the politicians and public personalities with their sashes and decorations, followed by the banners of various organisations – ex-servicemen, political groups, trade unions and associations of this and that. Further back, the contingents from the fighting services marched with their bands amid the rumble of the Army's tracked vehicles and gun carriages. Overhead, Mirages flew past in formation, making a giant Cross of Lorraine in the clear morning sky. Ahead of the procession, a lone police outrider, resplendent in white, had throttled his bike back and was having difficulty in maintaining the slow speed.

'What's all this?' Roisset said to the senior policeman. He ignored the CRS Colonel.

The man came to attention. 'Nothing, sir.'

'Who is manning your radio here?'

'Our radio?'

'Yes, man, your radio.'

'Inspector Dubosc.'

'I want him.'

'Yes, sir. At once.'

'Christ!' Baum whispered to Allembeau. 'The man's more interested in his dignity than he is in what we told him.'

A minute was lost while the unfortunate Dubosc was brought over. He saluted and stood stiffly to attention.

'Do you know who I am?'

'Yes, sir.'

'Who?'

'Commander Alain Roisset, sir.'

'Is that all?'

'I think so, sir.'

Baum was getting desperate. There was nothing he could do.

'Am I not also,' Roisset was saying, 'what you choose to call *a pompous prick*?' He almost choked on the words.

The man reddened and said nothing. He stood as rigid as a pole.

'I had the pleasure just now of listening in to your radio. There will be an enquiry, you may be sure. And you, my friend, will figure in it. Now, I want this pavement cleared.'

'But we are under orders, sir.'

'*I said I want it cleared!*' Roisset roared the words at them and seemed to take on substance and authority as his anger mounted. The CRS Colonel tried to intervene.

'I have my orders, you know.'

'You,' Roisset shouted, turning on him in his generalised and non-specific fury, 'you will kindly shut up! On the streets of Paris you answer to the *Préfecture*. And here on the spot, the *Préfecture* is me – Commander Alain Roisset. Now clear that pavement and let the DST men through. *Clear it!*'

An order was barked as the DST men advanced to the gate. The time was 10.11 and the head of the procession was a little over 100 yards up the avenue, where it had stopped for a moment to maintain its timing schedule. Now it slowly started to move forward again.

Roisset hadn't finished. 'I want your name,' he barked at the senior policeman. 'Isn't it Jospin?'

'Yes, sir.'

'And yours?'

The CRS Colonel considered refusing and thought better of it. 'Colonel Jean Roque, Second Brigade, CRS.'

'And tell me, Jospin, has anyone been in or out of that building site you seem to be guarding so lovingly?'

'A man came out about an hour ago. He was one of the watchmen.'

'You mean he said he was one of the watchmen. Am I right?'

'Yes, sir.'

'*Merde*!' Baum had heard the exchange and knew at once what it meant. 'Shit! That's one at least who's got away.' Then he nodded to Léon, whose field day this was going to be, whatever anyone might say to the contrary. 'In you go – fast!'

'Do we shoot?'

'You shoot.'

They crossed the pavement behind the line of police and attacked the entrance gates with their iron bars. In thirty seconds one of the bolts had been wrenched free and the big gate swung back on its hinges. As the puzzled police and CRS troopers stood watching, the small group of DST men in their shabby dark suits and clumsy shoes ran onto the site.

Ingrid had prepared the mortar and the lash-up which was to feed in the bombs. She knelt now on the concrete, waiting for the procession to reach the corner of the building site so that the first bomb would fall maybe fifty yards or so behind the leaders. There were certain public personalities in the front rank of marchers who were not to be harmed. She had regained her composure and now felt strangely calm – calmer than she ever remembered feeling during an action.

The entrance to the site was hidden from her by the corner of the new building and she neither saw nor heard the DST men as they broke in and fanned out over the works. Nor did she see the two sharpshooters climbing the access ladder of the tower crane. Their orders were clear: shoot to kill. 'If it moves, shoot it,' Léon had said. 'I'll tell you what to say if there's an enquiry.'

With their FR–FI sharpshooters' rifles slung on their backs, they raced up the ladder, pausing at every dozen rungs to search the ground below. About sixty feet up the kneeling figure of Ingrid came into view. Her back was towards them. They both turned on the ladder and unslung their rifles.

'I'll take his head,' one of the snipers said. 'You aim for the body.'

'Hey, wait a minute, it's a girl.'

'So what? They're all equal nowadays, aren't they?'

As they spoke they were taking aim.

Ingrid had placed one of the HE bombs at the top of the guttering. The smoke bomb might have been a useful diversion but now it was a luxury she couldn't afford. The mortar stood at the foot of the guttering, waiting for the bomb to plunge down towards it and onto the firing pin. She let the bomb go and grasped the base of the mortar as she had learned from the manual. The bomb started to slide down its track. This was it – the most effective political gesture that the movement had ever made. In a few seconds there would be the explosion, the cries and the panic. And then the *political* effects. That was it – to produce political results. Did not power reside after all in the muzzle of a gun?

As the bomb began to slide, both marksmen, almost in dead unison, squeezed their triggers. Ingrid's sudden movement towards the mortar caused the bullet aimed at her head to miss. The bullet from the other rifle, aimed at her heart, ripped into her shoulder at the moment when the bomb left the base of the gutter and plunged down towards the mortar's firing pin.

The girl was flung forward by the enormous thrust of the bullet. She fell onto the mortar at the very moment when the charge exploded and the still unprimed bomb burst out of the muzzle. It ripped into her chest, was deflected by her spine and buried itself in a concrete post immediately behind her. A half-second later it primed itself and exploded.

'My God!' said the marksman whose shot had hit home. He turned to his mate. 'My God! A girl! Oh, my God!'

Georges Wavre was summoned alone to the President's office on the following afternoon. He made his report on the events of the previous day and outlined a proposed course of action. There had been a great deal of activity throughout the morning that had not gone unnoticed at the DST. Guy Mallard, the Minister of the Interior, had been at the Elysée and afterwards the head of his personal staff asked Wavre to be available for a meeting at 5 p.m. Efforts by Baum during the morning to contact Commander Roisset at the *Préfecture de Police* had encountered curious confusions at the other end. First he was in but unavailable, then he was not in and not expected, then they contrived to lose the call twice. The DST heard from a friendly journalist that there would be a press conference at 4 p.m. relating to recent successful actions against the terrorists. It would be taken by the official spokesman of the Prime Minister's office.

The President treated Wavre as if he were some kind of opponent. He listened sulkily to the account of the previous morning's successful action in the Champs Elysées and soon interrupted.

'Yes, yes, I have a meeting shortly. Please limit yourself to the immediate questions. Do you expect any more arrests in the near future?'

'They are possible. We are after a man who is on the run. We have a description.'

Wavre saw no point in irritating the President still further with the tale of how they had captured the younger Pellerin, *alias* Brunot, and had had to let him go. He was probably fully informed on the subject anyway.

'All right. My office will be in touch with you.' And he turned to his telephone as a form of dismissal.

'I know the signs,' Wavre said to Baum later. 'I know them very well indeed. They are the signs of the State apparatus drawing back from what it has uncovered.'

'I have good hopes of picking up the man who escaped from the building site.'

'If it lasts that long,' Wavre said, almost to himself. 'Now we are out of the realm of security and into the jungle of politics, my friend. And in the jungle, as you know, everything has a nasty habit of closing in behind you.'

At 4 p.m., to a crowded press conference, the official

spokesman announced that during a failed bombing attempt against the parade, a terrorist had been killed thanks to the vigilance of the police and the CRS. Earlier, another member of the same terrorist group had been arrested by the police at the *Port de Javel*, where bombs and guns had been found.

'Were they Trotskyists, Maoists or what?' a journalist asked.

'Information so far leads us to believe they were an anarchist group,' the spokesman said.

'Where did they get their cash and weapons?'

'We have reason to believe they had contacts with the remains of the Italian Red Brigades. Some of their equipment was Italian. We are pursuing our enquiries.'

One of the journalists had good contacts at the DST. 'Will you comment on the rumour that they were Right-wing extremists?' he asked.

'That is patently absurd, given the targets they were attacking. There are no grounds for such reports.'

'What of the rumours of disagreements between the services responsible for security?'

'Totally unfounded.'

'Was the DST involved in the breaking up of the group?'

'Marginally. The DST's role, as you know, is limited to foreign subversion.'

The spokesman ended by expressing the Prime Minister's personal thanks to the police for their vigilance and to the Minister of the Interior and Prefect of Police for bringing the terror in Paris to an end.

'It had to be like that,' Wavre said later, reading the teleprinter sheets from AFP. 'They could never admit it was the Right because that would almost certainly lead to distinguished names - Pellerin for one. And any hint of dissatisfaction with the police is unacceptable politically in our country. Crime and violence is a very sensitive political issue.'

In the Minister of the Interior's office at five, Georges Wavre was filled in.

'Both the President and the Prime Minister want the

situation defused as rapidly as possible. For that reason, your friend Commander Roisset has been moved to a new post. He will be Deputy Director of the General Inspectorate of Police with responsibility for the south of the country.' There was heavy irony in the 'your friend'.

Georges Wavre smiled and said nothing. The Minister, expressionless, continued. 'The Prefect of Police came to see me today and we had a frank talk. I am satisfied with the outcome and he will be appointing his own deputy to replace Roisset, concerning whom he had some reservations.' He cleared his throat. 'I also have a personal message for you from the President. Further to your talk with him this afternoon, he asks me to say that the investigation he originally asked you to pursue is now to be considered closed. Do you understand that?'

'I do, Minister.'

'He says that any further investigations on that and on the bombers will be in the hands of the police.'

Wavre nodded. The Minister waved a hand. 'That is all, *Monsieur le Directeur*. Thank you for coming to see me.'

As Georges Wavre pulled his bulk out of the chair and made for the door, the Minister coughed. 'Oh, yes, there was one more thing.' He coughed again. 'The dossiers.'

'Yes, Minister, the dossiers?'

'Yes, your dossiers on the, er, personages involved one way and another in all these matters. I don't need to mention names right now, but I wish to see them, please. Have them sent to me first thing in the morning.'

'Does that include any members of the Government, Minister?'

'It does. As I say, anyone who came within your ambit during these investigations.'

'Very well.' And Georges Wavre made his ponderous way back to the DST offices next door.

To Baum he said, 'About the dossiers, we have had that kind of request before, Alfred.'

'We have indeed.'

'You know what to do?'

'I do. Everything to be duplicated?'

'Everything.'

'Some – editing?'

'Whatever is needed to defend the integrity of our archives.'

Baum nodded.

'Ministers come and go, Alfred, but the archives go on. I leave it to you.' There was a pause. 'Tell me, Alfred, *mon vieux*, do you have an opinion after all this on the leakage?'

'I would prefer to call it that strange hybrid, a hunch which is also a certainty.'

'Tell me.'

'Well, that miserable individual Pichu, in the course of spewing out his poison about his great benefactor, the Minister of Defence, told us one thing of interest. On a hunch – always on a hunch, you understand – I asked my Inspector to find out casually from Pichu where his Minister was the other day when we told Mallard we were holding Pellerin's son and asked him for a directive. You'll remember he asked for fifteen minutes, then he told us he'd contacted Pellerin and we'd best release his son right away. Well, Pichu told the Inspector in his innocent fashion that on that afternoon his boss was not at the Ministry at all. He claimed he was with a woman somewhere, absolutely incommunicado. But that may just be our Pichu putting the boot in. Anyway, it confirmed my view that it was Mallard who, above all, wanted us to draw a blank on the investigation. And that, together with my suspicions that he knew Hemminge from the old days in Beyrouth, is enough for me, even if it wouldn't be enough for a tribunal. Also, the psychology of the initials was wrong from Pellerin's point of view. Too easy, for such a wily old bird, that ploy of using Mallard's initials. Much likelier to be a double bluff by Mallard himself. Much likelier.'

He paused, reflecting. 'And consider what a distasteful operator the man has always been politically, though it is not my place to say so.'

'I will overlook it, Alfred.'

'But does it matter anyway?'

'Yes and no. No, because no one will do anything about

it. Yes because I prefer our archives to contain the truth even if outside they persist in living a lot of lies. It's a neurotic thing I have about the archives.'

'But how am I to put a hunch – even a hunch which is a certainty – into a man's dossier?'

Wavre grinned. 'That, I am pleased to say, is your problem and not mine.'

On the Tuesday, the American Ambassador was summoned to the Quai d'Orsay, where the Foreign Minister received him with a good deal of warmth and some very fine sherry which, in deference to his guest, he served with ice cubes.

'I am very pleased to see you, your Excellency. I hope you and Madame have been keeping well?'

They had, the Ambassador said. He was going to be cagey with the Minister. He was still smarting from his encounter with the President and if they were returning to the attack, he had plans to cut the encounter short. But the Minister's amiability seemed to be a fixture for the duration.

'It is good of you to come at such short notice,' the Minister offered next.

'My pleasure,' the Ambassador said briefly. What the hell was going on here?

'I asked you to come,' the Minister pursued, looking carefully into his sherry glass as if he expected to find a frog there, 'because we are organising these modest celebrations this year, you know.' He paused, as if he had little confidence in his own words. 'Yorktown, you know.'

The Ambassador did not know but did not care to admit it. Was he supposed to know about Yorktown? If so, why had that asshole of a First Secretary not briefed him?

The Minister, who was also shaky on Yorktown, nevertheless pressed on. 'Yes, we plan some events, some public expression, you understand, of the solidarity we feel with the United States in regard to the successful collaboration of your General Washington and our own Lafayette at the siege of Yorktown.' He paused. 'Virtually ending the

American War of Independence,' he added. He had been briefed and the thing was fresh in his mind. 'Two hundred years ago this year.'

His office had searched doggedly for an anniversary – any anniversary – since the Prime Minister's call that morning. Something that would make a sudden gesture look half way authentic. They had considered and rejected the birth and death dates of distinguished artists, philosophers, *littérateurs* and politicians and were getting desperate when someone had come up with the defeat of the British at Yorktown. It had a sufficient touch of authenticity.

The Ambassador had made his money in Florida real estate, and having handed a million of it to his Party, now found himself Ambassador to France, which was what his lady wife had wanted. History was not his subject, and feeling insecure, he limited himself to nodding judiciously.

'As part of these celebrations,' the Minister was saying, 'we wished to express our sense of solidarity with the United States in various ways, and that would include the granting of decorations to a number of distinguished personages. It is within my competence to make recommendations, you understand.'

The Ambassador understood, was feeling more relaxed, and ventured an 'Of course.' He drank some of his sherry. It was not a drink he particularly appreciated.

'I imagine,' the Foreign Minister said, 'that your colleague Monsieur Rolf Hemminge who has given so many years of distinguished service here in Paris, particularly in the realm of communication and the arts, will soon be reaching the end of his posting and returning home. It would give us pleasure on such an occasion to award him the Legion of Honour. As part of these modest celebrations.'

The Ambassador was unaware that Hemminge had any plans to depart and he was shrewd enough to grasp what the Minister was driving at.

'I don't know,' he said. 'But no doubt he'd appreciate the honour.'

'We like to make such awards as a token of our appreciation for services to Franco-US understanding,' the

Minister said. 'When a period of service here has drawn to an end.'

The Ambassador nodded.

'It could be awarded at a suitable ceremony,' the Minister said. 'By our Ambassador.' He sipped again. 'In Washington.' He coughed. 'Soon.'

The Ambassador nodded again. He had no time for Hemminge anyway. He didn't like gays. If they wanted him out, he wasn't going to cry 'foul'.

The Foreign Minister rose to his feet. 'It was very good of you to come,' he said. 'My respects to Madame, and I hope we shall have an opportunity soon of meeting in a more informal manner.'

'Me too,' the Ambassador said, and took his leave.

'I should have liked more length to the nose,' Baum said, 'and perhaps the eyes are a little full. But the ears are very well set and the whip is excellent. Also, that is a good coat texture. And I like his temperament.'

He smoothed his hand over the cat's back and moved on to the next exhibit. 'A fine Red Cameo,' he said. 'The nose leather and pads are a good pink and that is a splendid coat. Note the sparkling silver, lightly dusted with pink. Very fine. But the chin's a little bit shallow. Do you not agree?'

He was among his friends at the annual show of the Cat Club at St Cloud. The office and its nonsense seemed very far away. By his side, Estelle tried to look knowledgeable but her thoughts were elsewhere. It seemed in the last week as if a great weight had been lifted from her Alfred's mind. He complained no longer of his liver, he was sleeping better, and he'd been keeping more sensible hours. In reply to her timid enquiries he had merely said, 'A mystery was solved and you know how I hate mysteries.'

That evening friends were coming to dinner and she had splashed out on a fine *truite saumonée* which she was cooking with tarragon in the copper fish kettle that Alfred had arrived home with the other day. And Alfred had released from his modest stock a good Vouvray.

It would be a pleasant evening.